EXACTLY ME

an office romance filled
with heat, heart & haha

Ingrid Voss

Book Cover by Kylie Sek

Developmental Edit by Britney Waldrop

1st edition 2023

Print ISBN: 978-0-473-67932-3

CONTENT NOTE

This book is a lighthearted and humorous love story, but it contains some strong language and intimate scenes that are meant for a mature audience.
There is the mention of the loss of a family member as part of backstory, but it is not lingered on.

If you are sensitive to any of the above, please read mindfully.

CHAPTER 1

NORA

My hand squeaks as I swing myself around the wet lamppost. Droplets of rain land on my face like a thousand icy kisses.

"Whee," I say, defying Martin's scowl, then stop to test a new dance move, landing a foot in a puddle of brown, slushy snow.

Damn, my new *I-just-got-a-bonus* boots.

"Nora, you're making a fool of yourself," he says in a low voice, shooting a glance at the crowd scattered outside the kebab place and down toward Bergen harbor. People in various states end Saturday night in a similar way, ignoring the cold of a Norwegian February night. "What is it you're trying to do, anyway?" Raindrops sparkle in his short black hair as he turns back to me and takes another bite of his lamb wrap.

"I'm tap dancing. Can't you see?" I hold his gaze as I drop my heel and step my toe in an exaggerated move, thudding on the cobbled street, before I twirl to make my heavy wool coat fly out.

"Jesus." Martin stands at the edge of the building, rubbing his forehead with his free hand. "Didn't you just turn thirty-two?"

"What? A thirty-two-year-old can't have a late-night boogie?"

He narrows his eyes at me, wrinkling his nose. "Not on the street. And you're not dancing. You're a drunk bat struggling to take flight." He waves his kebab toward me, sending pieces of lettuce flying. "You're such a weirdo," he scoffs, making my stomach sink.

He makes me feel ridiculous.

"And you're a buzzkill. Remind me why I called you?"

"Because I'm hot and you like orgasms," he answers quickly and flashes me one of his most charming grins.

"Don't flatter yourself, Martin Nguyen." I lean on the lamppost. It's cold against my shoulder, even through the thick coat.

"You don't find me hot?"

"I do."

He stares at me, blinking. I stare back until his eyes widen in realization.

"Fuck off, what's all the moaning about then?" A wrinkle forms on his forehead. The male pride is wounded, and I stifle a laugh.

"It's enjoyable. I just don't climax like you," I answer, to leave no room for doubt. Martin slumps, frowning. "Don't worry. It's not you, it's me." I shrug and close my coat in response to a gust of wind. It's sort of true.

"What if you'd let me ... you know." Martin wiggles his eyebrows and licks his upper lip.

"Nah, I've got my tools," I say, and mask my discomfort with a chuckle. Leaving out that it's too intimate for me and I don't trust him to understand.

"Why *did* you call me then? I don't hear from you for months and you call out of the blue, already drunk, telling me to meet you at the bar. Not just for drinks and a kebab, I presumed." He throws the half-eaten wrap in the trash next to him and stuffs his hands deep into his coat pockets.

I once hoped Martin had something kind and sensitive under his slick top layer, and I only needed to peel it back. Turned out he's onion through and through. So why did I call him again tonight?

I'm alone.

Tonight, the loneliness was unbearable.

He pouts, glancing at me from under a knitted brow. What am I doing here? Seeing him is a waste of time. It won't make a difference. Not tonight, and not in the long run. He might even make it worse with his rude jokes and frequent frowns.

The light drizzle turns into heavy rain, and the sounds of shrieks and splashing footsteps surround us.

"I'll head home. Thanks for meeting up." I turn and unfurl my umbrella against the wind.

"That's not the way to your apartment. Where are you going?" he shouts after me. With a tight grip on the rubbery handle, I fight my way against the weather to the night bus. It'll take me to the only place I want to be right now. A place I won't be able to call home much longer.

***

With immense relief I open my mom's front door, and a comforting heat envelopes me as I step into the hallway. The familiar, lingering aroma of wood-fire is mixed with something new I can't pin down. I shake the rain out of my long curls and curse this Norwegian coastal town. It must be the only place it rains upwards. And back and forth.

I discard the umbrella in the corner where a basket should be, but the hard thud tells me it's gone. Mom must've packed it already. Hope the sound didn't wake her. It's late. But I didn't want to go home to my cold apartment tonight. I need to wake up here. Need to tell Mom what I'm thinking of doing next. See her reaction.

I pat the wall behind me for the light switch and, with a loud flick, the room comes into view along with the source of the smell I didn't recognize. Cardboard boxes line the wall, and there's a row of black plastic bags under the stairs. They're blocking off the shoe bench I need to perch on to remove my boots without falling. I tiptoe over and poke one carefully. It's too soft to sit on. I sink down on the floor and lean back on the bag. Oh, that's kind of comfortable ...

***

Thud!

I jerk upright, and the plastic bag rips off my face like a band-aid. "Gah!" I rub my tender cheek and groan. A pincushion has replaced my brain, and it's moving around in my head.

"Oh, good morning," my mom's singsong voice sounds from above. I groan in response. "Sorry, did I wake you? I tried to be quiet," she adds.

"It's okay. But please stop shouting," I say, my voice hoarse. Slowly, I turn toward her, trying to avoid further movement of the prickly cotton ball. Not successful.

Ouch.

I get so easily hung over these days. A couple of years ago I could stay out drinking till two a.m. and spring out of bed to kettlebell class at six-thirty the next morning. Now, I can't even look up without hurting, and the pale light spilling in through the narrow window tells me it's past nine already.

"How's my Nora-kitten?" Mom chirps as she floats down the stairs. Her usual outfit of black activewear is today accompanied by an assortment of colorful shawls. They billow behind her as she descends. "I was a tad surprised to find my grown-up daughter in a pile in the hallway, but always happy to see you." She stops in front of me.

I stand with a whimper and a lot of effort, and stretch out to let Mom remove my still damp coat. After draping it over a box to dry, she turns back and pulls me into a hug. It's an extra long one, and I lean into her embrace. I need it more than ever. A mild scent of mildew meets my nose, and I pull back to review the source.

"What's up with these things?" I flick the shawls and golden threads shimmer in the light.

"Oh, I found a box of old memories." She turns quickly and gestures for me to follow her.

Is she blushing?

"Oh yeah? What memories?" I smirk as I follow her through to the kitchen. "Anything naughty?"

"Christ, Nora, why does your mind go there first, of all places?"

"Just your face. But I guess I don't want to know what you and Dad did that makes you blush like that."

"Pffft." She waves a hand at me as she rounds the kitchen island. "Coffee?" She puts a pod in the machine without waiting for a response—the fact she found me sleeping in the hallway might speak for itself.

I slide up on a barstool and we stare at the

coffee dripping. The loud drone of the machine fills the room.

"How was last night?" she asks when it's quiet again and hands me the steaming mug of black gold. I breathe it in deeply. I love the smell of coffee. Scents can evoke so much emotion. Coffee is comforting. Familiar.

"The girls canceled last minute." I take a sip. It's too hot, but I need something to stop the lump forming in my throat. *I got drunk alone and called Martin instead.* I don't tell her that.

Sigh. The girls. My three besties from way back when. We rarely see each other anymore. Life gets in the way. *Their* lives, mainly —partners, fur babies, human babies, house renovations. There's always something that's more important.

Last night was supposed to be girls' night for the first time in over five months. A delayed Christmas get-together, which was the delayed Halloween hangout. Will it be Easter before I see them?

So sorry, the dog fell asleep on my lap and I couldn't move for hours and my phone was on the other side of the room. Now I'm too tired to get dressed and am not in the mood after all. Rain check?

Oh shit, was that today?! I thought it was next weekend. Sorry. Kids and no sitter :(

Hey grl! Hubby took me to dinner!! Drink since four!

Making more friends here in Bergen wasn't on my agenda after returning from London seven years ago. Didn't think it needed to be. I finished my Finance degree and moved back, finding everyone had shacked up while I was gone.

It didn't matter at first. I was immersed in my exciting new job. And as my friends got increasingly fused to their couches and partners, I poured all my time into work, exercise, and the futile search for Mr. Right.

It's not that I can't be alone. I can enjoy my own company. Cuddling up with a romance movie or novel and a bowl of popcorn. Daydreaming about my future meet-cute and subsequent happily ever after. Dancing to YouTube tutorials.

But these activities have lost their joy over the last months, or even years. I can't pinpoint when I started feeling this way, but all I see stretching ahead of me is more of this. Endless alone time.

Mom presses her lips together in a thin line, obviously unsure of what to say. I'm not telling her that last part. Mari Gundersen is many things to me. Sweet Mom. Quirky Mom. BFF Mom. But I don't like saying *it* out loud. Not to Mom, not to my friends.

I'm lonely.

If I tell them, I'll always wonder if they're with me out of pity, to take care of me, rather than because they actually want to. I'll be the sad, single friend everyone's passing between them on holidays and Saturdays. They've got enough on their plates as it is. And I don't want Mom to worry while she's away.

So, it's just me, myself and I.

And Dee.

The last message I got was from her.

Dee: Have you decided yet?

"Why are you smiling at your phone? Is it a boy? Is it Martin?" Mom asks, wiggling her eyebrows. "Anything going on?"

"Nah, I'd never date him. Handsome, but heartless—only good for one thing."

Mom grimaces.

"Too far?" I take a sip of my coffee to hide my smirk.

"I know I've encouraged you to meet different men before settling down, but you shouldn't be with *heartless* men, Nora. Jesus Christ. It's better to be alone than with someone that isn't good for you."

"I don't want to be alone all the time, though. That's why I'm going on so many dates. Trying to find that man."

I never imagined myself being alone in my thirties. My dreams have always been to share my days with someone. Preferably with a man who makes my life more colorful. More interesting. More fun. I've seen it in my friends; how they light up around their other halves. I saw it in my parents. And every rom-com ever.

I want that.

I'm just one half now and I ache for that other

part.

"Not everyone is as lucky as you—finding the love of your life already at sixteen," I say, poking my mom's arm. She clears her throat and gazes into her coffee. "Sorry. I didn't mean to make you sad."

She shakes her head and gives me her tight-lipped smile and brave eyes before emptying her cup. It's quiet for a beat. How often does she get sad like that, being on her own all the time? Dad died over ten years ago.

"You never met anyone in the office?" Mom moves to the sink to wash her mug and talks over her shoulder to me, shouting to be heard over the running water. "My friend Karen met her wife at work, and they still love having lunch together."

"Nah, I had a fling with Dan in IT a few years ago and haven't dared call the help-desk since."

Mom lets out a snort as she wipes her mug dry with a towel. "I'm sure it can't have been that bad," she says as she turns to put it away. I contemplate telling her that 'Yes, when a man eyes your vulva like it's about to talk back', it's *that* bad—but I don't want to traumatize her. It was traumatizing enough for me.

"The message is from Dee," I say instead, with a surprising tickle in my stomach. Could this really be happening? What will Mom say?

Deepa Ladhani. My friend-soulmate, if that's a thing. My sister from another mister. We met at university, lived in the same halls of residence, and practically had to be removed at the hip when I moved home. It was hard to leave, but the trainee program for the largest fund manager in Norway had been too big of an opportunity to miss out on.

Dee has asked me to move back several times since. More often in the past year. Possibly because of my increased whining. She's the only one I've opened up to.

[September]
Dee: I think it would do you well to come back.

[December]
Dee: You don't seem like yourself. How are you not even excited about Christmas? Come to London!

[January]
Dee: Hey. And I mean that in that loud way people say HEY! If I have to hear another drunken voice note about how lonely you are, I will come to Norway and drag you here myself.

"Have you decided about what?" Mom asks.

"About moving to London. Dee will have a spare room soon, so I need to decide."

Her face lights up. Just as I hoped.

"That's a fantastic idea!" She claps her hands together. "What's your answer?"

Her genuine joy for me makes me smile, but I don't dare to match her enthusiasm until I know for sure.

"I want to go. I'm done here. Especially with you moving. I'll talk to my boss tomorrow. Our main software provider is based there."

"Software? But you're a portfolio manager."

"Yeah, and it's ..." I weigh my words. "Pretty bleak."

Fucking dark, more like it.

"Staying on top of the news to understand the market developments, it's ... I haven't found the right coping strategies. I can't switch off." I tap my temple. "If I work for the software provider, I can pivot my career and be a consultant, rather than start from scratch. I'll be a shoo-in."

There's no need to sell it to her. But I'm ready to persuade my boss to help me out. Mom takes a deep breath, absorbing what I've just said.

"I guess it'll be a Gundersen-family goodbye to Bergen," she says as if it's already decided. Her eyes meet mine again, this time with a shine to them. It makes it more real.

"Seems like it." I pat her hand and look around at my childhood home. My big brother moved to Oslo not long after our dad died and Mom has been saying this place is too big for her ever since.

"I'm leaving two weeks earlier than planned. Did I tell you?"

I shake my head, waiting for more information.

"Got my flights booked for the end of April instead. T-Adventures convinced me to visit Argentina and Chile with them first, instead of flying straight to Peru. I'm so excited!" She does a little shoulder shimmy, her gray bob swaying, and I cheer with her.

I'm so proud she's finally doing it. Fulfilling her dream of seeing the world. She's been watching travel documentaries for years, and her bucket list of places to go is forever growing.

"What's your timeline if you get your job? When will you be off?" Mom asks.

"At least three months." I grimace. "Visa application and notice period ... but what's a few months? I can help you out with the last bits. Say goodbye to the old house together before we both start our new phases in life."

Allowing the enthusiasm I've been trying to suppress to bubble up, I flash her a huge grin. It doesn't matter what my manager says tomorrow —I'm moving to London.

CHAPTER 2

JAKE

My thumb hovers over the call button. The twinkling lights of Midtown Manhattan and the pink glow of the sky behind it remind me it might be too late. It's nearly ten in the evening in France. I'll wait. Nobody wants disappointing news before bedtime.

A knock on the door disrupts my thinking, and I turn around.

"Hey, Jake."

"Ava, I thought you'd all gone for your Friday drinks," I say and make a point to check my wristwatch.

When I glance up, I catch her scanning me up and down and I chew my cheek, pretending not to notice.

"Heading out now. Wanna join?" she asks, leaning on the doorjamb.

I sit down at my desk and wiggle the mouse to turn the screen back on. "No, thanks. Have a good weekend." I turn to my screen, clicking on nothing in particular on my desktop.

"You sure?"

I meet her gaze and give her a small smile to be polite.

"Yes. Have fun."

She shrugs and straightens up, putting a hand on the doorknob. It's the same every time any of them ask. I've never been big on socializing. Why do they still try?

"Hey, the team and I ..." she starts in a soft tone I've not heard before.

Damn. They know.

"We're sorry you didn't get the promotion."

The exec team said they would announce *next* week. But I'm not surprised it's out. Here at HercuSoft, secrets circulate the office at lightning speed.

I chuckle and rub my chin to stifle my smile.

"Why? Because it means I'm still your line manager?" I know I'm demanding.

She frowns at me.

"I'll be honest. You could be a bit more involved with the team. But we recognize how good you are at your job." Her comment leaves me dumbfounded; I didn't realize it was a big deal to them. "So ... she got it because she's an 'old friend' of the CEO, right?" Ava uses air quotes to emphasize her point.

I can't lie to myself. I wish there's some truth to that. But having seen what such rumors can do to a woman, I don't want to fuel the fire.

"Bullshit. She's fucking brilliant."

"You think so?"

"I know so."

I cross my arms and lean back in my chair. A move that makes Ava glance down again, if only for a second.

Fuck's sake.

This is another reason I don't go out with the team. All it takes is one person who believes they're worth the risk. It makes it hard to relax. Ava has the same stare Heather had. She wants something. I can't have the wrong people thinking anything is going on again.

There's shuffling in the office behind Ava and a thin voice calling her name.

"All right, have a good one, boss."

Boss. I scoff inwardly. Head of Development, but not CTO.

I nod to her and pick my phone up as she closes the door behind her. I'm glad everyone's leaving, finally. Now I can sit here in peace and contemplate how to explain to my dad I've fallen short of his expectations. Again.

Letting myself get distracted instead, I flick through my Instagram feed and find my sister's last post—her new house in Primrose Hill. Sometimes I wish I'd gone to London with her after university, or even to France with my parents—Mom's favorite country after moving around for decades.

Tonight, I feel so far away from them.

When I open her profile, those big brown eyes we both have sparkle at me from several of the photos on the grid; in front of various major landmarks, laughing with her husband, and a recent one from what looks like a conference. I click in on the post. She's in front of a stall with her law firm's branding, flowing chestnut brown hair and a sleek black pants suit. Immaculate as always. Her belly is a visible bump.

Protect and propel your tech startup's success with expert IP legal guidance. Build a strong foundation for growth and stay ahead in the competitive tech landscape. #IPProtection #TechStartups #LondonTechWeek

It triggers something in me. Maybe I've not lost at all. Could this be the change I need to do the work I've dreamed of, but on a smaller scale? At least it's a plan for improvement and not simply acceptance of the status quo. And if I'm closer to her, I can be part of her life and see my niece or nephew—if she lets me.

***

Mom's face fills the screen as she leans forward to adjust the camera. Although it's only been a couple of weeks since our last video call, I'm relieved to see she looks the same. As if she'd suddenly age and remind me how long it's been since I saw her in real life. Her brown skin is still taut across her high cheekbones. Her shoulder length hair still black with only a wisp of gray. She moves her lips, but there's no sound.

Every time.

"Tu es en mode muet, Maman. Clique sur l'icône de microphone." I point toward the bottom of the screen and laugh as she gingerly clicks multiple icons that clearly aren't the ones to unmute. Her mouth moves again, asking if I can hear her, and I shake my head. "There's Dad, he knows." I switch back to English, as Dad never learned any of the languages spoken around us over the years. His engineering brain is only good for numbers, not words, he always said.

White-haired and smiling, my old man joins my mom in the frame. Lit up by the blue sheen from the screen, his square face looks older than his sixty-eight years.

"What's the problem, Roshani?" he asks my mom. His South English accent remains distinct, even after forty-odd years of working and living across the globe.

"I can hear you now," I say at the same time as Mom tries to explain. She must have accidentally found the right button.

"Good morning, son. What's the news about the promotion?" Dad asks with raised eyebrows.

Damn. Straight to it. I hate to let him down. He thinks I'm the best at everything. Hopefully, he'll like my new plan.

"Robert, let him say hello first," my mom says, contrasting my dad's short vowels with her long

American ones. “I’m surprised you’re up at five-thirty on a Saturday. Are you okay?” she asks.

“Early bird.” I shrug. Didn’t sleep. I was up researching tech startups, but they don’t need to know that. “I have some news,” I say, and my dad’s eyes widen with expectation. “I’m moving to London.”

“You’re what?” Mom asks in a higher pitch.

“Yeah, I don’t want to work for a large company anymore, and London is a booming tech hub.”

So is New York, but London has my sister.

“That’s wonderful, sweetheart. How exciting!” Mom says, beaming at the camera, but not meeting my eye. I can never get used to that aspect of video calls. “Did you know your diaper-buddy Mark is in London?”

“Hmm. From Germany?”

“Yes, Lothar and Else’s son. Do you remember them?”

“Oh, yeah. Else taught me pencil drawing.”

“That’s right!”

Mark and I were inseparable for nearly five years until Dad’s work took us from Germany to Indonesia and the Beckers moved to London.

“They’re so lovely. Oh, get in touch with Mark, will you? I’ll get his details. Sage is doing some work for him, actually.” Mom immediately gets her phone out.

“What happened with the promotion? I thought being the CTO of HercuSoft was your goal?" Dad interrupts, his flexing jaw hints at the disappointment I didn't want to see.

"It was."

"You applied this time, at least? Not wasting your opportunities again?"

"Try that again, Robert, with a little less accusation. So he had different priorities for a while," Mom says strictly to the side of his face. "It's not a crime to give love a chance."

I flinch. I don't deserve her sweet thoughts. Love wasn't part of it.

"It's fine, Mom." I desperately want to change the subject. "I applied but didn't get it. Sorry." Staring at my dad, I chew the inside of my cheek so I don't reveal my embarrassment.

"Don't apologize to *us*. I just hope you gave it your all."

"I know. Do or do not, etcetera."

"We only succeed in life by going at our goals with everything we've got."

The mantra I've heard since I was in elementary school.

"It's a blessing in disguise. I realize I can do so much more for a startup or a struggling business. It'll be good, Dad. This is the role I'm meant to have."

The thrill of change, of progress, bubbles up in me. Last night, I spent hours researching companies in London and found countless prospects that will allow me to fulfill my career goals. The relentless focus on the role

I once squandered made me blind to other opportunities.

"I'm so pleased for you, son." Mom claps her hands together over her heart. "Your passion shines through."

I beam at her.

"Will you come to see us, finally?" she asks.

"Of course."

I give Dad a moment to speak, but there's nothing. His eyes are moving as if studying the screen.

"I'll come after my Norway trip," I say instead.

"Norway?" Mom asks.

I chuckle, knowing it's kind of silly, what I'm about to tell her. "Do you remember the Slow TV I sent you a link for? The long train ride across the mountains?"

They nod.

I have it on in the background when working from home. It's soothing. "Mid-May I'll fly to Oslo and take the train to Bergen. I'll take my sketchbook." I shrug, not sure if I mean it, but it makes my mom smile.

"Why wait till May?" Dad asks with a frown.

"I'll need to ride out the notice period and sort out my apartment."

Looking around, I automatically do a quick assessment. I can sell most of it, send some, and find a caring new home for my plants.

"I can't wait to hear what Sage thinks about it. She finally moved in to her Primrose Hill house last week. Did she send you photos? Very fancy. Right by the park."

"I saw it on Instagram. How's the baby-bean doing?"

"She's growing beautifully. Did you not see the 3D ultrasound screenshot last month? From the twenty-week scan? The little girl is pouting!" She mimes what she must have seen in the picture, but then her smile fades. "You always ask us ... Do you not speak to your sister?"

"It's hard to find the right time, Mom. We're both busy."

"Oh, okay." The sadness in her eyes is obvious and my lungs feel too small. We were all so close before. Christmas together each year was a minimum. Then I fucked up, and I've been hiding —first behind the travel restrictions and then work—so I wouldn't have to face them. It hits me now how much I miss them. Would they look at me like that if they knew the real story? Sage has been avoiding a real conversation with me for over three years.

"I'm eager to see how you get on." Dad has finally found his words. "The company that gets you will be so lucky, having someone who goes the extra mile." He gives me that proud Dad expression and I chew my cheek again.

"You know it, Dad. I'll leave it all on the field."

CHAPTER 3

Three Months Later...

NORA

"Oh, Bryant," I whisper into his mouth, and his kiss deepens. The rush of emotions settles in my now burning core. He stops to fling his hat to the side and rip his shirt off, exposing his tanned skin and washboard abs. Just as I remember him from the days at the ranch. I take his callused hand and put it on my inner thigh, sliding it up toward my wetness. "Touch me," I demand.

I grip my book and bite my lip so I don't sigh out loud.

I want this. Raw passion. True love.

Then I notice it. A tingling sensation. Not the one threatening to form in my pants region, but the one on top of my head.

Someone is watching me.

In my peripheral vision across from me, I make out a shape. A tall, broad-shouldered man-shape. He's in dark jeans and a black T-shirt, leaving light brown, solid arms bare. The instinct to check him out properly is overpowering. When people move at the final boarding call to London Gatwick, I glance up and he catches me looking.

His dark eyes are captivating, and I'm stuck.

Oh.

Adrenaline hits me. I'm hot and cold at the same time. When a woman in a flapping dress passes and snaps me out of it, I jump up and rush down the line.

That was intense.

***

Ugh, I have the middle seat, but at least it's by the fire exit, so I've got plenty of room for my long legs. I kick off my Converse shoes, stuff my purse and jacket under the seat in front before leaning back to continue my book.

My stomach rumbles, reminding me of the small breakfast I had. They better have a delicious airplane panini for me.

A person stops next to my row. I turn to see the magnificent man-shape from before putting his carry-on in the overhead compartment. His well-fitted jeans hint at muscular thighs underneath, and it takes all my willpower to stop ogling him before he sits down.

"Hey," he says in my direction with a deep and raspy voice. It's as if he hasn't used his vocal cords yet today.

His shoulder pushes me partway into the next

seat and a waft of something clean and manly, like cedarwood and mild cologne, meets my nose. I hold myself back from leaning in to sniff him more deeply.

"*Hei*," I answer, trying to angle my head to catch his eye, but the proximity makes it hard. "*Skal du på weekend-tur til London?*" I ask, just as he leans to stuff his tablet in the seat pocket in front of him. The movement of his broad torso pulls me along with him.

"Sorry, I don't speak Norwegian."

He's American? Yum. A hot one to boot.

I'm about to translate my question when someone clears their throat above us. A sizeable man points at the window seat, interrupting the start of what could've been a pleasantly awkward transit conversation with the yummy man.

"Sorry, sir," Mr. America grumbles and gets up. He slides out into the aisle. I swivel my legs over to let the newcomer through, and he glowers at me. Gesturing down, I'm trying to say *there's plenty of space*, but he doesn't seem to agree.

The aisle is busy with other passengers putting their luggage away, so I'm forced to squeeze up next to the American. Despite him turning to make more space, I have to stand sideways up against him. He's tall, but so am I — towering five foot seven over the ground. He must be at least six foot one.

Mr. Window Seat folds his jacket and puts his stuff away, taking his time, so I glance toward the warm man beside me. His delicious, dented chin is just above eye-level, and I'm very close to his solid pecs. His scent fills my nose again when I breathe in and I'm flushed with heat.

Oh gosh.

I'm certain my nipples harden and look down. Yep. My nipples are saluting him, ridiculously obvious through the thin fabric of my bra and top. Maybe he won't notice.

I let my gaze move up to take in the rest of his face. Dark brown eyes, deep as wells, framed by long eyelashes. A tight-lipped grimace. With that expression on such a striking face, he could be a classic pained romance hero. Wonder what lies behind it? A lost love? Unrequited love? No way. Maybe he's the 'other man'. And it's not a pained expression, simply a grumpy frown.

Distracted by his presence, I jump in fright when he touches the back of my shoulder. The warmth of his hand sears through my cotton long-sleeve, giving me goosebumps and a rush of adrenaline that hits much further south than it should.

"Sorry, didn't mean to scare you. You can sit," he says, gesturing with the other hand to the seat. I blink. My brain is temporarily out of order.

He raises his thick, perfect eyebrows at me when I don't move.

"Oh, right."

I scramble into my seat, still flustered by the shock he gave me. He sits back down, his arm and leg presses against me, amplifying the feeling from before. I squirm to get comfortable, but every time I move, my side rubs against his and it gets worse. Bah, this will be a long flight.

CHAPTER 4

JAKE

Thank fuck I get to sit down again. That was painful. How can I get so hot from standing next to someone?

Wonder what she was thinking. I felt her eyes on me the whole time.

It was so hard not to glance down and absorb every detail. Those cheekbones, those pink lips. They were right there in the corner of my eye.

When I sat down in the waiting area earlier, she caught my eye immediately. I stared at her like a creep, but something about her made it impossible to look away. Something soft, yet incredibly sexy. I noticed how her blue cotton top hugs her toned arms and small round breasts. How she sat with her knees wide and feet crossed at her ankles. So relaxed. So unbothered. I noticed her dark blonde messy bun, that looks like it's hiding long, wild curls. And how she held her book tight in one milky-white hand, twirling a loose curl with the other, immersed in the story.

The way she bit her lip when she was reading made my mind go places. Inappropriate places. When she caught my eye, it was like time froze. I could get lost in her face and happily be nowhere else.

I want to see more of her now, but it's hard to do unnoticed when she's right next to me. Trying to angle my head so I can get a look at her face again, her protruding nipples come into view. Jesus Christ, as if I wasn't struggling enough already.

I shift in my seat to pull the jeans down and get into a more comfortable position, but it's impossible to avoid bumping into her again. Her shoulders and knees are everywhere.

"Sorry," I mutter, and she squeaks something in response. The man in the window seat has turned away already, which I learned this week is pretty common for Norwegians. They don't tend to talk to people they're next to. Not on buses, trains, and especially not in elevators. Potentially in a café or bar. There seems to be a loophole if you're on a mountain or alcohol is involved. Considering this is a ten-thirty a.m. flight, that won't be the case here, thankfully.

Small talk is high on the list of my least favorite things to do. Especially now I'm hungry, and tired from an active week. I steal a peek at the intriguing curly beauty next to me.

If *she* wants to talk, I'll do my best.

Oh. She's got her book up again.

That settles it.

I put on my headphones, set them to noise cancellation and close my eyes, letting my arms drop into my lap and stretching my legs out under the seat in front. Despite all the jokes from my friends about how much I love tech, this podcast should help reduce my still-threatening jeans bulge; help take my mind off the warm arm and leg pressed up against my left side. It's like she's on fire.

She's shuffling around. *What is she doing?*

I sense someone idling in the aisle, but I can't hear anything through my headphones. I don't want to.

Now she shifts forward in her seat. Her arm bumps into mine and her knee pushes against my leg. When I open my eyes to check what's going on, she's leaning across my lap, handing her book and a pile of stuff over to the flight attendant. I squeeze my eyes shut until she's done, not wanting to look at those lean, sexy arms so closely. And definitely not her breasts. Nope.

She sits back, and a puff of air sends a delicate scent of sweet vanilla and flowers my way and my pants tighten again.

Goddamnit.

CHAPTER 5

NORA

Crap. I gave the flight attendant everything when she told me we can't have loose items in this row during take-off. I should've kept my book, silly me.

Mr. America is sleeping, or pretending to. Manspreading like he's the only one here. I glance down without moving my head. Wonder why he can't put his legs together. Is there something in the way? The thought of him feeling the same rush as me makes me tingle.

Jesus. *Am I in heat or something?*

I need something to do. I can't sit here with only my thoughts for company. Scooting forward in my seat, I turn and study the American's face. He's more relaxed now, revealing full lips and a prominent Cupid's bow. He's stunning. I shake myself mentally to snap out of my trance and poke his arm gently to ask to come past. It's muscular, but softer than I thought. No reaction, though. I poke his leg.

Nothing.

"Hello?" I try.

He must be out cold. I can climb over his legs, I guess. There's extra room here, so I won't be right in his face.

I step over him, holding on to the folded-up table and seat in front. As my right leg lands in the aisle, I'm in a high lunge over his knees. His legs twitch, making me jump and lose my balance as I try to take the left leg with me. The table comes loose, and I fall sideways into his lap.

"What're y—" He grunts as I land on him.

"Oh, my god!" I scramble and twist on top of him, trying to find my footing to stand up again. "Sorry, the table is stuck." I try to push it up, but it won't budge.

I'm sitting on his fucking lap. Jesus Christ.

He grabs my upper arms, making the adrenaline surge in me.

"Please stop moving," he says in a low, strained voice. "Just—Ah." He holds me hard so I can't wriggle. "Push the table in and then lift."

Oh. The table has been pulled out. I push it back into the correct position and lift it up. When I lean forward, he lets out a low groan and clears his throat.

Holy shit. That's not only his seatbelt I'm sitting on.

I push off the handles as quickly as I can and bounce onto my feet.

"I'm so sorry," I say when I regain my balance

in the aisle, unable to ignore the lingering sensation of his warmth on me and the intense feeling between my legs.

He straightens up, pulling on his jeans, and takes his headphones off. “I’m so sorry … Uhm. Sorry I spooked you. What are you doing, anyway?” He glances up at me with big black eyes. A crease forms between his eyebrows.

“You were sleeping. I need my book.” I point up and shrug apologetically. He nods and presses his lips together.

As I stretch to open the hatch and locate my book, I sense his gaze on me as strongly as if he’d touched me, and it sends a shiver through me.

“Can I come past again?” I ask with a sheepish grin after closing the hatch, waving my book.

He takes off his seatbelt and stands up this time. Is that an outline of an erection in his jeans? He’s not hiding it. Or does he not realize I can see it?

Shit. I’m staring at his crotch. Stop staring at the man’s crotch.

I edge past and glance up, meeting his dark eyes again. I’m fully aware my nipples are about to poke him. Bah, what a day to choose a soft bra. His gaze doesn’t waver, he’s not looking down. He breathes in deeply through his nose and grumbles something that may have been ‘sorry’, and turns to make his way down the aisle. Several heads swivel to follow the tall, gorgeous human. His butt is sensational. Oh gosh, I’m terrible. Objectifying him like this. But how can I not enjoy watching such a beautiful specimen of a man?

***

Seventy-three minutes of staring into my book. I've not read a single page, and I've not eaten as I must have blanked out when the flight attendant came around. It seems leaving Norway has made me a randy goat and incapable of normal human brain activity.

I've tried to come up with something to say or ask that's worthy of him removing his headphones again, but I don't function on an empty stomach. And it doesn't help to have your blood rushing at every touch of an elbow or knee.

When the plane finally lands, we do the classic awkward shuffle, politely nodding and gesturing to let the other go first. And we leave the plane with no additional salutes of body parts.

I bolt toward the restrooms. I've needed to pee since the seatbelt light on the plane told me I wasn't allowed to. My bladder is evil like that.

Perhaps I'll run into him again at the passport control and say something clever—as I imagine I'd done earlier if I was being myself. Truth be told, it would probably be more silly than clever. But at least it would be something.

While waiting by the luggage carousel for my suitcase a few minutes later, I change to my UK SIM-card to text Dee. It's fiddly and I drop the little tool several times, shaking from hunger and adrenaline. I glance up in between, looking around for a tall, dark shape. Nothing yet.

Me: I've landed. Seems I need to get laid. Will tell you all about it when we meet *facepalm*

By the time I have my suitcase, I still haven't seen him. I've probably lost him.

Aw. I'll never see that magnificent shape again.

I stop at the Cornish pasty cart by the train station. The delicious baked, buttery scent reminds me I'm famished. At this hunger level, I can't decide: cheese and beans, beef, or onion? I end up buying all three before rushing down to the platform to catch my train to central London. I cut through a small group to perch by the wall and sort out my things before the train—

Wham!

My paper food bags go flying as I run into someone, and our bags mix on the ground. As I bend down to find mine, cedarwood and manliness hits my nose and I know who it is I'll see when I look up.

CHAPTER 6

JAKE

"I'm so sorry," she breathes. Her eyes meet mine as we're both crouched down. We're close in the bright daylight, and only now do I notice she has freckles across the bridge of her nose. Green eyes.

My pulse races, and it makes me pause.

Damn.

"I'm sorry," I grumble and gather the scattered bags. Seems we went to the same pasty cart. "You have three?"

"I'm hungry." She meets my eye again, as if in defiance.

"No judgment, just checking none are missing." I shrug.

"I'm not sure which ones are mine now," she says as we stand up, her voice shaking.

Seeing how frazzled she is, I'm glad I didn't walk up to her at the luggage carousel as I contemplated doing when she was on her phone. She'd probably have throw the damn thing in the air from shock.

A part of me wants to tell her to take them all and get lost. I've never been this affected by anyone and it's making me unsettled. Work has been my focus for the past few years and will be for the indefinite future. There's no room for distractions.

And she feels like one.

From the second I laid eyes on her in Norway, I've struggled to control my reactions and my imagination.

"I presume you're heading to town?" my mouth says before my mind can argue, gesturing toward the train arriving next to us.

"London Bridge," she squeaks, not looking at me directly. Did I make her that uncomfortable on the plane?

The train's squealing brakes forces me to take action. I move toward it with all the paper bags in one hand and my luggage in the other. "Let's figure it out on board."

"Oh." She scurries behind me to the doors now open. The people that stood waiting file in before us and I turn to help her with her massive suitcase.

"Here, let me give you a hand."

"Thanks, I'm okay. You worry about your own stuff, mister." She fans my hand away and gestures toward my suitcase on the other side. I'm surprised by her reaction, and at my skin prickling from the near touch, so I remain silent. "I do things myself." She holds my gaze with a smirk as she flings her suitcase into the train and rams a guy straight in the knee. "Oh, my gosh, I'm so sorry." She jumps on board and checks on the man.

I hoist my massive suitcase in carefully, no need for more injuries, and roll it into the luggage rack. I spot a free table seat and stride over.

As the train moves away from Gatwick Airport, she manhandles her luggage, attempting to get it into the rack next to mine. I could help her, but an educated guess says she'd refuse again. She stops and blows the curly tendrils out of her eyes and resumes, trying a different way. The guy she rammed now gestures to her suitcase. I bet she won't let him help. She shakes her head and waves a hand.

Hah, knew it.

After finally succeeding, she lifts her head and scans the train car. I'm easy to spot and a hint of red appears on her cheeks when she does. It does something funny to my heart rate, and I scowl inwardly at my biochemistry. Her eyes narrow as she makes her way toward me. What is my face doing?

She plops down on the seat in front of me and looks through the bags on the table.

Good, I don't want to talk either. Not at all.

But I do wonder what her name is. And there's something so charming about the way she talks. Like many Norwegians I met while there, she sounds almost American, but with a slight Scandinavian lilt.

"I'm Jake," I say, despite my better judgment. It's not exactly the best way to avoid conversation.

"Oh. Sorry." She looks up. "I'm Nora. Nora Gundersen." I get a smile for the first time—a close-lipped smile that doesn't entirely reach her eyes—as she extends her hand for me to shake. I look at it, and back to her face, before taking it.

"That's very formal," I say, holding it for a beat longer than I should. It feels good in mine.

"Hah. I guess we Vikings don't know what to do when we meet people—surprise attack, or awkward formal introductions," she says, pulling her hand back with a sheepish grin.

"Or in your case, an attempt at both?" I say, letting my mouth tug slightly at the sides. She blinks. Her cheeks go red again. Does she blush when she's embarrassed or annoyed?

After a quiet moment, she peers into the bags again.

"These are mine," she says, her tone clipped. She moves three of the bags to the side, takes a pasty out of its bag and bites into it—with gusto. Flaky crust flies everywhere. She has crumbs around her mouth and an expression of genuine pleasure on her face, as she chews with her eyes closed. I'm transfixed. I've never known pasty to be an aphrodisiac.

A moan escapes her. "Mmm."

She opens her eyes again, looking at me. "Oh, my god. This is amazing. I was starving," she mumbles through a mouthful. A hand comes up to hide her mouth as she continues munching, humming with satisfaction.

"Hm." I shake my head, unsure of what to say. My imagination conjures up pictures of what I could do to make her moan more like that. And yet again, there's a flush of heat in me. It's not the fun kind. It's the raging *'I've not had sex in years'*-kind, and I search for a distraction through the window.

Trees. Blue sky.

I've not been with a woman since Heather. I've wanted to, a couple of times. But the overriding part of me tells me it's not a good idea. Bad things seem to happen each time. Heather was the last of a series of unfortunate events. No, that makes it sound like it happened *to* me. I made it happen. I make terrible decisions.

It's for the best. I'm fine alone. I've got my work, and hopefully my sister too.

"Sorry if I was rude before. I get grumpy when I'm hungry," she says when finished, brushing crumbs off her face and the table.

"Hm," I say and continue staring out the window.

"What's *your* excuse?"

My eyes cut to hers. A hint of a smile plays on her lips.

"I've had a long day," I answer. A long three

years, more like it.

"It was a *hard* journey," she deadpans. I glare at her, waiting for confirmation she's joking. She glares back. So she noticed.

Shit.

"I can't help but feel I'm rubbing you the wrong way," she says, and this time I catch her stifling a smile. I press my lips together to keep myself from laughing in relief. She's joking about it.

More trees and blue sky.

"I want to apologize about the whole lap situation," she says and wrinkles her nose.

"You don't have to," I respond quickly. "For what it's worth, I wasn't trying to … I don't know. I'm sorry I made you uncomfortable." I breathe out loudly and rub my forehead. She chuckles. This is a weird conversation.

"You didn't," she says and scratches her eyebrow. "If it makes you feel better, I spent the rest of the trip clenching my thighs together, hoping for turbulence."

I let out a bark of a laugh in surprise but quickly recover, rubbing my chin. She looks at me as if in shock at my sudden reaction; her green eyes wide and pink mouth frozen in a small O.

CHAPTER 7

NORA

I've had a minor heart attack. Yep, I'm pretty sure that's what just happened. He laughed, and it nearly killed me.

His tense expression opened up for a second into a wide, bright white smile. I glimpsed those full lips again. Little wrinkles formed on the sides of his vibrant, brown eyes. For a fleeting moment he transformed into a warm, kind-looking man.

The thin line is back now, and he looks out the window. I sense he doesn't have any interest in talking to me, but I'm curious about him. What is he thinking about?

The train stops at East Croydon. The sound of rustling and shuffling departing and arriving passengers is loud around us. I pretend to stare at the platform outside while letting my indirect vision take him in. My heart races. I feel the questions rise to the surface and bubble over.

"Was that your first time in Norway?" I ask

when the train moves again. It's not long till we're at London Bridge and I have to say goodbye to this view.

"It was."

"What did you do? Why did you go to Norway?"

"Why not? It's spectacular."

"If you're into nature and spending lots of money, I guess."

He lets out a huff of a laugh without showing me that smile again.

"I went to explore. Took the train from Oslo to Bergen."

"How was it? Did you know you can follow the journey on YouTube?"

The corners of his mouth move up, almost imperceptibly.

"It was even better in real life. And I experienced your national day. That was something."

Oh, he sounds almost excited.

"I love the seventeenth of May. Did you see the parades? Eat lots of ice cream and hot dogs?"

"Yeah. It was good."

I pause for more information. He's still not looking at me properly; only a glance in between. I change the subject instead, as he doesn't seem interested in sharing any details.

"What are you doing in London? Next stop on a big summer adventure?" He doesn't respond right away. His jaw is working hard. Is he chewing his cheek? I continue, “I’m moving here.” I beam, picking at another pasty despite feeling full enough after the first one.

He hums; a deep sound. Then he finally turns to face me again and picks up one of his pasties. “Me too.”

“That’s so cool. What a fun coincidence.” I grin properly for the first time all day, and the corners of his mouth twitch ever so slightly as his gaze intensifies. I’ve never seen eyes so fierce. He seems to search for something in mine. I guess he didn’t find it, or it’s all in my head, as he turns away again. Must be loving that view.

“I think we’ve stopped,” he says, peering out the window. The speaker above crackles and a distorted voice announces there’s a disruption on the tracks.

“What part of London are you staying in? I’ll be in Hackney. London Fields. Do you know it?” I ask gingerly. We’ve got lots in common based on this new information. We’re both immigrants and single. How do I know he’s single? I guess I don’t. A girl can dream.

Stop it, Nora. A man this good-looking will have women chasing him left, right, and center. And if he grew up like that, he’ll probably be an arrogant skirt-chaser. Not unlike the worst men of my past.

Yet ... he seems more reserved. He’s not flirting. Hmm.

Either way, I wouldn’t mind seeing him naked.

Feel his weight on me.

"Camden," he answers, yanking me back to the present. "Staying with a family friend."

"Fun! You've been to Camden before?"

"I have."

Wonder what part of Camden he'll be in. Probably the fancy part. He looks well off, in an understated way. His style is simple yet refined. Everything he wears screams high quality, but nothing ostentatious. A wristwatch with intricate clockwork details, a well-cut black V-neck T-shirt without a logo, clean nails on beautiful hands, and styled hair—just long enough to run my fingers through and hold on tight. Mmm.

"What?" he grunts, catching me staring. I should stop ogling him. Poor guy. If reversed, I'd consider him a total creep.

"Sorry. Nothing. What do you do for work?"

He rakes a hand through his dark brown waves and rubs his neck. The move makes his biceps flex and I need to check in with my face to make sure I'm not drooling.

"I'm a CTO—that's a Chief Technology Officer—for a growing tech company."

"Nice." I nod. "I'm going to work for a tech company, too. I'm a senior consultant, FYI. That means For Your Information."

I've coaxed a small smile out of him.

He holds his hands up. "Apologies for assuming you didn't know what a CTO is."

"I suppose not everyone does, but I couldn't help myself." I grin. He answers with a smirk, and we fall silent. The train jolts back into motion and the Shard and our destination looms up ahead.

"What are you reading?" he asks, gesturing to the book on the seat next to me. Thank heavens for discreet covers. Although, what's there to be ashamed of?

"It's a sexy cowboy romance." I decide to be honest and flash him a sly grin.

"Sounds riveting," he says in a level tone, but with raised eyebrows.

"Very much so," I answer, ignoring his blatant sarcasm. "It's my escapism."

"From what?"

"Hmm. Everyday life, I guess. Relentlessness." I've said too much. He's frowning at me. "Hah." I open my mouth to excuse the comment, but stop myself. I won't bother pretending I was joking. He doesn't care. He's just making conversation. "Are you reading anything?"

"The Lean Startup, by Eric Ries."

"Any good?"

"Mesmerizing," he says, his eyes are intense again. I chuckle at his apparent joke, but he doesn't flinch. I can't figure this guy out. One moment he's staring out the window, as if I'm not even here, next he's looking at me like he wants to eat me.

I don't mind the latter.

"Can't wait to head out tonight. Might go to Camden now you mentioned it."

Just leaving that there.

"That's nice." His eyes meet mine, but I can't make out his expression.

***

I stand on the platform and watch Jake lug his suitcase out of the train. It's enormous.

"Need a hand with that?" I ask and grin at him.

"Funny."

I don't want to say goodbye, despite his rough demeanor and allergy to full sentences. He doesn't stop when he reaches me, but keeps walking toward the exit. I'm certain he sends me a sideways glance, so I roll my suitcase next to him, trying to keep up with his long strides.

"Do you want to meet up in Camden Town later?" I ask. What's there to lose at this stage?

"I'm not going out," he mutters over his shoulder.

Our suitcases thunder on the ground as we make our way through the ticket barrier. I veer toward the elevators for the underground train while he heads for the exit.

"Aren't you taking the Northern Line?"

"What?" he grumbles and turns back to me.

"To get to Camden? Come, it's this way."

He hesitates. "No, I'll take a taxi." He looks like he's thinking hard, his brow furrowed and jaw flexing. "Nice to meet you." He turns and walks off, so I talk louder.

"I'll be in Camden later if you change your mind!"

He waves.

CHAPTER 8

JAKE

I stare at the laptop screen. Willing my brain to work. Must. Do. Research. All I see are green eyes and freckles. And that smile. Her entire face lit up.

Fuck. What a smile.

Focus, Jake.

She asked so many questions. Was she interested, or is she one of those rare Norwegians who like talking to strangers on trains? It was hard to tell. I, of course, did the classic move of holding back. Yet she still wanted to meet me again.

It was probably only physical, though. She said I'd turned her on. I let out an involuntary groan at the memory. I'm not a stranger to women hitting on me, but the thought of *her* thinking of me like that—while sitting right next to me—drives me wild.

"Dammit." I slam the lid shut and get up to stretch, strolling barefoot into the sun-filled backyard.

Was she serious, though? Does she want me to find her? She could've just been funny about it. Some of her comments were my kind of humor, but I was so baffled, it didn't sink in until later.

What haunts me the most is her face when she said everyday life is relentless. There was a flicker of sadness in her eyes. I wanted to wrap my arms around her and tell her I'll make it all right.

I squeeze my eyes shut and rub them. *Cut the crap, Jake.* What makes me think *I* could make anything better? Knowing me, I'd probably make it worse.

I let the sunlight shine through my closed eyelids and zero in on the sound of the birds. The occasional car. Someone clattering in a kitchen a few houses down.

Mark's apartment isn't in Camden Town as I thought. It's at the edge of Camden borough, next to Primrose Hill. And it's not an apartment. It's a four-bedroom house. He's obviously underselling his situation when talking to people.

I slide the phone out of my pocket and dial Mom.

"*Bonjour, Maman.*"

"Jake. How was your flight?"

"Uhm." Nora's voice pops into my head; '*it was a hard journey.*' I chuckle to myself. "It was good, thanks. I'm at Mark's now. Did you know he lives near Primrose Hill?"

"No, isn't that something?"

"Do you have Sage's address?"

"Of course, I'll send it to you. What's your plan now? When will I get to see my son?"

"I've got two weeks until I start work, but need to do more preparation and find a place to live. Marseille might be too far this time around. Would you and Dad want to come to Paris for a few days instead? My treat."

***

"Camden? Why do you want to go there? There are better options in Mayfair," Mark says, opening two glass bottles of beer in his rustic, expansive kitchen. The sound echoes under the tall ceiling.

"A girl on the train said it's good."

"A girl, eh? Didn't take you long." He hands me one bottle with a smirk. The dew has already formed on the outside; it's so cold. "I don't know. It's not my jam."

"How about dinner in Mayfair and head to Blues Kitchen for some live music after?" I suggest.

"Someone's been Googling," Mark says, raising his eyebrows. It's my best guess of where I might run into Nora. It's an American place, so perhaps she assumes I'll go there. Why do I have this urge to find her? What will happen if I do? I can't take her home only for the night. It's not what I want anymore. And I don't have time for more now with this new job.

I just want to see her.

I don't even have to talk to her.

"Fine, let's do it," he says after thinking. "I'll make a booking for us at Hakkasan. You like Cantonese?"

"Sure." I sip my beer and we saunter out to the patio. "This place is amazing, Mark. I'm assuming your company is doing well, then?"

"Yeah, I sold it a few years ago. Who knew fitness tech would become such a hit? Bought this house and a couple of others that I rent out. Reinvesting in small tech companies." He shrugs as if it's nothing. I'll need to Google his company again. I'm usually on top of what happens in the world of tech, but I've missed the news about the sale.

"Fuck. Congrats, man. What are you doing now? You said you were in the office?"

"I advise fellow entrepreneurs. Identify optimal solutions and help them navigate evolving tech and market needs." He takes a swig of his beer and shrugs again. "I didn't enjoy the management side of running a company. Prefer the tech aspect."

That's the lifestyle I want to get to. Do the most interesting jobs only. He's a few years ahead of me, but the future I want for myself seems even more realistic now. I have to nail this role, and it'll be within reach.

CHAPTER 9

NORA

My suitcase rattles behind me down the uneven street. After looking for the right number on a long street of identical homes, I finally find Dee's place.

It's a charming English brown-brick terraced house with green window frames. I'm glad this is it. The one three doors down has a broken toilet and bits of a mannequin in a cart up front where this one has pink rose bushes.

Dee greets me with a joyful squeal, jumping up and down. She's still in her sleepwear—an oversized Nirvana T-shirt and black shorts—revealing her toned, golden legs.

"You're here!" She makes a move to run out, but a quick look at her fluffy purple slippers tells me I'm doing the running. She stretches her arms out and wiggles them to hurry me up, her long black hair bouncing. I let go of my suitcase and sprint up the three steps to wrap my arms around her.

"Woah, hello muscles," I exclaim. I exaggeratedly paw her upper back and shoulders before I lean my cheek down on her forehead and squeeze her properly.

"Yup. You've got a gym buddy now." She squeezes me back as we sway. "Come, I've got cocktails."

"Ah, you know me so well."

I swing my suitcase over the step and into the narrow hallway, and roll it to the base of the blue carpeted staircase.

"Collette's upstairs—the landlady. She pops down from time to time. Mostly if she hears the cocktail shaker or smells popcorn."

"Sounds like a person after my own heart."

"Yeah. I usually leave these doors open for her when I'm home." Dee gestures to the double doors leading in to the living room.

I put my shoes under the wall mirror and look around at the many paintings around it. Dee follows my gaze.

"Colette painted all these."

They're fairly abstract, but I recognize a pink Eiffel Tower, and one that might be a face.

I turn to the lounge area. It's a feast for the eyes. There's a floor-to-ceiling shelf covering the back of the room. Trust an editor to have a wall of books. There's the occasional plant and trinket in between, and fairy lights draped across the top. A massive, green L-shaped couch stands in front of the bay windows.

"Wow, this is perfect, Dee." I walk around slowly, making sure I haven't missed a single detail of my new home. The white kitchen has a breakfast bar, and I spy the familiar ingredients for Dee's special Prosecco mojitos ready for my arrival.

***

"Cheers, my friend. Welcome home." Dee lifts her glass minutes later from her reclining chair on the patio.

"Cheers. Those words have never sounded better." I clink mine to hers. The warming rays of the late May sun caress my face as I relax back in my seat next to her. I breathe in the scent of late spring in London—mint from the mojito, dry grass, and the hint of burned skin as I'm part ginger and it's already been two minutes.

"Now, what the hell was your message about?" Dee asks with a smile. I tell her about Jake, what I've named 'the lap dance' and our journey in from the airport.

"Quite the start to your new life," Dee says with a grin.

"Tell me about it. And I don't know what possessed me on the train. I kept letting words fall out of my face. Every silly comment I was thinking came straight out." I stick a flat tongue out. "Bleh. Like that."

"That doesn't sound too abnormal for you."

"Maybe not to *you*, but I've known you for

nearly a decade. I rarely behave like my silly self with strangers. Must be my reinvigorated London-self."

"You keep saying 'silly' like that. *You*, my intelligent, funny, considerate, trustworthy friend, are not silly." Dee gives me her serious expression. "Unless you're doing it on purpose, of course," she adds quickly with a grin.

I scrunch my mouth up, embarrassed. Classic Norwegian; not able to receive a compliment. "Now you're the silly one."

She raises her eyebrows at me and sips her drink with a glint in her eye.

"You wouldn't believe the electricity between us, though. I've never been so turned on simply being near someone," I continue, to a snort from Dee. I hide my face in one hand, sipping my mojito with a straw from under it.

"Literally never?" she asks with what sounds like genuine curiosity. "What about that security guard you pulled with you into the student bar accessible toilet?"

"Hah. Oh, Mick. He was begging for it. Standing around in a uniform like that. It was just for kicks back then, though. I liked the adventure of it. But I don't think anyone got me proper *hot*." I grimace. "Not like today. Sheesh." I fan my face.

"Hm. No one in Norway lately either?"

"Nah. You'd know it. Casual sex lost its appeal many years ago. And I've told you all my dating stories."

"Indeed, you have. My voice note library is a treasure box of blackmail potential." She wiggles her eyebrows at me.

"Careful. I know where you live."

Dee chuckles. She sips her mojito with a smile still on her lips. I stare ahead into the small garden patch. Tiny insects dance on the tall grass, catching the light.

"Don't stress about meeting anyone right away. Enjoy London," Dee adds after a quiet spell.

I hum, thinking. The sun is warm on my face.

"I start work on Monday, so I might as well do the dating thing right away—use my new life momentum. If I'm ever to find Mr. Right, I need to keep looking. Not getting any younger." I stir my mint leaves, pretending it's no big deal.

"Pfft, you're still young. Take your time. There's always someone around here, so you're not alone, at least. And I find even the city itself to be a delightful companion. There's so much ..." She waves a hand, looking for the right word. "History. Art. Color. Food. Tons of personality."

I sigh and turn to her.

Her eyes are closed as she basks in the sunlight. She might be right. The one year I had here in London to complete my masters was the time of my life.

"Maybe," I say finally. "I wonder if Mr. America will enjoy London as much."

"Interesting segue." Dee smirks. "Can't get him

out of your mind?"

"He was so hot, Dee," I wail.

"Was he interesting? Kind?"

"Hmm. I can't say for sure. He traveled in Norway, so that's sort of interesting. He didn't say a lot. Either way, he was …" I mime broad shoulders and me drooling. Dee rolls her eyes at me.

"Isn't it the type of man you *explicitly* told me not to let you waste your time on?"

"Did I say that? You're extrapolating." I lean back again and sip my drink through the silicone straw, the final slurp making a noise.

"Ahem." Dee has her phone in her hand now. "I quote: 'going through and deleting old photos before starting my new life, and I realize how soul-sucking Martin and some of my dates were. Make sure I don't waste time on a heartless hottie ever again.'"

"That was ages ago."

"It was Tuesday."

I snort, and choose to ignore both her and Tuesday-Nora.

"I told him we're going out in Camden."

"Huh. Why Camden?"

"He said he's staying there. It's still fun, isn't it?"

"Bit much on a Friday. After I turned thirty, everything is." She grimaces. I know what she means. "If we go early, it might be more like the good old days." She pauses for thought. "All right.

Let's get this uninteresting hot American man out of your system."

"I think you mean *into* my system," I say, wiggling my eyebrows, receiving a snort and another eye-roll in response.

CHAPTER 10

NORA

We stand on the bridge over the canal, looking out over Camden Lock. I can't believe I'm back in London. I lean on the brick railing and sigh loudly. What a wonderful view. The sky is bright blue. The hanging birches framing the lock are a vibrant green. The graffiti on the surrounding walls is popping. It's like someone put a filter on the world and it's all enhanced.

The area's brimming with people; the sun drawing everyone out from their regular hiding places. Some are in blindingly white shirts with their sleeves rolled up, straight from the office. Others in sparkly tops and flowing hair, ready for the Friday night out. Dee and I are in the latter group this evening, and my royal blue floral romper suit matches the colorful surroundings.

"My gosh, I love this place," I say, pushing back my long curls that are being swept forward in the breeze.

"What?" Dee puts a hand to her ear.

"I love this place." I shout this time. She can't hear me over the cars and buses roaring on the rough roadway behind us and the buzz of voices coming from the lock. She points for us to go down into the market area.

We're met by a waft of barbecued meat, cinnamon churros, incense, cigarettes, curries, arepas, and perfumes. All scents dancing in the light breeze, hitting our noses at different times. I'm in heaven. These are the smells of my memories; of markets with friends, of sitting on a ledge with the sun in my eyes, of eating a falafel pitta and laughing so hard I have chickpea crumbs in my nose for hours. The scents of London.

***

Sitting by the window in one of the restaurants lining the market square, I eat my rosemary chips while looking out at a man and a woman closing the tarp on the fronts of their stalls. A couple of tourists with 'I heart London' caps saunter around, cameras at the ready, probably wondering what they just missed. Most people are now crowded on the other side of the lock where the sun still reaches.

"What's up with the cheesy grin?" Dee's loud voice startles me.

"Am I smiling? I enjoy being here."

"And you have some cheese right there." She points at the side of my mouth.

I tilt my head back and cackle. Of course I do.

"Where do you think your American buff would go out? What was his style?" Dee looks out over the market space as well, as if to find the answer there. "Hey, show me his Instagram."

"Only got his first name." I shrug. "Hmm. He looked kind of ... polished. Where do polished people go?"

"Mayfair. Soho. If you're equating polished with posh?"

I sigh. It's impossible to say. You can find any type anywhere in London, I recall from my university days. Which is one of my favorite things about this city.

"Why don't we focus on finding *you* a man instead? It's a bit of a stretch running into Jake, even though he's fairly large and I have a knack for bumping into people."

Dee clears her throat conspicuously.

I turn to her abruptly. "What! You've met someone?" There's no hiding the shock on my face or the guilt spreading on hers. "Why didn't you say anything earlier?" I playfully smack her thigh.

"I don't know." She bites her thumbnail.

"Come on. Tell me." I brush the salt off my hands, place them on my knees and turn toward her to show I'm all ears.

"I guess I'm still getting used to it being official. It's only been a couple of months. We were so back-and-forth in the past I didn't dare say it out loud before." She finally meets my eye. "It's Ajay. Still. Again."

I stifle a gasp and disguise it as a small *oh* instead.

Ajay Gupta. Dee's kryptonite.

How she used to fawn over him in university. If he was nearby, she'd drop everything.

"Oh, wow. Have you seen him loads since we graduated? You've not mentioned it." I hate how accusative I sound, but I share everything and thought she did too.

"Not for ages. I bumped into him at a party last year and we stayed in touch. There's been nothing to tell until now."

My surprise is obvious, but I try to shake off the frown that's formed on my face.

"He's grown up. I've grown up. It's different now," Dee adds.

"How's that?" I ask, making it higher pitched to make up for my tone earlier.

"He's invited me to his dad's birthday in three weeks. He holds my hand in public. It's definitely official this time. Not like before."

"Hmm. Okay, I'll admit that's different." I try to be supportive. I know I need to find a balance between saying exactly what I'm thinking and letting it be.

Dee nudges my knee. "Come on. Give him a chance. I am."

"Fine, but allow a friend to be skeptical of the man who—at one point—had broken your heart more times than he'd made you come." I raise my eyebrows at her. Ajay used to behave like Dee's boyfriend one day and show up at a party with another girl the next. Absolute asshattery.

"Pfft. He's rectified that. If you must know," Dee says into her wine glass, and a hint of pink forms in her golden cheeks.

"Nice. Ajay's learned some new tricks?"

"Oooh, yes. But I don't want to share details of our sex life now we're dating."

"Understood." I lift my glass to my lips and pause. "You're happy then?"

"I am."

I put the glass down again and turn to her, angling my head. "Do you love him? Or did you? I never heard you say it."

"It's a big word." She swivels her wine thoughtfully. "I'm not sure I loved him all those years ago. But it hurt like hell when he kept screwing me over, so maybe I did ... a bit." Dee turns away quickly, letting her hair fall as a curtain down the side of her face. "Maybe I do."

I sense her fear through her words and how she grips her wine glass tightly. He's got her heart in his hands and she's exposed. Or I'm projecting. Maybe I'm the one who's afraid. The memory of her large eyes filled with tears is fresh.

***

We check out a bar near the lock. The area is still bustling with a crowd of people, shiny from sweat and red-faced from the sun. Their eyes are heavy after hours of drinking. It's even louder than before, with everyone shouting rather than talking and speakers blaring music from all angles.

Dee goes inside to get drinks for us while I snatch a table outside overlooking the canal. A redheaded man in a disheveled shirt saunters over with his pint and a sideways smile. I should've known better than to sit alone like this.

"Hello, love." He has to speak loudly for me to hear him. His accent is northern, so calling me 'love' might be natural, rather than sleazy. I don't like it, regardless. I give him a close-lipped grimace and raised eyebrows as a greeting and turn away.

Take a hint.

He says something I can't make out and I shake my head and shrug. Instead of going away, he comes closer and speaks even louder, spit flying across the table.

"How's your day been?"

"Fine," I say.

"Wha'?" he bellows and leans closer. His ear and head well inside my personal space.

"No, thank you," I shout into his ear.

"No, I asked 'how's your day been?'"

I get up and make my way toward the bar,

meeting Dee in the doorway.

"Already?" she asks, nodding toward the guy. I roll my eyes and shake my head.

"Not my type. Let's go inside." I nod toward the bar area and accept the wine glass Dee's reaching out to me.

"He's not bad-looking."

"I refuse to let my happily ever after start with someone drunkenly spit-shouting at me."

Dee shrugs and turns back.

The noise level is equally bad inside. We stand at a high table and take turns shouting into each other's ears. We finish our wines fast. Once back outside—and far enough away to hear anything at a normal volume—my inner ear is still thumping and I feel my thirty-two years of age more than ever before.

When did London become so loud?

"How the hell do you meet someone in a bar when it's like that?" I'm still shouting. Dee laughs and hooks her arm in mine.

"You don't." Her naturally loud voice is clear over the noise of Camden High Street. "Everyone's on Crosspath these days."

"What's that? Some kind of drug?"

She stops dead in her tracks. "You don't know Crosspath? Have you been living under a rock back in Norway? It's the newest dating app!"

I shake my head.

"I tried Tinder once, but maybe Bergen is too small? After swiping past two colleagues and a friend of my brother, I deleted it."

Dee laughs, takes my arm and leads me down the street again. "Right, we're checking one more place for your American, and if we don't find him, we go home and I'll open up a new world for you."

I smile in response, happy she's eager to help me with my seemingly never-ending search for love.

The Blues Kitchen is, if possible, even louder. The sounds of trumpets and drums from the live band, along with heavy heat from warm bodies and food, hit us squarely in the face as we open the doors.

I'll need a couple of intense drinks to get into this groove, but I've lost the urge. It's been a long day. And even if Jake is in here tonight, I won't find him in this crowd.

CHAPTER 11

JAKE

The band is on fire. I stand along the wall, enjoying the sounds of trumpets and trombones blasting across the room. The accompanying bass drums send vibrations through me. Mark was right. This place is loud. But it's also amazing. As long as you're not trying to talk to anyone.

Mark's head is visible above most of the crowd as he makes his way back to me. He hands me an Old Fashioned before he steps aside and gestures to two glamorous girls.

Ah, crap.

"This is Anna and something. Lisa, I think." He has to speak loudly despite being so close his breath is on my ear. "This is Jake. A-me-ri-can," he shouts toward the girls, enunciating each syllable. They nod and smile in response. I clink their glasses and gesture that the band is great. Another nod.

They're gorgeous. At first glance. Bright

white teeth. Long eyelashes. I study Lisa or Something's face in the dim light. She's flawless. The spotlight from the stage moves across the crowd in intervals. It creates shadows across her face and lights other parts up. It makes her look like a doll. An increasingly creepy doll. Unblinking. Smiling.

She's not real. I don't know what I'm looking at.

"Are you okay?" Lisa or Something asks. My face must be revealing my thoughts. I rearrange my expression to a happy one and give her the thumbs up. Not a move I normally do, but it works when sound doesn't. She touches my upper arm and gives my biceps a light squeeze through my shirt. I feel weird. Awkward. If this was years ago, I wouldn't be out of my element here. But it's wrong for me now.

Mark leans in toward the other girl's ear. She laughs at whatever he says. His free hand hovers near her lower back. I glance at the girl in front of me. She's focused on the band now, bobbing her head.

They don't know me, though. I could follow Mark's lead. Get some much-needed release. Weirdly, jerking off in the shower seems more tempting.

My lungs are suddenly empty.

I need air.

I excuse myself to the girl and communicate to Mark that I'll be back before edging my way through a sweaty crowd to the more open restaurant area. Once out of the throng of people, I breathe deeply and let my shoulders drop.

What's going on? I'm having a great night with Mark. Have I been a hermit for so long I get a panic attack from being hit on? Ugh. Memories of Heather squeezing my biceps that same way flash across my mind.

If only I'd said no then.

In between the barbecue smell and alcohol fumes, a hint of sweet flowers meets my nose. Nora pops into my head and everything else disappears for a moment.

What's she doing there?

Twirling her hair and biting her lip. She's not reading a book, though. She's looking at me.

My brain is foggy and the intense noise level of this place makes it hard to think. I narrowly avoid crashing into the server on my way out. Once outside, I stop and take another deep breath, letting my head hang back as I stare up into the starless, pitch-black sky.

I sit down on the window ledge and lean my arms on my knees. It's been a long day, and three hectic months preparing for the move. It's crashing down on me now I'm finally here. I should go back to the house. Get some sleep. So far there's no sign of Nora and I hardly know what I'm looking for. She's probably not in a messy bun and cotton long-sleeve.

I rub my neck and groan to myself.

A loud laugh breaks my train of thought. I look up instinctively to find the source. The silhouette of two girls is clear against the streetlights. They're walking arm in arm, tilting their heads back, laughing. Sounds like they're having a good time.

I sigh and get up. Mark's here and not in the comfort of Mayfair because of me. It'd be a dick move to run away now on our first night out.

The noise and smells from inside hit me like a truck when I open the door. I'll need another strong drink to cope and be a good sport, but will have to come up with a nice way to let Lisa or Something down. I don't want her.

CHAPTER 12

NORA

No. No. Oh gosh. Double no.

I keep swiping. It's hard to stop. I should go to sleep. It's late and I've been up since dawn traveling.

Dee went to bed after showing me Crosspath and I'm curled up under the quilt of my new bed. In my new home. Looking for Mr. Right.

This dating app allows you to choose between the standard photo swipe, or swiping on profile alone; their picture only available *after* matching.

I tried the profile-first setting for a while, but I'm surprised how much looks matter. I'm ashamed, despite not being super picky when it comes to it. Or am I? No, they had terrible profiles too.

Oh, here's a nice-looking one. Preston. Wide smile, light brown hair.

I swipe right. It's a match. *Yikes!*

I open his profile.

Chartered Accountant. Wow, he's got a lot of hobbies. Piano, guitar, running, art. I'm a complete slacker in comparison. No chance he'll find me very interesting. But I can improve. What to write?

Me: Hello :)

***

"*My* first memory of a man was at the end of World War Two. I had just turned ten then." Colette grasps her whiskey glass with a wrinkled hand. It's steady, and her voice doesn't waver, despite her many years. And her many whiskeys. "We celebrated the end of the war with bonfires up on the hill overlooking Sheffield."

Dee and I lean forward, eager to hear more.

"It was a delightful May evening. Gordon, a boy from our street, he must have been twelve then, took my hands, and we twirled and twirled and fell over on the grass. I kissed his cheek. I remember it like it was yesterday. His face was wet and salty from sweat and tears of joy. He was the most handsome boy I'd seen." She looks at us with her pale blue hooded eyes and chuckles.

We remain silent, willing her to continue.

If you'd told me a few months ago I'd spend a London Saturday night at home, listening to an old lady, I'd say you were batshit. But there's nowhere else I'd rather be. Colette's stories are wonderful and plentiful.

"By the time I was ready to court, it was the fifties. A boy asked me out on a date. It was different back then. He had to ask my father for permission. None of this." She gestures to the phones on the table and puts her empty glass down.

Dee gets up. "Espresso martinis?" she asks to a united *Yes* from me and Colette.

"I bet you had men lining up for miles to date you," I say, not finished with Colette's reminiscing. I imagine her young. Blond waves and bangs. She has that classically beautiful face, touched by time and a long life lived well. She has short hair now—white and stylish. It suits her square chin.

"Hold on, shaking commencing," Dee shouts from the kitchen before making a heck of a ruckus with the metal and glass cocktail shaker. Once finished, I catch Colette's eye and raise my eyebrows.

"I suppose I could choose, but the man had to ask. I liked this one, so I'm glad he did." She smiles wistfully.

"How did you meet him?" Dee asks from the kitchen while pouring the espresso martinis into three coupe glasses.

"I first met him when my friends and I went out dancing. The bop was the big thing. Rock and roll was new here then. Ah, the excitement."

"Oooh," Dee and I chime in unison.

"But our date was at the cinema."

She chortles and accepts the drink handed to her, full to the brim with dark, gorgeous liquid and a beige fluffy layer on top. She raises it carefully to her mouth so as not to spill and takes a sip. The drink leaves a line of foam on her upper lip.

"He had to look after his little brother that day. We bribed him to sit in the front so we could kiss in the back." She giggles and wipes her coffee mustache with her free hand.

"What happened next?" I ask and sip my drink.

"I never thought my first man would be the one I'd end up with, but he was perfect for me. We were going steady for a while and then we got married."

She pauses to drink her martini.

"He died when I was in my early fifties," Colette continues. Dee and I break into a sigh that she waves off. "I've been single and thriving almost as long as you've been alive, and probably had more men than you can count." She sits upright. "So, show me that *app* and let me have a look at those boys you've found." She leans forward and grabs my phone. With an unsure finger and some help from Dee, she navigates into Crosspath and flicks through my findings. Correction: finding. Singular.

"He's a handsome chap," Colette says, peering down her nose at the phone. "Can you only talk to one at a time?"

"Let me see." Dee takes the phone from her. "Nora. He's a hunk. And from looking at the profile, you didn't choose him based on that. Accountant who plays the piano and listens to jazz?"

"Well, I want someone with proper hobbies. Let him rub off on me. I literally had nothing to put on my profile. Exercising and dancing to YouTube videos don't count as hobbies, do they? Who's going to choose me based on that?"

"Did you not want to try out the new setting? Seeing the profile first?"

"I already did."

"And?"

"I matched with two guys."

"Where are they?" She's getting impatient.

"I deleted them. Not my cup of tea."

"Seriously? Despite your strong preference for broad shoulders, I've never known you as picky. You've dated all kinds of men over the years."

"Yes. But." I wave a finger to show I'm about to make a point. "One was missing a tooth. The other was really, *really* short." I emphasize my point, holding up my index finger and thumb.

"That's a bit judgmental. They can't help it."

"I guess I'm shallow. Sue me. It's hard when it's right there in your face." I pout, knowing how I sound. "It's not like the profiles were everything I was looking for, either. I appreciate I'll need to compromise to find Mr. Right, but it's not great to start like *that*."

"Let me help. I'll swipe on some I think you'll like."

I grumble. "Colette, please check them, too. Something tells me you have an eye for quality men."

They huddle over my phone, pointing and giggling. I finish my martini and frown at them over the rim of my glass. Not being in control is hard, but I don't have to commit to whomever they find, so what's the harm?

"What're you looking for in a man, duck?" Colette asks in a soft voice, peering over my phone at me.

"I hardly know, to be honest. A man with cool hobbies so we can have fun together? Ambitious but not only working? Likes food, but is healthy. Taller than me. Someone I can fall in love and live happily ever after with. Simple." I grin.

"A sense of humor? Someone who you can be yourself with?" Colette adds with raised eyebrows.

"Of course. Hard to tell from a profile, though, isn't it?"

"Just take your time, Nora. You won't fall in love on the first date," Dee adds while swiping.

I don't want to say anything because she's probably projecting. It's taken Ajay years to be with her officially and he's not said he's in love yet. I'm a firm believer in my intuition. I might not crush on the guy instantly, but if there's no spark right away, I'm certain I won't find it later.

That might be why I've never been properly in love; I always find a reason not to see them again. *Or* I've simply not met the right one yet.

"Here's a few. You've already got a message from one." Dee hands the phone back to me and a ripple of excitement shoots through me.

"Hmm. A self-proclaimed geek who loves a good cocktail and a run. Interesting combo." I open the photo and find a blond man with a playful expression and hypnotic hazel eyes. "Oooh. Hello, Mark."

CHAPTER 13

JAKE

"Awesome, that must be it." I point up ahead at the building with an intricate full-wall mural of a person in a colorful headdress, and turn back to see Mark glancing up from his phone. He lights up when the bar and people on the grass across the canal come into view. They're drinking, laughing, and basking in the sun, which is soon high in the sky.

"How did you hear about this place?" Mark asks as we enter the building and take it all in. There are pink umbrellas over the bar, a wall of yellow flowers, and a mannequin with a green lampshade for a head in the far corner.

"Google. Supposed to be good for Sunday brunch," I say. I searched for where the locals go and Hackney Wick came up in an article about the most vibrant neighborhoods of London. I may also have recognized the name from what Nora said. She lives somewhere nearby. Not sure what reality I live in, where I think we'll just bump into each other again in this massive city, but it doesn't hurt to increase the odds. Canal-side in 'the Wick' is supposed to be *the* place to go for a lazy Sunday.

"What can I get you?" Mark leans on the bar, looking at the selection, and frowns. No cocktails? I learned from our Saturday night out he likes his elaborate drinks.

"Just a club soda for me. Two nights in a row is enough for me these days. And I'm going to my sister's for dinner."

Mark chuckles. "Right. A soda water and an IPA, please," he says to the bearded bartender. "And the food menus."

We sip our cold drinks in silence, sitting on wooden benches on the balcony overlooking the canal. Red and green bunting sway in the breeze overhead.

Mark gets up to go to the restroom and I stare out at the world. The grass across the canal is bright green, and the sky is a strong blue. It's a perfect day. This is a magnificent spot. A ping from Mark's phone makes me turn automatically. His lock-screen lights up with a notification from an app I don't recognize. It's the word on the screen that makes me pause—a lizard brain reaction.

Crosspath: **Nora**

What the fuck?

Mark comes back, and the lizard is still in

control, effectively triggering my fight reflex.

"What's this?" I hold up his phone and he furrows his brow, probably at my rude tone, but bends down to see what I'm referring to.

"Crosspath." He takes his phone back, his eyes searching my face. "It's a dating app." He sits down. "Why are you asking?"

"I've heard of the app, of course. But the name that popped up. Nora. Is she new?"

"Yes, we just matched last night. She's said as much as 'hello' so far."

"Can you show me the photo?" I'm still gruff and I curse myself. Mark's not in the wrong, and Nora is a common name.

"Here." He holds his phone up and the adrenaline rushing through me pools in my stomach.

It's her.

Green sparkling eyes, freckles, large curly hair, broad smile. She's fucking stunning.

I can't say why it bothers me, but I don't want him to talk to her. Definitely not date her.

"Do you know her?" Mark asks, and I look up from the photo to catch his eye. Would he care if I told him the truth? It's not like I have any claim to her.

Nothing happened.

A whole lot of …

No. Not nothing. Definitely something. Something happened to *me*, at least.

It's like my heart has been beating quietly for

so long I forgot it was there. Since I sat down in the airport on Friday, it's been racing off and on. My body has reheated after years in cryosleep. It's probably because our encounter on the plane is the closest I've been to a woman in a long time.

Maybe that's why I want to see her again so badly. Check if it's me. Is it time to forgive myself and open up again? It didn't feel like that in the bar. So is it only Nora or simply the abnormal transit situation?

"Kind of," I finally answer and stir the ice of my club soda with the sprig of rosemary they stuck in there to make it more exciting. "We met on my way here. Had a bit of a ... thing, I guess."

"Is she the girl from the train? What a small world."

"Yeah."

Mark sits still with his phone in his hand. He's watching me. Should I tell him not to see her?

"I can delete her. If it matters to you," Mark says calmly. Ugh, he's so nice.

Fuck.

I don't have time for dating now, regardless of how I feel. I'm about to travel to see my parents. Find an apartment. Start my new job. But I don't want him to either. The thought of him taking her home, stroking those arms, kissing those pink lips. Assuming he'd get that far. After this weekend, I have the impression he gets whomever he wants.

"Yeah. Thanks." I run a hand through my hair

and rub my neck. "Why are you even on this app? You have women practically waiting outside your door."

Mark shrugs. "I've set the app to show me based on profile first, so I know they have something in common with me when they match. Makes a change from the bar scene."

I finish my drink and glance at the phone in his hands, taking a softer tone now to match his. "You'll skip her?"

"No worries, mate. I'll delete her now," he says, his thumb moving across the screen.

"Wait." I hold a hand up.

What if never find her?

"I didn't get her number. Can you … leave her there?"

***

I follow the curved street down. Each house looks like the next—columned awnings, bay windows on the side—except they're in different pastel colors. It's like a cute movie. I'm half expecting that English guy Hugh-whatever to open a door and dance down the street. I find the one she described and knock, heat rising in me. Fuck, my palms are sweating. What if this all goes to hell like the last time we spoke?

The green door opens and there she is.

"Hey, sis."

Her face breaks into a pained smile and tears

pop from her eyes as she flings herself onto me, wrapping her arms around my torso. I'm taken aback, but hug her tightly.

"Bloody hell, Jake. I've missed you." She's sob-laughing loudly into my chest, her accent clearly tilting toward British English now. "I'm sorry, I'm full of breastfeeding hormones and everything makes me cry so hard." She breathes in through her nose to compose herself as she pulls back, wiping her wet cheeks. "Come in. Meet your niece."

The unmistakable smell of our mom's chicken curry greets me as I enter the narrow hallway.

"How do you have time to cook like this with a newborn?" I say with a low voice as I follow Sage into the vast living room and open kitchen area, assuming the quiet of the house means the baby's asleep. "Not that I'm surprised—you never could sit still."

"She sleeps a lot. I put everything in the slow cooker these days." Sage grins and gestures to the bassinet standing by the side of the couch. "She's in there. Want some water or tea before dinner? Ryan will be back in an hour."

"Water's fine, thanks," I answer as I sneak up next to the bassinet and take in the sight of the incredibly small shape. Her teeny belly moves up and down. Sage returns with two glasses of water in her hands.

"She's beautiful. Looks like Ryan, actually. A beautiful wrinkly pink Ryan. Is it weird to say that? She has your eyes."

"Her eyes are closed."

I turn and beam at my sister, who still looks like she's holding back tears.

"I can tell, anyway. She's got our big, round brown eyes. What's her name?"

"Undecided."

"Hello, Undecided," I whisper to the sleeping bundle, receiving a snort from my sister. Undecided's tiny baby breath is just audible and makes my heart swell. "I'm your uncle and will carry you around a lot and make you watch Star Wars before you're eight."

"In your dreams," my sister whispers.

"Don't listen to her, she's gone to the dark side," I say and Sage huffs and nods her head for me to join her.

We sit down on the couches by the large bay window. Sage curls her legs up under her and I sink down on the opposite couch, facing her. The leafy tree in the front yard shields us from curious eyes of passers-by.

"If I'd known you wouldn't slam the door in my face, I would've come as soon as the borders opened." I study her as I say it. She seems genuinely happy to see me, so this could be it. I finally get to say what I should've, years ago.

Don't fuck it up again, Jake. No excuses.

"You're lucky I'm drunk with prolactin and oxytocin," she says with a sideways smile and leans forward to grab her water. I fidget with my hands in my lap, looking at my cuticles.

"Will you forgive me?"

"Forgive you? For what? Being an asshole or not calling me for over three years?" she asks, pressing her lips together.

"You didn't call me either," I say calmly; careful not to ruffle her feathers, but unwilling to take the blame for the near radio silence.

"I gave you plenty of opportunities to talk." She pauses for a beat, then groans and runs a hand over her smooth hair, sliding it down the long dark brown ponytail as she breathes out loudly. Even as a new mom, she looks impeccable. "No. You're right. It was easy to leave it to you. I was building the firm. The years flew past. And I guess I wanted to see if you were going to try harder to show you were sorry."

"I was sorry. I *am* sorry. That's why I stayed away. That and work. I still feel like shit. Ashamed, embarrassed ... You name it." I scoff at myself. Even though I didn't hurt her directly, she took offense. She was livid. Said she expected better of me. I suppose I did too.

Sage lets out a long sigh and shifts forward on the couch to look me in the eye. "As much as I enjoy seeing men suffer when they do something wrong, you're my little brother, and you're a good guy. You need to get over it and forgive yourself, too."

I hum, still fidgeting with my fingers.

"How is she?"

"Heather's fine, Jake." Sage sits back, sitting crisscross on the deep white couch. "She's a capable woman who found a new job. She has a boyfriend too. You're probably the one worse off."

"How would you know how I am?" I frown as I grab my glass. I never thought of it as worse off. I kept my HercuSoft job, my colleagues, and friends. Got a slap on the wrist for unprofessional conduct. My current celibacy is a choice.

"I've been cyberstalking you, and asked Mom for news. Don't look so surprised. Despite you going incommunicado, I still cared."

A storm of emotion brews in me, and I do my best to hide it. *I* was incommunicado? *She* was avoiding *me*. Could we have made up a long time ago?

"You have *two* posts on Insta in the last few years. Your new home gym and a bowl of sludge," she adds.

"That was homemade parippu. Mom's recipe," I say.

She raises her eyebrows in surprise and nods. "Still. You don't seem to have a life outside work and the gym. Mom is worried, by the way. She keeps asking me how you are. She's over the moon you're making a change. I mean, you were never gregarious, but you didn't use to be such a loner. Have you even been out with a woman since?"

Undecided squirms in the bassinet and we go quiet.

Have I not had a life? Work, exercise, the occasional night out with the guys. Loner? Maybe compared to in my twenties.

"How's her sister?"

"Great. We're still good friends. No drama. You didn't answer my question."

"If I've been on a date?" I ask, stalling. I've not talked about this with anyone. I decide honesty is the best way forward if I want to rebuild our relationship. "No. I've sworn off women for a while. I kept fucking up."

"Seriously? Heather was over three years ago. You must be going insane." She raises her eyebrows and stifles a giggle.

"Jesus, Sage." I laugh and look away. Not talking about my sex life with my sister.

"What do you mean, you *kept* fucking up? What happened?"

I sigh. "I don't have *a single* positive memory of the last ones I dated. There was one I thought I liked, but she was sleeping with other men and I simply didn't care. Didn't even flinch when she told me. What a waste of time. Somehow she still got upset I had been 'stringing her along'. I don't know. Maybe I did it all wrong."

I'm saying it all out loud. It feels so good to talk to someone finally. Hear the words make sense as I say them.

"With the next woman, we had a pregnancy

scare after dating for a couple of months. Only a scare. But we both freaked out and realized we didn't want to be together and definitely not have a child together. It was my fault. Could've been a disaster for her. And then Heather …" I groan and run a hand through my hair, rubbing my neck. "Let's just say I've made too many bad decisions, but I don't anymore."

"Because you're avoiding *all* women?"

I shrug and decide not to tell her about my last date. It could sound like I'm looking for pity. The image of my yawning dinner companion is fresh in mind. Starters hadn't even arrived yet, and I already bored her. Do I only have work to talk about? Was I ever very interesting?

"Aren't you lonely? Don't you want to share your days with someone?"

"I'm fine." I pick at my cuticles. Time flies. Life happens. I haven't stopped to consider whether I'd need to share it with someone.

"I can't remember you ever dating *one* person longer than a few months. Surely it's not all down to bad decision-making. Tell me I don't have the wrong impression of you. You were never a player, right? Heather wasn't one of countless young women?"

"No, can't believe you have to ask that."

"You're right, sorry. I know, really. But it's good to hear you confirm it." She holds a hand up.

"Things just never stuck. People like what they see, then they get bored with me."

"Bullshit. I've known you my whole life and you are *not* boring. You haven't found the right one, is all. Promise me if you meet someone you like, you don't swear her off immediately?"

I blow air out, puffing up my cheeks, and nod to please her. Nora's face appears in my mind, but I'll get over that soon enough. Once I busy myself with apartment hunting and work, I'll be back to normal.

"Sis." Getting to the crux of it. "Is this us getting back to how we were? I've missed you."

"Sounds like you're done taking advantage of young, innocent engineers, so I think we're good. You've repented." She sips her water. The glint in her eye over the rim of the tall glass adds a touch of playfulness to the heavy words.

"I didn't take *advantage* ..."

Her eyes narrow. Damn, why did I have to go there?

"Let's not do this again." Her voice is strict now. Lawyer voice. "You held a position of seniority over her—both in terms of title and a substantial age difference. She was twenty-*four*, Jake. You were her boss's boss." I can't stand that look of disgust flashing across her face. I suppose it won't help mending our relationship to add that she wasn't all innocent. If Sage can forgive me for fucking up her friend's little sister's HercuSoft dream, I should be okay with it being this way.

CHAPTER 14

NORA

I get to the office building and take the elevator to the sixth floor. Rosie, the HR manager I've been speaking to on video calls from Norway, greets me with her arms outstretched. She shakes my hand with both of hers so vigorously it makes her short, black curls bounce.

"Welcome to Upturns."

She looks up at me with round blue eyes and a wide grin. The red lipstick makes her skin and teeth look extra white.

It's my first day at work *and* I have a date later; this might just become the Monday to redeem all regular, rough Mondays.

"Follow me. Let's breeze through first and I'll introduce you properly to your team afterwards. Some are away, visiting clients." She waves around in the general direction of the corner section. "We're nearly fifty now. Growing steadily."

They've decorated the space with green

plants, contrasting the standard white walls and gray carpet. The London Eye—the iconic Ferris wheel—and river Thames dominate the view from the floor-to-ceiling windows. It's spectacular.

The consultants look immersed in their work —eyes glued to the screens, headphones on. My new manager, Sean, waves. The bright ceiling light reflects on his shiny, balding head as he moves.

The next part of the office is packed with people of all shapes and sizes. Rosie points at them quickly as she names the teams; development, support, and IT. They sit hunched over their keyboards, heads bent low. The tapping sound of fingers on keys is a constant buzz.

"That's Manuel Garcia's office there, the CEO and founder. He'll be back later today. Make sure you say hi. He's elated to have you on board directly from a client."

"Oh wow, sure," I respond and she continues.

"That's mine, door always open. And that's Howard's office there. He's the business development side of things. Contracts and negotiations. Anything Manuel hates doing." She cackles to herself. "He's out for the week."

All the offices are large, with glass walls and wide desks facing outwards around an area set up with a whiteboard, couches, and colorful ottomans. Looks like a casual meeting space.

"And this one?" I ask and point at the last office she didn't mention. It looks empty. No plants or pictures like the others.

"Ah, that's for our new—"

A petite woman with olive skin and a brown pixie cut shows up next to us, poking Rosie on the arm.

"Rosie, sorry to interrupt. Can we move our meeting? I need to go. Client issues." The words fly out of her mouth with a hint of an Italian accent.

"No worries. Say hi, first. Nora has finally joined us from NordInvest. Nora, this is Sara. She's been with us almost since the beginning, so you may have crossed paths."

"Of course, Nora, lovely to meet you. I've been on the other end of your emails."

I shake her tiny hand.

"Nice to put a face to a name." I keep it short, sensing her urgency.

"We'll catch up later. *Ciao*." She walks off with a wave.

"Anyway," Rosie says, angling back to look at me with a huge grin on her face. "What was I saying? Yes, we have a few new starters joining in two weeks."

I grin back, eager to get into it.

"That's it. Let's get your new consultant team to join us in the kitchen for some pastries! And Nora—" She lowers her voice. "Take it easy today. It'll get busy quickly. I heard they need you at

Zyclon right away and it might be a hard one." She gives me a reassuring pat. They're a similar client to my old company. What's so hard about it?

CHAPTER 15

NORA

I'm meeting Preston at a wine bar near the office. It's a cramped and dark place, so I'm happy to find a table outside in the courtyard.

I had a short first day—mainly spent eating pastries, drinking coffee, looking over shoulders, and waiting for my laptop to be set up. I spent the last hour walking around the area, seeing sights and killing time.

Now my feet hurt, I'm a little sweaty, and very hungry.

While waiting for Preston, I get a bowl of olives and red wine. I let my gaze glide across the other patrons, not looking at anything in particular. The wine is acidic, but tasty, and a cherry flavor fills my mouth.

There's that gnawing in my stomach I get before a date. All the worries. Will I be able to relax and be myself? Will he like me if I do?

A string of memories from dates gone bad flash before my eyes. Frowns. Awkward laughs.

Heavy silences. Feeling foolish. Saying the wrong thing. Eating too much or too fast.

Gah. I hate dates!

And what if he's my Mr. Right, but I'm not what he's looking for? Can I handle being hurt like that? Not wanted?

I need something to do. These thoughts are going nowhere useful. I open Crosspath to reread Preston's profile and check his photo again.

Preston, 33, Chartered Accountant.
The adventure of life is to learn. The purpose of life is to grow. The nature of life is to change. - William Arthur Ward

Music - listen to John Coltrane, play Beethoven, or possibly one day Kaikhosru Sorabji's 'Opus Clavicembalisticum' :P
Art - paint some, see some. Love David Hockney
Food - oysters in a restaurant, roll sushi at home
Health - my third marathon coming up!

Mine is pointless in comparison. He obviously matched me based on my photo.

Nora, 32, Senior Consultant
Wine a little, laugh a lot
Everything is better with cheese
Alt-rock and synth pop

That's it. What else do I write? What do I want another person to read and find interesting? It's not exactly impressive that I can almost play 'Sheena is a Punk Rocker' on the ukulele. Or that I follow the steps of an ultra-beginners tap dance tutorial on YouTube nearly without mistakes, but with plenty of cursing. What would that teach them about me, anyway?

I sit, musing, with my phone in my hand, when Preston suddenly stands in front of me. He looks like a shiny ad for blue suits and leather satchels. He removes his pilot glasses, revealing blue eyes with tiny pupils adjusting to the light.

"Nora?" He waits for me to nod and stretches out a hand. "Preston. Nice to meet you."

It's soft. I study him as he pulls the tall chair out from under the table and sits. His movements are smooth and swift. He smells like fabric softener and I'm suddenly extremely aware of my own salty scent.

"Am I late?" He gestures to the remnants of olives and nearly empty glass of wine.

"No, I was early. Went for a walk and got hungry."

"Nice day for it. Top-up?" He glides off the chair at my nod, strides across the area, and bends his head, elegantly swooping through the small door to the bar.

We only exchanged a couple of messages on Crosspath before this. I hate texting strangers. Nobody can convey their sense of humor or personality over text—it's a complete waste of energy.

"How do you find time for all these hobbies of yours?" I ask, genuinely curious, when he's back in his seat.

"Well." He huffs into his wine glass and sets it down instead of taking a sip; apparently his response can't wait. "I don't do them all at once."

His wide grin shows off his perfectly white teeth. "Actually." He shifts in his chair as if to get comfortable for a long conversation. "Over the last decade or so, I've found one or two things a year I want to learn and I focus on that. I do a course, I define a fixed goal, and then I set out to accomplish that goal." He gesticulates a lot, his hands chopping the side of the table.

"Right." As if to counter his movements, I keep my hands in my lap. "What was your painting goal, for example? Learn a certain technique?"

He chuckles softly, as if my suggestion was silly. Maybe it was. What do I know?

"For each new skill, I have a *proper* goal, something with stakes. I booked myself in for seven pieces at an art exhibition via a friend. I had to learn to paint—acrylic painting, of course, it's *very* difficult for beginners—and make a collection. All within six months."

I take a slow sip of wine. Sounds dreadful to me.

"My piano goal was to play 'the Flight of the Bumblebee' for an audience." He puts a hand on the stem of his glass, getting ready to pick it up.

"Hm." I swivel my wine. Keen to keep the conversation on him, as I have little to add. "Do you enjoy these activities that you do? Painting, playing the piano—"

"And guitar," he interjects, again interrupting his wine from making it into his mouth.

"—and guitar," I repeat.

"I enjoy accomplishing something. Learning new skills."

He's annoying me, and I'm not entirely sure why. Is it because he makes me feel unaccomplished and wayward in my approach? Or because I think there ought to be a level of emotion and joy in doing things, and he seems to lack this. He's a collector of skills. Should one not take some pleasure in the *journey* of learning?

"What about you?"

Damn, I was quiet for too long. Now I have to perform. He swivels his wine, sniffs it, and finally takes a sip. Haughtily. I bet he's been to a sommelier course and knows everything about all wines.

"Oh." I realize I'm staring and shift my gaze to my glass. "I dabble in this and that." I sit up, realizing I've been slouching.

"Dabble?" He cocks his head and looks at me.

"Yeah, doing a bit—"

"Oh, I know the word," he says with a smirk. "But I find people use it when it means they're not *really* into whatever they're dabbling in. Give me an example of something you do."

I'm stunted. I stare at him open-mouthed for a moment while he sips his wine again. Annoyed he potentially has a point, and flabbergasted at the abruptness.

"I do kettlebell exercises. Run," I say finally, thrilled I came up with something true. I stuff an olive in my mouth.

"Marvelous. Where do you run? What's your PB for 5k?"

My what for what?

"I run in the park … to music. I love it," I say while chewing my olive.

"Ever done a marathon?" he asks. I shake my head. "Half-marathon?"

"Did a *movie*-marathon more than once. Watched eleven Star Wars movies in one weekend."

He sends me a quizzical look over the rim of his glass.

"And the Lord of the Rings." I point at him with an olive. "Extended version. Now that's a hell of a marathon."

He sips his wine quietly while I pop the olive in my mouth. My movie accomplishments are apparently not worthy of a response.

"And I'm learning Spanish," I add and swivel my wine the way he did, but I go straight for the sip.

"Aaah. *¿y como te va con eso?"* he asks. Then he smirks as I sit here, opening and closing my mouth like a goldfish. *"Por tu expresión supongo que no muy bien."*

Show-off.

***

I leave the bar with a small wet patch on my cheek from where he kissed me. It feels cool as it dries in the breeze. Watching him walk down the street is a relief. His backside looks better, mainly because it means I don't have to listen to his front side anymore. I drag my feet toward the tube station, with my dignity shattered and a conviction that I'm lazy and utterly useless. How will an intelligent, interesting man ever find me intriguing?

I slump down in a seat on the train.

It turned out Preston ordered sharing platters when at the bar, and I got stuck with him for an excruciating three hours. The conversation continued in much the same way as it started. Him asking about things I want to learn and about my approach. And me babbling, stuttering and, in the end, grunting responses, getting caught in my attempted embellishments because, of course, he knows everything.

I argued that at least I enjoy the activity itself, whatever it may be. Playing the ukulele. Dancing around. This made him scoff, for the umpteenth time, and he said I would enjoy it more if I was better at it. If I learned the technique. Honed my skills. He got wired about signing me up for ukulele classes, and a concert at the end of the year. I've never run away from a date before, but it was close today.

My phone vibrates as I have reception again, the District Line entering overground tracks.

Preston: Thanks for a lovely date. If you'll let me, I can help hold you accountable. Let's play some ukulele! Here's a link to a

—

I close my eyes and put my phone away. I need Dee and Colette.

***

When I get home, I find Dee is at Ajay's, so I walk up the stairs and carefully knock on Colette's door, hoping I won't wake her if she's sleeping. She wrenches the door open before I can put my hand down.

"Why are you creeping around like that outside an old lady's door?" She cackles. "Come in, come in. Tell me what's going on." She waves her hand for me to follow. There's a slight hobble to her gait, but she's quick in her movements.

"Night cap?" she asks, standing in front of a little bar cart by the kitchen.

"Sure, thank you," I respond and plop down on the couch, unaware of how deep and soft it is. It swallows me whole. As I try to wriggle my way back up from my velvet sinkhole, Colette turns back with two tumblers and laughs at the sight of me. She sets them down and gives me a hand, rescuing me from certain couch death.

"Should've warned you about this old thing. If I ever go missing, this is the first place to look."

I perch on the edge instead as she hands me the glass. Whiskey? The peaty smell is powerful and welcoming, confirming my suspicion.

"Tell me, what brings you here? Weren't you

going out with that chap this evening?" Colette leans back in a chair opposite me.

I tell her about the date and she nods along, tutting and humphing in between. I brush the fading blue fabric in a circle next to me on the couch as I speak.

"What do you think? Am I boring for not having these hobbies and skills? Should we not just enjoy what we're doing? Do we have to be *good* at everything?"

"Hmm," she says, tilting her head side to side. "You're definitely not boring, duck. You need to find a man who complements you. Same outlook, but doesn't have to be the same interests. Preston sounds very wrong for you, but he'll be great for someone who wants to be encouraged like that."

"I guess." I thought I wanted to be encouraged. Motivated. To be with someone better than me who could improve me. But he made me feel crap.

"As for whether you need to be *good* at a hobby …" She blows out air. "It all depends on *why* you're doing it. It sounds to me this young man has certain goals. Your reasons may be different. Like you said, you run because you enjoy it and he runs to be fast." She stops for a beat and sips her drink.

"Personally," she continues, "with my painting, for instance, I take pleasure in the journey. And in conveying my vision, my emotions ... in evoking something in myself, or others."

I nod along vigorously. This is what I mean.

"However, this became easier as I learned the right techniques. My first paintings were a complete mess and hardly what I meant for them to look like. There's a painting of a nude downstairs that looks like the Eiffel Tower!"

I snort into my whiskey.

"I can't imagine painting anything if the goal is simply to finish it."

"Exactly." It's a relief to have someone make sense. She's put into words the thoughts that were jumbled up in my brain and I couldn't put it together.

"Well. I want to tap dance. But I overthink the steps and don't have any rhythm. Did a tutorial a gazillion times but I still can't get it right." I scoff at myself.

"Why tap dancing?"

"It looks fun. In musicals." I shrug, picturing Gene Kelly dancing and singing in the rain.

"They probably practiced quite a bit."

"It doesn't have to be tap dancing. I don't know how to dance at all. I just flap about when I'm at home and thinking it'd be better if I had some proper moves to do."

"If you want to learn, learn. Whatever it is. But remember why you're doing it. If you want to dance to have fun, make sure you focus on that."

"I suppose it's a goal in itself. Pleasure. Joy.

Probably not a Preston-approved one, but I shouldn't care about others' opinions, right?" I'm feeling wiser simply sitting here with her.

"Right. You do you, as they say. Don't start a hobby because you try to impress some man. Hey, are you familiar with the kitchen dance?"

"No?"

"It could be our thing—me and my daughter. We would dance in the kitchen when cooking or eating at the breakfast bar. Happens still, on occasion. We flail, kick, twirl, and laugh." She smiles wistfully. "Dance as if no one is watching, that chap Mark Twain said." Colette raises her glass to me.

"That's a nice saying." I clink hers with mine and empty it. The alcohol burns my throat on the way down, leaving a warm, comforting sensation in my stomach. "Where's your daughter now?"

"She's in Guernsey with her husband. He's retired and their kids are abroad. Spread all over, all three of them." She gets up from her chair and takes my empty glass from my hand. "Another one?"

"Ah, no thank you. I have work in the morning. Thanks again, Colette. I needed the reassurance."

I look forward to my morning run. A run I will enjoy simply for the sake of it. But I might give tap dancing a proper go. Surely they have actual classes here in London. I owe it to myself to try.

It's like with my dating, try different dances and I'll eventually find the right one. Once I've settled into this new 'hard' client I'll squeeze it into my wonderfully busy London schedule.

CHAPTER 16

NORA

"What's your poison?" Dave, the IT manager, booms across the group. He's a tall and solidly built man with black hair and an end-of-the-week beard.

"White wine, please." I learned from the first round that one does *not* specify the wine or level of dryness when one is not paying. I contemplate doing a round only to avoid getting the sweet Pinot Gris, but a round for over ten people is a bit much to pay for a slightly less shitty wine. I keep my musings to myself; I'm here to socialize with my new colleagues. Best not to start it off by trashing their favorite wine.

The guys opposite me erupt into a cheer. "Hey, look who it is. Just in time for the next round." Dave's voice travels across the commotion and I turn to see who he's talking to.

It's a tall man with sleek golden blond hair and a suntanned, pointed face. He must be Howard, the business development guy who's been out all week. The other consultants have said it's not common for him to be out that long. There are whispers of him having been abroad, and of big new clients.

"The prodigal son returns." Manuel gives him a hug. "Looking forward to our catch up later. I got your email." He raises his eyebrows conspiratorially and gets a pat on the shoulder in return.

"You bet." Howard turns to Dave and points at him. "Beer, please," he says and inevitably walks into the circle. He points at me now, with two stupid finger guns. Pulls the thumb triggers. "You're new." He shuffles Sara over so he can stand next to me. "I'm Howard Conrad. Director of Commercials and BD. You must be ...?"

"Ah," Manuel chimes in from the other side of the circle. "Howard, this is Nora Gundersen. She's our new superstar consultant. From NordInvest. She's been at Zyclon only a few days and Ashton can't stop raving about her."

"Hello." I wave awkwardly, not used to this kind of introduction. "Nice to meet you. I've heard you've been out getting us some new clients?"

"Just some super confidential stuff." He winks at me. Ugh, I hate winks. He's giving me the heebie-jeebies.

"I suppose you can't tell me more then." I try to lean across him to catch Sara's eye or jump into another ongoing conversation.

"You'll hear soon enough. I think Manuel will tell everyone when the new CTO is in."

I cough on the last sip of my wine.

"New CTO?" No way. Could it be? Surely not. "What's his, or her, name? If I may ask."

Howard nods. "Top secret for now." He raises his eyebrows and I'm sensing a smidgeon of exaggeration. It seems he enjoys being in the know. "He's a familiar name for us who read about these things. It'll make sense when we let you in on the latest." He winks again and I cringe inwardly.

Howard's mouth is moving once more, but a group of people behind us burst into a birthday song and I can't hear him. I don't want to hear him.

"Sorry?" I put a hand to my ear. Why do I have to be polite?

"I said, where's your drink?" he leans in, talking louder. The group quiets down.

"Oh, Dave's getting it. Looks like he might need some help." I jut my chin toward the bar, hoping Howard will be the type who will show off with his kindness as well as his privileged insights.

"Nah, he'll just go in and out," he says and wobbles on the balls of his feet, hands in his pockets.

"Got to use the ladies'," I say quickly and dash.

When I come back out of the restroom, Howard's by the door. I won't be able to avoid him. Bah. I try to edge past, pretending I can't see him.

"Hey." He nudges me and leans on the doorjamb, effectively blocking my way. "So, what's your story? It's great to have someone with your experience on board." He grins. His round gray eyes are unblinking and he cranes his neck down. Inching closer. It feels like he's flirting and I'm not a fan.

"Uhm. Yeah, thanks. I'm glad to be a part of the team. It's fun to be out socializing with people."

My youngest consultant colleague, Leith, presses past Howard and sneers, "Get a room, will you."

Howard chuckles. I scoff incredulously but don't say anything as I spot the opportunity to escape now Howard has stepped aside.

"Oh look, my wine is waiting for me." I rush outside into the large circle of fabulous co-workers who're not potentially hitting on me.

***

The sun has set without me noticing it getting darker. The big circle has split up into smaller groups and I lean against the windowsill on the side of the pub with Sara. She's having a cigarette, waving it animatedly as she talks.

Sara Pecorino, my potentially new work friend, has been at Upturns since they were only ten people in a tiny office down the road.

"Speaking of dates," she says out of the blue,

lighting her cigarette again—it lost its ember in a particularly enthusiastic hand gesture. “Are you seeing someone?”

“Nah. I’m on Crosspath. If that counts.”

“I met a man there. He fucked me on the kitchen counter of his Richmond mansion and then sent me home with his private driver.”

She shrugs and blows out a big cloud of smoke. Yep, she’s definitely friend material.

“I wouldn’t mind some of that. My last date was more like a bad job interview.”

Sara huffs and shakes her head. “That’s what I hate about dates. All the pretending. You won’t tell your date you’d eat the *whole* pizza. And that you want to fork a lemon meringue pie into your face after, as well. But no, you’re stuck picking at crumbs on the plate, pretending you’re full because women don’t eat. Bullcrap!” She waves a hand.

“Hah, exactly. I love a great meal. It’s why I’m still squishy even with all this exercise but what’s the point if you can’t enjoy food? Wonder how many dates have been turned off by that?” I ponder loudly.

“Fuck’em.” She shrugs, then steps on her cigarette and pushes off the windowsill. “I gotta go to the loo. Wanna come?”

“Yep.” I don’t want to stand outside by myself. We make our way into the bar. It’s packed now. The air is humid, reeking of armpits and stale beer.

We edge our way through the tall, sweaty crowd toward the ladies' room in the back. There's only the one toilet, and there's a queue. It stinks of old urine. I'm not *that* opposed to waiting by myself. But I stay by the door and try to be as inconspicuous as possible, so no one takes my standing alone as an invitation.

Oh, this old painting on the wall is very interesting. *Whistle, whistle.*

A clammy hand lightly grasps the back of my upper arm. I look around to see the cold eyes of Howard again. His eyelids are drooping, but he doesn't slur as he speaks. His voice is clear in my ear.

"I wish I could take you home with me."

He looks at me with a grin that says exactly that. It's sleazy, and completely inappropriate. Which is what I should tell him, in words, but right now all I can do is let my eyes do the talking. He lets go of my arm, winks—despite my dagger-eyes—and edges his way out.

When Sara returns, I mouth 'I'm going home' before she can reach me.

She shakes her head and points at her watch. "Too early!" she shouts above the noise and drags me to the bar, where she orders us two drinks each before I can protest. They arrive quickly; a tequila shot and a Prosecco. Oh gosh.

"*Dai, dai.* Come on." She waves her hands at me to get ready to drink the shots together.

"For you," I say and drink it in one big gulp.

"Baaah." I shake my head as I bite the lemon, and Sara laughs. At least I'm entertaining.

"This Howard guy, does he hit on everyone, or should I feel special?" I ask and drink my Prosecco to kill the taste of tequila.

She scoffs. "Fucking Howard. Tell him *no* clearly or he'll never stop. There are a couple of dev guys who'll get a bit handsy after a few drinks, but just tell them *no* or go to Rosie."

I nod and give her the thumbs up.

"He mentioned a new CTO starting. Do you know their name? Howard said it was 'top secret.'" I make air quotation marks. Sara shakes her head.

"He's probably forgotten the name." She laughs. "He's American, I think. Rosie said someone's coming from New York. They've waited for him."

My heart lunges in my chest. How many American CTOs recently moved to the country? Am I excited? Nervous? Why do I care? I scull my Prosecco to distract myself.

"Let's go dancing." Sara pulls me along after we finish our drinks.

We skip and shimmy through Trafalgar Square, but slow down after almost crashing into someone. People are scattered across the area—eating chips and singing loudly. One guy runs through, flapping his arms, shrieking like a seagull. A woman chases him, doing the same. How late is it?

"Is there anywhere that will let us in now?" I ask.

"Oh, yes," she says and picks up the pace until we reach a thumping place on Haymarket, an otherwise quiet street.

Once inside, I immediately regret it. It's by far the loudest music I have ever heard. The bass is changing my heart's rhythm. It shakes my soul. What on earth are we doing *here*? Sara points at the bar.

There's Dave and a couple of IT guys. I didn't notice them leaving earlier. Damn, there's Howard too. His Cheshire Cat grin visible across the room, his teeth reflecting the strobe lights.

"They always come here after the pub. Never-ending party," she shrieks into my ear and runs toward them. She flings herself into Dave's arms. It seems a familiar move to him. His massive hands fall comfortably around her tiny waistline.

I follow her slowly, trying to be nonchalant, not wanting Howard to think I'm here for him after what he said, or that I'd want him to mirror Dave. I can be pretty blunt with guys when I have to, but he's a director at my new workplace, not a random I'll never see again.

"Champagne!" Sara shouts, and a glass is handed to me. Howard's eyes are on me. Surely, he won't do anything in front of the others. I clink everyone's glasses without meeting his gaze. A hand appears on the small of my back and I pretend to need something from my purse to move away from it. I drink my champagne quickly, looking anywhere but at the group, and then mime to Sara that I'm leaving. She nods and gives me the thumbs up.

Before Howard makes another move, I sneak out and head toward the bus stop, mind racing.

Is it possible the man who's made me hotter than anyone before—the man I gave an accidental lap grind and talked the ear off on the train afterwards—is going to work where I work? I'm both mortified and exhilarated. Is that possible?

CHAPTER 17

JAKE

The air is heavy with the delicious gym sock smell of melted Raclette cheese. I stroll slowly on Rue Mouffetard and it's exactly as I remember. Paris distilled. Farther down, I'm met by a variety of earthy and pungent scents wafting from the many small shops and stands lining the cobbled street. There are colorful displays of fresh vegetables, fruits, a selection of cheeses, and saucissons. The merchants shout prices to customers and greetings to fellow vendors. There's the sound of coffee machines grinding beans, people chattering, and tinny music playing through an open shop window. Edith Piaf's distinct voice travels above the noise to me. She doesn't regret anything, she sings. Goosebumps spread across my arms. It's such a powerful tune and I'm reminded of what *I* regret.

In front of me, my parents walk arm in arm. My mom points toward a shop, and Dad whispers something into her ear that makes her giggle. They've been together since they were in their twenties. I'm close to forty already and my family thinks I'm a loner. But I'm sure I'm doing the right thing. Focusing on work first. Not making bad decisions that affect others.

A friend told me once: I can have everything I want in life—just not all at the same time.

Focus is key to my success.

My stomach churns. Ever since last Friday in Camden, I've had this unease in my gut. I think I'm nervous about this role—about failing now I've finally been given the reins.

"Jake. *Par ici, mon chéri*," Mom says, turning to me and guides me by the arm into a quaint bistro with red and white checkered tablecloths and wooden furniture. I'd forgotten how narrow, low, and petite Paris is. Or I didn't notice before. I was a gangly teenager back then. Now, I'm a giant, bumping into tables, excusing myself again and again. I straddle a miniature chair, hoping it'll hold my weight.

"Why don't you stay with Mark and relax for a week?" my dad asks after we've ordered our food. I've got a confit duck coming and am salivating at the thought.

"As great as Mark's place is, living with a grown man and his active social life will be ... too hectic."

Mom chuckles. "He's rather busy, is he?"

The humming, graying waitress arrives with bottled water and a basket of bread. It smells freshly baked and my stomach rumbles.

"We went out for dinner and drinks both Friday and Saturday, and he had drinks for lunch yesterday, too. I haven't been this tired in years and he said it was a quiet weekend. I won't be able to keep up."

"Good. Focus on what's important to you. You got your dream role, now you can give it your all."

"Mm-hmm," I agree through a mouthful of bread. I'll have to.

"Oh, honey, you must have time to live as well."

"Sage said that too. What do you mean? I'm fine."

"Work. Exercise. Technology news. And what is it you have, your little plants?"

"Peace lilies, mostly. I'll have to get new ones."

"Now that you're in a new job and a new town, please make time for other things. You love food. You love drawing. Meet someone."

"One thing at a time, Mom. I need to ace this role and there's a lot to do, and a lot to learn. It can't be done within a regular workday. I'll see Sage, Ryan, and the baby as often as I can, though. And visit you."

"My brother should've had your attitude. Make sure you keep it," Dad states clearly. My late uncle seems to come up whenever there's an idea of slack or not 'giving it your all'. He always pushes, or 'encourages', me and my sister to aim higher and work harder.

His face falls, and he runs a hand across it. Mom rubs his upper arm, giving him a tender look. We let him go through it. Every time.

"He was intelligent. He could've done anything. *Anything* he wanted. I struggled my way through my engineering degree; he breezed through it. Just like you, Jake." He rubs his eyes gently and breathes. "He was an arrogant arse."

"Robert." My mom moves her hand to grab his.

"I remember, Dad. He didn't have a career to fall back on when he lost all his money. I'm clearly not making his mistakes."

Ignoring me, he continues.

We had this conversation when I left AbbleTech for HercuSoft—a smaller and less known company. And when I didn't apply for the CTO role last time it became available.

"Instead of taking the opportunities right in front of him, the good solid roles, he had to gamble in currencies and investments. He wanted anything but the nine-to-five. He thought he knew something we *peasants* didn't. Thought he was above holding a proper job. Working hard."

"Many people do that, Dad, and it pans out. He was very unlucky."

"He was overconfident and careless. And the downtimes of the nineties hit him like a wrecking ball. He lost everything. And then he went and got himself hit by a bloody bus." He waves a hand angrily at nothing in particular.

My uncle was on a bender after receiving some bad news and wandered into the street. It was deemed an accident, but my dad blames himself for not being there, and curses his brother just as much.

My duck arrives along with my parents' steaks, and I dig in while he continues. Dad needs to work through his guilt whenever this topic arises.

"I tried to offer help … Bastard was too proud." He shakes his head, his thin white hair waving like silk. "I was in Indonesia then and had my mind on you all. That's why I kept pushing myself, getting those promotions. Working hard. I didn't want to end up like him, and I needed to show you kids how important it is to put in the effort."

I glance at my mom and am surprised to see a frown where there's normally a gentle, empathic expression. Is she as concerned about me as he is?

"Don't worry about me. Neither of you. I'm doing well. I won't take unnecessary risks. Plus, I've got savings and investments from many frugal years and selling my apartment."

Dad rubs his eyes. "Just work hard and stay safe, son. These financial markets are fickle. You don't want to be out of a job."

"I hear you, Dad." I'm pleased with my decision *not* to tell him my contract has a six months' probation period. And that it depends on me writing a technology strategy that helps lock down an investor. If I fail at this, I'll struggle to get a chance with another company.

No pressure.

CHAPTER 18

NORA

Me: Have you seen him yet?

Sara: Negative. I have not sighted the great American Eagle yet.

Me: You're making a terrible impression of a dork

Sara: I'm just trying to fit in

Me: Let me know. I'll be there as soon as I can, definitely in time for the meeting

Sara: Rosie brought cake

Me: Yaasss. Just need to sort out whatever Ash called me over for

Sara: Ash? Is that what you call the Night King?

Me: What? The main White Walker from Game of Thrones? I get the icy eye reference, but what's the rest? It's not like he's the leader of the undead, these peeps are nice

Sara: He's scary and rude, you'll see it, eventually

Me: Hmm. More like a commanding Superman imo

Me: Over and out. He's here

I quickly shut down the office chat window before the tall figure appears next to me. Ashton Alexander, Global Head of Investment and

Equity for Zyclon Group and a notorious client. I've been here nearly two weeks and I notice he's the demanding leader type—be quick or be gone—but so far he's not half as bad as my colleagues implied. I think it's because I made a good first impression by ironing out some of their kinks, and can handle his slightly rude but meant-as-funny remarks.

Despite being on good terms with the client, I shouldn't blatantly chat on the clock, though; they pay plenty for consultant time.

"Morning, boss man," I say in a singsong voice and swivel my chair to look at him. His brown, lightly graying, tousled hair softens his eerie White Walker eyes. All men are normally checked through my happily-ever-after-filter, but I shelved him off as client immediately. And having met his girlfriend at the Zyclon drinks last week, further shuts down my biological, as well as my emotional, responses. I don't have an interest in someone else's man.

"Good morning, Nor," he says with his Scottish lilt and leans on the back of the chair next to me, clutching his takeaway coffee cup. There's a mischievous glint in his eye.

"What's up?" I ask, cocking my head.

"What's with the hair today? Did you get caught in the rain?" he asks, grinning now.

"I did, actually. Surprise shower on my walk in." I laugh and pat it down. It's completely wild. "What's *your* excuse?" I flash him a playful grin as he moves a hand up to check his thick mane.

"Oy." He laughs. I reach into my bag for a hair tie as he sits down next to me. It's going up in a high bun, then. My classic curly bird's nest.

"How was your weekend? Did you try out that speakeasy place I mentioned?" he asks.

"Absolutely, thanks for the tip! It was amazing. Loved the style, and the *volume*. We could actually talk," I say with emphasis. He nods in agreement. After a relaxing day in the park, Dee and I met a couple of her friends for a girls' night out—a break from the Mr. Right hunt. "What about you?"

"Cycled around Richmond Park. Did some running. I'm old and boring."

"Nah, I wouldn't say boring." I wait for the reaction, trying to keep a straight face.

"Oy, again. Am I paying you for this?"

"You walked straight into it."

"Maybe. Don't tell the team you get away with these things. I think they fear me and I kind of like it that way," he says in a low voice. "They call me the Night King. Oh, don't give me that look. I'm sure your colleagues have told you."

"They would never," I answer, doing my best to keep my poker face. He furrows his brow at me.

"Anyway," he says—catch up complete. His face changes back to boss expression. He didn't ask me here to talk about the weekend. "Thanks for coming over through the rain this morning.

I know you can remote in, but I prefer if you chat with Finn in person. It's important we get this right." His voice so low it can't be heard across the office. "I'm pretty sure he messed up the reports for the quarterly review, and he's blaming your tool again. Before I complain to Upturns once more and look like a fool with a huge bill in my inbox, can you go through it and check? You're obviously some kind of wiz with this."

"Sure thing. I have to head back for an all-company meeting to greet our new CTO at eleven. If I don't figure it out straight away, I'll come back after."

"All good."

I take twenty minutes to find Finn's mistake and run him through it, and shoot off an email to the Zyclon team. My trick is to explain how to not make the mistake again without making Finn look bad. The corner of my screen flashes orange and Sara's name pops up again. It makes my heart race. Why am I so certain it's him?

Sara: The Eagle has landed

Sara: If I wasn't sitting on a cushioned chair, I'd be sliding right off it

Me: *blush*

Sara: You better get here fast to get a front-row seat. OMG. Rawr, I love a dented chin.

Dented chin?

Me: Packing up! What color hair?

Sara: Brown. Darkish.

It has to be him!

Sara: He's a sexy suit commercial come to life, that's for sure. Great face.

Sara: When I say face, I mean butt

CHAPTER 19

JAKE

"You remember Howard and Rosie." Manuel gestures for me to take a seat around the large boardroom table, across from the slender, blond man and the pale, black-haired woman I met last week.

"Nice to see you again," I say to them both as they stand to shake my hand.

"Coffee?" Rosie offers from a metal carafe and I accept as Manuel takes a seat at the head of the table. It's a novel experience from my former twenty-strong leadership meetings. Weird, but I'll get used to it. Each of us has a wide range of responsibilities that in bigger companies are covered by several people.

"We're delighted to have you here, finally. It's been a long time coming, replacing our old CTO." Manuel whistles and Rosie makes a noise of agreement. Sounds like it might be messier than they let on during the interviews, but I can handle anything. "Since we last spoke, Howard has confirmed four significant investor interests. He'll take you through it this afternoon. Basically, they're eager to see the plans for expansion into the private sector. We're still growing in our current segment, but we're too vulnerable. If we lose large clients like Zyclon or NordInvest, or any of the mid-range ones, we'll struggle." He rubs his chin as he says this. There's a hint of nervousness to the gesture. Or am I imagining it? "Your initial challenge will be to make our products easier to set up and use, so our new users can adopt them without the cost of consultants."

"Are you looking to have two products so we can keep the consultant revenue stream?" I ask and Manuel nods.

"Something like that. But we don't want to maintain two separate ones, either."

Talk about getting straight into it. They take me through their findings and I'm loving it. My brain fires on all cylinders. This is my scene. I'm already strategizing in the back of my mind while they talk.

"Where do you suggest we start?" He folds his hands on the table. As the founder of Upturns—an entrepreneurial finance expert with an affinity for tech—I'm certain he has a clear idea. But he's also an excellent people-reader and knows I didn't come here to be told what to do.

"I'll review the current systems, aligning our efforts with the direction you've set. Considering our small team and confidential objectives, it's best for me to speak directly with clients and consultants. If we need to rebuild to support both growth and expansion, let's do it efficiently."

"Sounds good. Howard will confirm the meetings, but you've got roughly six weeks. It's tight, but the entire company will support. And your team has been operating without a CTO for over eight months—they can handle you being divided." Manuel locks eyes with me and I nod in acknowledgement.

Six weeks. I'll need to plan this out properly so I don't miss anything.

There's rustling and laughing from the area outside the meeting room, and we all turn to look.

"The team is getting ready for the all-company session." Rosie nods toward the group behind me. "I'd like to announce something once you're finished with your introduction."

"Sure," I respond and she smiles as she gets up. I turn back to Manuel. "What do they know about the plans?"

"It's a fact that we're growing. Bringing you on hints that something will change, considering your past. But keep the investors and expansion under wraps until we're certain what it looks like."

"Understood."

"All right, let's head out. I'll introduce you to

the key people after the group session. We've got an outstanding new addition to the team, by the way. The *perfect* resource for your first steps," Manuel says enthusiastically while packing away his laptop. "She was a portfolio manager in Norway with NordInvest. Most of our successful updates were requests from her and her team," he adds, grinning. Goosebumps form on my arms at the mention of Norway.

"That's great. She's *Norwegian*?" My voice breaks on the last word and I clear my throat. I glance out the glass wall at the team gathering as we make our way out behind Howard.

"Yes." He juts his chin to my right and I follow his gaze. "She's up front and center, I can see. Her name's Nora."

***

There she is. Dark blonde curls in a high bun. Just like at the airport. Loose strands frame her lightly freckled face. She looks more sun-kissed than last time.

Of all the FinTechs in all of London, I had to choose this one. The only one with a person who's twice left me frazzled and, frankly, a little concerned about my bodily control.

Manuel's presence at the top of the room makes the group fall quiet instantly.

"Thank you all for joining. We won't take up too much of your time and I know you came for the cake." Everyone laughs. They seem to adore him; the way they look at him. Curious eyes flicker toward me.

"We have a few new starters today. You can see the most obvious one next to me here, but I want to give a quick shout out to the others first." Manuel names four new developers who pipe up from the crowd. He gives them a moment before the attention is on me. Good man.

"Please welcome our new CTO, Jake Fielding. He comes from over five years at HercuSoft, as their Head of Development, and another five years as a product manager with AbbleTech before that."

Heads nod, and there's a murmur at the mention of my former employers.

"The tech news readers among you may recognize his name from several successful product expansions in the past years." He smiles in my direction and continues with specific examples to the point when I no longer pretend to be embarrassed, but actually want him to stop. I'll take it, though. It's gratifying to see it reflected in others; the pride I hold for my work. Manuel gestures to me after finishing his lengthy introduction.

"Thank you for that detailed run-through of my resume," I say with a grin as an obvious joke to a low chuckle in the group. "It's all a team effort, though. I'd achieve very little on my own. So I'm thrilled to be here at Upturns. To get a chance to work with another talented team.

You've all been part of building these superb products. Clients are knocking down the doors, so now we'll ensure we're set up for continued growth and success." I scan the group as I talk—a diverse crowd, that's good.

I avoid looking directly at Nora, but in my side-vision, she's twirling her hair. Like she did when I saw her reading her book. Her 'sexy romance'.

What is she thinking about now?

Damn. Focus.

"In the upcoming weeks, I'll be conducting an assessment of our software suite to define our priorities."

My gaze finally lands on her. She freezes and her eyes widen. I can't avoid looking at her pink mouth and her lips part as I do.

Fuck. I'm in trouble.

I clear my throat and pull my gaze away, turning to Rosie for her announcement as my brain has gone blank.

"Tell us a little about *you*, Jake."

"Manuel covered the important parts. But I guess I can add ... I like cake." I shrug, receiving another round of laughter, a little louder this time.

"What kind of cake?" Rosie asks in a soft tone, angling her head.

"Dark chocolate," I say, keeping it simple. Saying it's best with a hint of pear and salted caramel could make me sound snobby. And why would they care? Ugh, come on Rosie. I'm done talking about myself.

There's shuffling and clearing of throats as neither Rosie nor I continue.

"You had some announcement?" I raise my eyebrows at her.

"Oh, yes." Rosie turns to the crowd. "Office day out in three weeks. Kayaking! Please respond to my email; I need firm numbers. And some of you complained you don't get to go to the consultant and client party the week after. But don't worry, you'll get pizza with your regular office booze this time!"

The team erupts into cheers and someone yells, "Pizza!"

Rosie laughs and waves, giving a thumbs up, receiving another loud cheer.

I should make a move, but find myself rooted to the spot. Nailed down by Nora's fierce stare.

CHAPTER 20

NORA

He's looking directly at me. Everyone's getting up to leave, and I'm stuck in his sticky gaze. Those intense eyes are staring deep into my soul. If I stay entirely still, maybe he'll look away.

Am I breathing? I inhale deeply to be sure, my chest rising as I do. His eyes darken before he finally looks away. Manuel has caught his attention and they're laughing, exchanging arm pats, and Manuel points at me.

Hold on, what? They're coming this way.

Aaaaah, what is my face doing? I try to smile. I think I'm smiling.

"Jake, this is Nora, the consultant I mentioned earlier. Nora, I was telling Jake how you will be the perfect person to help him with his user experience review."

"Really? Why?" It comes out higher pitched than I planned. Manuel laughs as if I was joking. I guess I know why.

Stay professional, Nora.

"Sorry, of course, yes. Happy to help in any way you need, Jake. Nice to meet you."

I reach out a hand to shake his and he takes it with a tense expression. Is that his thinking face or his resting face? Scowlface. The warmth from his hand travels up my arm and makes my hairs stand on end.

"And you," he grumbles.

Manuel pats Jake on the back of his arm again. "Rosie bought cake. Come. You're not the only one with a sweet tooth," he says with a grin.

"Sure, let me check one thing first and I'll be right in." Jake gestures to his office.

I head to my desk in a trance. How the hell am I going to do any work now?

It's okay. He's just a normal human. I'll get over it.

Get over what? It's simply my body reacting to him. Could be I'm supposed to be ovulating. Again, though? Surely that's what was going on when we met on the plane. Maybe he won't affect me this time. Except that rush when he looked at me earlier.

Ah!

And the shock of seeing his name on my screen.

Jake Fielding pops up on my office chat, blinking orange in the corner. I turn around and see him at his desk in his glass office. He looks normal. His Scowlface on. Not like his blood is on fire, like me.

Jake: Hi

Me: Hello

Jake: Funny coincidence

Me: Hilarious

Jake: ...

He's typing.

Still going.

I swivel on my chair to check what's going on. Manuel's in Jake's doorway. Looks like he got stuck mid-type. What was he about to say? I need to know. What do I *want* him to say? 'Come, let's make out in the hallway?' What makes me think he'd write anything personal? He wasn't interested in seeing me again last time. Why would he be now when we work together?

Disappointing, but not unexpected, his message reveals what I'd already concluded.

Jake: I'd appreciate if we could keep our plane meet between us

Me: Of course, don't worry

Jake: Thank you. Now cake :)

***

I barge into the kitchen, thinking it's empty, and a startled Jake turns around, spilling his coffee.

"Oh gosh. I'm so sorry." I rush to help, but he steps back and puts his mug on the counter before finding a paper towel to wipe his pants.

"It's okay, don't worry." He throws the paper

into the trash by the fridge and grabs his mug.

"Sorry."

"Are you having a coffee?" he asks, gesturing to the machine and giving me more than enough space to get past him without getting close.

"No, I came in to check if there was any cake left." I flap my arms awkwardly, pointing at the last piece sitting on a sea of crumbs in the open box on the table.

My stomach flip-flops at the proximity of him. He makes me nervous. They say one should picture someone naked when nervous, don't they?

It doesn't help.

Ugh, it makes it worse. I'm warm.

"Ah. Go ahead." He nods and shuffles his feet.

"Were you about to have it?"

"No?" He drags out the word, making it sound more like a question. "I want you to have it."

"Thank you, but now it feels undeserving. You were here first." I flap my arms again. Jesus, I need a dress with pockets. I never know what to do with my hands.

"Are you sure?" He finally breaks our awkward stand-off with a sideways smile that has my heart racing, and takes a step towards the cake as if to test me.

"I'll fight ya for it," I say quickly in my best Irish accent, and put my fists up before my brain can warn me it's silly.

He lets out a short laugh. "A bare-knuckle

boxing match, like in the movie?"

"Hey, you got my *Snatch* reference."

He nods. "It's one of my favorites. But better find something more legal to determine who gets the cake." He sips his coffee again, his eyes glinting over the rim.

"Yeah, I think it'd be frowned upon if we started pounding each other in the kitchen."

He coughs into his mug, nearly spilling again.

"What did I say?" I run it back in my mind. Oh, that could sound like a double entendre. I stare at him without blinking for a moment but, for once, I manage to keep a straight face—curious to see how he responds.

Jake clears his throat. "No, you're right, it would be frowned upon."

"Why did you cough like that?" I do my best to keep my mask.

"No reason." He looks so uncomfortable. I flash him a smile and his eyes widen.

"Just yanking your chain. I heard it in my head after I said it and was hoping you'd spell it out for me."

Jake laughs, shaking his head. I don't know why I keep doing this to him. These comments come too easily. I enjoy amusing him and he's doing a terrible job pretending it's not working.

He turns to put his empty mug in the sink next to the machine. "It might be best if you have the cake," he says when he faces me again. He's ready to leave. Did I take it too far?

"Don't give up so easily. Oh, I have an idea." I hold a fist up again. "Are you thinking what I'm thinking?"

"Uhm. Not sure I dare say. What *are* you thinking, Nora?"

"Bare—" His gaze flickers down for an almost imperceptible moment. "—knuckle rock-paper-scissors."

"Okay. Is it common to fight over cake in this office, by the way? Do I need to get used to this?" Jake puts a hand up to play.

"Nope. No idea what I'm doing. Just didn't want you to give up the cake too easily." I grin and he answers with a shrug. I want to keep him here, and surely he sees straight through it.

"Ready?" He counts down and when he reveals a rock fist, I have my hand open to represent paper. I automatically wrap my hand on top of his to show my victory. The touch brings back the overwhelming rush in me from when I met him the first time, and I pull my hand back as if I got burned. His eyes darken. Not a popular move, I gather.

"Again," I say, pretending it didn't happen, despite the blood rushing in my ears. "Three-two-one, go!"

Jake shows his scissors and I hold my fingers upwards and wriggle them.

"What is *that*?" he asks with a chuckle and a sideways smile. Oh, be still my heart. Almost a whole smile.

"It's fire," I answer. "Joey Tribbiani special." His expression is blank. "From *Friends*?" I add.

"I'm a *Seinfeld* guy."

He moves to cut my fire-fingers with his hand-scissors as Leith walks in and we both jump, pulling our hands back.

"Get a room, will you," he drawls, heading straight for the coffee machine, and raises his eyebrows at me when our eyes meet. He's got a chip on his shoulder, this one.

"We're fighting over the last piece. I think it's a tie," I say, keeping it light.

"No, it's all yours. Despite the cheating." Jake presses his lips together and ducks out before I can respond.

Damn you, Leith.

I put half of the slice on a plate and take it to Jake's office. When he sees it's me knocking on the open door, his eyes dart around. Is he nervous or looking for a way out? He's probably tired of talking to me by now and I'm keeping him from his work. I put the plate on the corner of his desk, and step back to lean on the door frame to indicate I won't stick around too long.

"Sorry, wanted you to have your well-deserved cake."

"Oh. Thanks."

"I don't cheat, by the way. I'm very rule abiding." I flash him a grin and add, "Except some rules need a little bending."

"Hah."

"Don't mind Leith. He said the same to me and Howard last week. Must be something about two people talking he simply can't handle." I shrug.

"Right." He doesn't look convinced.

I'm about to leave when I notice the client party invitation open on his screen. The black and gold is instantly recognizable.

"You got the email from Rosie. The Great Gatsby theme. Fun, right?."

He turns to his screen and back to me. "I guess. Will people dress up?"

"I hope so. Did you see it says casino? Sounds cool."

Why am I standing here babbling? His body's angled toward the computer. He's obviously not interested in talking to me.

"I don't gamble," he says flatly.

"Not a big risk taker?"

"Nope."

"It's with fake money."

"Ah."

"Moving overseas from HercuSoft to a tiny company like this could be considered a risk." I can't stop myself from talking. I don't want to look away from him. Wonder what the crease on his forehead means. Did I say the wrong thing?

"Maybe. But I've learned it's best not to."

"The hard way?"

His forehead crease deepens. Whoops, that was probably too personal a question.

"Sort of," he answers in his deep voice. He runs

a hand over his mouth and puts it back on the computer mouse.

"I don't mind some risk. I believe you have to make your own luck, though. You can't expect to win if you don't play. It's statistics. No risk, no reward and all that." I muse loudly, momentarily forgetting he's waiting to get back to work. He clears his throat and rubs his neck.

"I'll stop bothering you now." I grin and straighten up. "See ya." I stride off, already excited for our next kitchen run-in. I'll have to make sure it happens.

***

I've had more caffeine these last few days than last year in total. I'm practically vibrating on the kitchen chair, the phone shaking in my hand.

Jake is buried in work, mostly frowning at his screen, or in meetings with his different teams. He comes out for coffee. So, I've been trying to catch him in the kitchen again and then, needing an excuse to be there, I make myself an espresso, or a large cappuccino, when he might be lingering. We talk politely about work, but he's usually with another team member coming from or going to his next meeting.

The tension between us is palpable and I can't get enough.

Even when he's not looking directly at me, I feel his eyes on my skin. At my desk, my skin tingles like the first time in the airport, but when

I turn around to check, Jake's engrossed in what's on his screen.

I'm both terrified and excited about working with him next week.

It would help to meet someone else. This physical distraction in the office is only that—a distraction. It's not helpful to achieve any of the happily ever after scenarios I've conjured up. Several of them involve Jake. How could they not? He makes my blood rush simply standing nearby. But it's a smiling, dancing Jake I dream about, and from what I've seen of him so far, it's obviously a fantasy. The hint of flirtation I saw in him the first day has not made a reappearance. His face is stiff. He works every evening, and he's probably never danced in his life. His most colorful garment so far is a navy suit. He's not social; has lunch alone or with Manuel, or he goes to the gym.

Wonder if he prowls the streets for women at night like a dark, sexy vampire. Or is he all alone? A gorgeous man like that? No. Surely not.

Now my thoughts of a dancing, smiling Jake is a naked Jake. With that incredibly attractive two-day stubble he's got going on today. Oh, my word.

I'm shaken back to the present by Sara entering the kitchen.

She laughs as she strolls to the coffee machine. "Nora, are you okay? You have your mouth open."

"Oh, gosh." I wipe my chin. It feels like I'm drooling. "Lost in thought." I eat a piece of my daily dark chocolate, pretending that's what I was busy with.

"Any plans for the weekend?" Sara asks as she pushes the button and the machine does its regular spluttering and coughing.

"Exploring Hackney tomorrow. There's a food market there I want to try. And walk along the canals."

"How nice. Is it a date?" she asks just as Jake walks in, alone for once. He stops in his tracks, looking at each of us. I tighten the grip on my phone to stop my caffein shake.

"Sorry, don't let me interrupt." He holds up his hands and flashes Sara a smile.

He scowls at me and smiles at her!

Sara grabs her coffee from the machine and gestures for Jake to go for it.

"So, is it a date?" Sara asks in a lower voice, sitting down across from me. I glance toward Jake. That's where my eyes want to go. He's on his phone, waiting for his coffee, and I can't make out his expression. Why would he care?

"Yeah, it's a date. This super nice guy from Crosspath," I answer, louder than necessary and Jake turns away, facing the machine.

It's a lie. I'm going with Dee. I'm pathetic. Why do I want him to care? I can't believe I just lied. Playing games is not my style. Should I *woman up* and talk to him? Grow some tits, as they say?

Since the date with Preston, I've not found anyone remotely interesting on the app. All I see when reading people's profiles is bragging, annoying guys. The potentially interesting fitness geek guy, Mark, ghosted me after only two messages.

"Good for you. It sounds fun," Sara says.

"What about you?" I ask and my eyes follow Jake as he leaves without a word.

"Nothing much. Swimming in Hyde Park Lido," she answers. I hardly hear it. My mind left the room with Jake.

***

I continue my break after Sara leaves, sufficiently distracted from work and eager to find a *real* date so I'm not a complete liar.

Using the profile-first setting of Crosspath, I swipe left. Skimming through.

Blergh, blergh, blergh.

Does everyone run bloody marathons these days? What happened to liking food and drinks and comedy shows?

Ooh. That's exactly what this guy has on his profile.

Nathan, 35, General Manager
Seeking a partner who appreciates the basics: tacos, cocktails, laughs, and movies! Nothing fancy, just good times and splendid company.

I swipe right. We're matched! I'm nervous about seeing his picture and get annoyed with myself. It shouldn't matter. Letting my thumb rest on the screen, I close my eyes and swipe once more. Slowly, slowly, opening my eyes; a face comes into view.

Hmm. Not half bad. Brown hair, thick eyebrows, and a broad white smile. A tad mousey, but I'll put my judgmental side away. He looks and sounds nice.

Me: Hello

Nathan: Hello! Wow, your eyes are beautiful.

Uh-oh. Cliché as first line? Danger, danger. He'll get three chances.

Me: *vomit*

Nathan: Exactly, they're vomit green. Thanks, I struggled to put my finger on it. Hey, I hate texting, I'm not funny in writing. Wanna grab a drink at the Mexican place in Southbank at six on Monday?

Me: Sounds good. Monday Funday is a new thing.

I put the phone down, and it buzzes again. This time it's not Nathan.

Martin: Hey, I'll be in London in a few weeks. Keen to keep me company?

CHAPTER 21

JAKE

Nora's desk is next to the kitchen. And she drinks a lot of coffee. I've tried to avoid being alone with her in there after our first encounter. That stunning and annoyingly adorable dork made me drop my guard immediately. But Leith reminded me how dangerous it is to do so. I'm grateful it happened so quickly. Before anyone else noticed the crackling air between us.

It's been easy enough to stay away from her since. Work has me preoccupied and I only go to the kitchen when I'm with someone else on the way to a meeting.

When she's near, I feel pulled toward her. She's impossible to ignore. I *feel* her next to me.

I try to avoid staring at her so I only look at her briefly, in between. Just long enough to give her a curt smile. Trying to be pleasant, but not inviting.

She's been in the kitchen for a while now. I drum my fingers on my desk. Waiting. I need a coffee.

Ah, Sara walks in.

I won't be alone with her if I go now. I spring up from my desk and head over for my post-lunch caffeine.

"Is it a date?" Sara's loud voice rings from the open kitchen. Is she talking to Nora? They both freeze as I walk in.

"Sorry. Don't let me interrupt," I say, as casually as I can, and smile politely at Sara. Nora's shoulders are bare today. In a split second, the vivid image of me pulling down the strap of her top and caressing that lightly tanned, freckled skin pops into my head. My body threatens to react, but I focus hard and distract myself with the noisy coffee machine.

They continue talking about Nora's date. With a 'super nice' man. Her voice is clear over the hissing of the machine next to me and I make a face inwardly. *Super nice*. Who wants 'super nice'? I grit my teeth, staring at my phone, pretending not to listen. It's not my business. Wonder how long she'll be single if she's actively dating now?

It's good, though. It'll reduce this insane tension between us if she's with another man. The thought makes me cringe. I shouldn't care. But I do. I want to be the one to make her smile that way she did on the train. Make her laugh that heartwarming laugh I've heard from the kitchen when she's in here. It's should be *my* name she calls out in pleasure, grasping the sheets of *my* bed.

Dammit. Am I upset that she's going on a date, or at myself for feeling something about it?

My coffee finishes and I exit as quickly as I can, doing my best to hide the agony I'm sure is plastered on my face.

I dread spending next week by her side.

CHAPTER 22

NORA

After a long day fixing issues at Zyclon instead of HQ with Jake, I arrive for my Monday dinner-date hungry and sweaty. It's a scorching summer day. My face is hot, I bet I'm red, and my curls stick to my forehead.

A brown-haired man sits at a wooden table in the outside area of the colorful restaurant, overlooking the bustling Southbank waterfront.

"Hi, you must be Nathan," I say breathlessly, and he gives me a bewildered expression. "You look exactly like your picture. From Crosspath? I'm Nora."

I reach out my clammy hand and regret it, but he's already grabbed it with a hint of a grimace.

"Oh, right? Nice to meet you. You look … warm."

"Sorry. Yeah." I fan my face before I sit down next to him and stuff my laptop bag away. Hope I don't look appalling, despite my 'warm' appearance.

"The server came before, so I took the liberty to order some nibbles," he says, beaming. It looks genuine and is reassuring. I'll try to relax now.

"That's perfect, I'm famished." I'm still out of breath from the power walk down here. It's like there's not enough oxygen in the air when it's warm like this.

"Did you run here?" He has a hint of dimples. Is he cute? I can't decide.

"Almost. Didn't want to be late."

"Yeah, no worries, only eleven minutes," he says, looking at his wristwatch and I laugh, which he answers with raised eyebrows. He said he wasn't good at conveying his humor in writing, but it seems he might have some issues face to face as well. I'll give him the benefit of the doubt.

"Right. Sorry." I laugh again. Awkward start. "How was your day, mister general manager? What are you the manager of, by the way?"

"It's just general manager. It was good, very busy. I manage a popular restaurant." He points backwards at the Mexican place we're at.

"Oh wow, this place is great. Nice." I look around pointedly. "So, we're on a date where you work? You don't mind them seeing you?"

"I like these tacos." He points at the menu. They must be good.

"I love tacos. Can't wait to try some."

The server arrives as if on cue, and my stomach makes a loud rumbling noise. On her tray are four small tacos, a bowl of corn chips and tomato salsa. I can already tell I'll need more —morning kettle bell exercises makes me extra hungry all day, and I didn't have time for a substantial lunch.

"Excuse me, can I order a few more tacos? The pork carnitas, and the beef. And the eggplant. Oh, and the guacamole. Your sour beer, is it fruity?" She nods and shrugs, good enough for me. "I'll have a pint. Thank you."

When I turn back to Nathan, he's scowling in my direction but shakes it off when my eyes meet his. What is he thinking? I need sustenance to chat. Don't want to be grumpy Nora on a date. I hover over the corn chips.

"Were they to share?"

He nods and I munch a couple down.

"Baja fish?" I ask and stuff a taco in my mouth before he answers. Half of it makes it in before I realize it might be too much in one go, and I bite off as daintily as I can, trying to shield my chewing with my hands.

"Mmm. So good," I say as I finish the mouthful. "Compliments to your chef."

Nathan eats a taco as well and I nibble on a chip instead of the next taco, not wanting to be seen as gluttonous, despite my vow to myself not to eat less on a date for show.

"What do you do for work? What's a senior consultant?" he asks.

I explain our software and what I do for the

clients; a short version, as I'm aware few people find my line of work interesting. The word 'finance' makes most people cringe.

The server arrives again and exchanges pleasantries with Nathan that I don't listen to. I'm busy taking a long sip of my cold, fresh beer, which I end with a happy groan as the server leaves.

"Delicious. I was so thirsty." I grin and Nathan raises his eyebrows while sipping a colorful cocktail through a straw. He grabs one of the fresh tacos.

"The problem-solving aspect is my favorite part. Not simply following a set to-do list. I'm sure you have loads of that here."

"Absolutely." Nathan tells me about the ins and outs of managing the restaurant while I sneak another taco. They're so small. How many are you meant to eat? I never know for sure. He talks and talks and I nod along, making sounds of agreement and interest, while having a third taco. That's still less than half, I note. We can always order more. Nathan is fairly slender. Perhaps he doesn't eat much. If *I* worked here, I wouldn't be doing much else.

"You've got quite the appetite," he blurts out, but smiles and sips his cocktail again.

"Oh, do I?" I can't tell if he's being flirty in a tactless way or just rude. His attention to my eating makes me feel awkward. Can I not eat more now?

"I'll be right back." I stand up to go to the restroom instead and realize a group has been seated next to us on the long bench and I'll have to lift my leg up to get out. Not a brilliant move in a bodycon dress. I could swivel, but there's not enough legroom. Crap. I hate shared seating like this.

Nathan gets up to give me space and we're face to face. Nearly crotch to crotch. I half expect my body to tingle, being so close to a man.

But there's nothing. Not a single spark.

How odd. I've been such a horn dog since I got on the plane to London. Well, except with Ashton, but he's got a girlfriend. And Finn, he's only twenty-five. Howard—ew. Dave—nope. Preston—no, sir. Seeing Martin's message last week only gave me the chills. I've not even answered him yet.

Hmm. Have I not been out of the ordinary after all?

Is it only ... Jake?

Nathan breathes in audibly. Does he feel anything? I catch myself not caring either way.

My intuition kicks in. This is dead in the water.

All I think about is how my body would react standing this close to Jake again.

***

"Hey Mom, how's Costa Rica?"

My mom's face is pixelated on my screen, but my brain can fill in the blanks. It's so good to hear her voice.

This is a much better way to spend my Monday night—feet up, popcorn in a bowl on the couch next to me, and Mom on my laptop. I left Nathan early and am pleased.

"Must be nice to sit on your butt in the sand finally after all that trekking?" I add.

"Oh, I'm going waterfall rappelling. No sitting around. I'll sit when I get to Mexico."

"Jesus, Mom, gotta take care of yourself, too."

She waves a hand at me. I can't see it on the screen, but I recognize the shoulder moving and the eye-roll that usually goes with it.

"What's happening there? Have you seen Jake again?"

"I will. I had to go to the client's office today. But he's booked me up for the rest of this week and next to teach him about the tools."

"Does he still seem like your Martin type?"

"Not sure yet. I call him Scowlface for now; he never smiles properly at me. He seems to be the only one that gets my blood rushing, though. Bah. Can't seem to focus when he's near."

I tell her about my date with Nathan and anything else I may have missed in our WhatsApp exchanges.

"Is this a crush? I don't even know him. I think it's just physical. How did you know with Dad?" I ask in a small voice, hoping for some Mom wisdom.

"Oh, Nora." She chews her lip and screws up

her eyebrows.

"Sorry, Mom, I don't seem to understand what makes you sad."

"I'm not sad." She exhales hard, making her cheeks puff out. "I'm guilt ridden."

"You're what?" I pause the handful of popcorn on its way to my mouth.

"There's something I never told you. Johan didn't want me to because it ruined our romantic high school story and special anniversary date."

I'm quiet, mind racing. What is she about to tell me?

"Your dad and I broke up. For over a year, until we met again for the last year of university."

"What? Why?"

"I went abroad. And I wanted to be free. Alone." She takes a sip of her bottled water.

"You studied abroad? And were you—*alone*?"

"For most of the time. But I met a man in Chile. Pedro. He had my blood rushing like your Jake does. Mm-hmm."

"So Dad wasn't the love of your life? Love at first sight?"

My gut clenches. I don't like not understanding. Their story has always been so clear. It's been one of my reference points for true love.

"He was. But I only knew it for sure once I'd experienced something else. Being alone. And having that animalistic urge for someone. Pure lust and passion," she says with her eyes closed.

"Okay, thanks Mom."

"Too much?" She laughs, repeating one of my standard comments to her. "Now he wasn't this *heartless* type you talk about, but he was a free soul; not meant to be tied down. Oh, the memories." She clutches her throat as she gushes about Pedro. I have a sudden realization of where her colorful shawls may have come from.

"Men like that aren't meant to be husbands. He had other women. Other priorities. Once I was back with your father, I knew it was where I belonged, but our relationship was better for it."

"You think Jake is my Pedro? But I don't have someone like Dad. I don't *need* a Pedro."

"You'll find your Johan when you least expect it, but it doesn't hurt to have a little Pedro in the meantime."

"He's the CTO, though. Could be a bad idea."

"I'm all for work flings. He's not your direct manager, is he?"

"No."

She shrugs and presses her lips together. "Where else to meet someone when that's where you spend most of your time? Doesn't sound like this app of yours works very well? Nor the bars. Anyone in the gym?"

"I've not looked. I'm not so keen on talking to men when my face is purple."

There's a commotion in the background and my mom turns around.

"I've got to go, kitten! It's time to head out.

Speak soon. I love you."

And she's gone.

The house is quiet. Dee is at Ajay's, which isn't normal for a Monday. Maybe they're ramping things up.

It's time for me to dig out my tools and get some Jake-thoughts out of my head. This better help with tomorrow.

CHAPTER 23

NORA

"What is it I can show you that's most helpful to you?" It's Tuesday. The inevitable show-and-tell week has started and Jake is closer to me now than he's been since the plane. How will I stay professional through this? No groping the new CTO in the office.

What my mom said echoes in my head, though. Wonder what Jake would say to that.

"I'd like to learn how you use the suite. Is it intuitive? Any problems?"

"How much time do you have?" I ask with a sly smile.

"That bad?"

"Nah, but there are a few complicated areas that confuse people and it's easy to make mistakes."

Jake sits on the chair next to me and seems reluctant to move closer. It's probably for the best, but I can't imagine he sees the details from there. I click through, explaining, and he inches closer. The heat emanating from his large body is getting stronger. My left side is burning. I turn my head to see his face; he's squinting at the screen. The numbers are tiny, and he leans in to read as I point to the monitor. The scent of his cologne is mild but powerful. I'm not sure what I said out loud and what I was thinking.

The little vibrator session yesterday obviously didn't make a difference. My heart is working in overdrive to send oxygen to the brain as well as servicing whatever the hell is going on further south.

"So what does this do?" he asks, pointing to the screen. His arm grazes mine and my entire core is on fire. How am I supposed to stay professional with this damned man-magnet right here?

He wheels a few inches away. Does he read minds too? "Can we get this up on a bigger screen in a meeting room? I can't see without crawling into your lap."

"Wha-what?" I splutter.

I would love that. His face in my lap, especially. Oh, gosh, don't go there, Nora.

"I wouldn't. I meant—"

"Of course. Let's use the boardroom." I gesture toward the corner of the office. It'll ensure maximum space between us. As we walk, I glance down quickly to remind myself what I'm wearing. My nipples are hard. It's not too hot today, so I'm in my favorite pink pencil skirt and a black blouse.

No visible nips, phew. I've been wearing my padded bras since his arrival, just in case, and they seem to do their job.

"The boardroom is taken. Any other rooms?" Jake asks.

Yes, but they're smaller and more private, and I don't think I can handle being with you in there.

I can't say that.

"They're not great. Let's head over to Zyclon instead. Lots of people you can talk to and you can meet the key client."

***

The air in the back of the black cab is heavy with the driver's cigarette stink and exhaust from the traffic, but a hint of cedarwood is a welcome relief. I angle my face toward Jake so it's the main scent I breathe and now I don't want to breathe anything else, ever again. It's intoxicating. His large hand relaxes on his knee next to me. I already know it's soft yet strong from his handshake. It's beautiful. I've never noticed hands before, but his are ... attractive.

"So you're from New York?"

"Partly," he answers without turning to face me.

"Did you grow up somewhere else?"

"It's a long story."

"We've got time." The traffic is moving slowly and I need him to talk to distract me from my thoughts about his hands and where I want them.

"Well ..."

"Start from the beginning. Are your parents from New York?"

He looks at me now, and the frown on his forehead deepens before it relaxes and disappears.

"My dad's English, actually. From Devon. Moved to the States to work as a robotics engineer after graduating. Met my mom. She's Sri Lankan American." His voice has a lighter tone to it than when he talks about work.

"Ooh, how did they meet?"

He chuckles and answers in the same relaxed tone. "In a bar. She worked there while studying psychology."

"Oh wow, so did she become a psychologist?"

"Yes, eventually. Long story not so long; my dad accepted an expat role which took him around the globe. My mom paused her career and doctorate plans so we could all come with him."

"All? Siblings?"

"One sister. Four years older than me."

I lift my eyebrows at him. There's no way I can tell how old he is.

"She's forty-one." He smiles when I nod, doing the math. "Anyway, we spent the early years in Germany, then Indonesia, France, New York, and finally Edinburgh. Mom finished her doctorate there. I did my software engineering degree, then moved back to New York nearly ten years ago for my AbbleTech role."

"That's it?" I ask, tongue-in-cheek. He smirks and tilts his head—a 'you asked' kind of expression.

"Sounds exciting. You've lived all over! Where's your sister now?"

"She's an IP lawyer here in London. Got her own boutique law firm."

"Wow, that's awe-inspiring."

I recognize the intersection we're coming into; we're getting close to the Zyclon office.

"It is. Big footsteps to follow in."

"Your parents must be so proud to have such high achievers as kids."

He hums in response.

"Do they live here too?"

"They're in the south of France."

"Dreamy."

We're at a red light a couple of blocks away and I squeeze in another question. I'm enjoying the bass of his voice and finding him increasingly interesting.

"Do you speak other languages?"

"French."

"Oh là là."

He chuckles. "Some basic Sinhalese from my mom. My sister and I went to international schools and spent most of our days with other expat families. American or British, mainly. I only picked up some words here and there."

"All right." The taxi driver pulls up to the curb below the tall glass building and I'll have to pause my interrogation.

***

"Thanks, everyone. This was most illuminating. Quite a lot to take in," Jake says with a grin and raised eyebrows to the Zyclon team gathered around Finn's desk. Over the last two hours, I've watched him listen intently, nodding his head, and asking pointed questions. But he also laughed and made them laugh. Is this Client-Jake or Normal-Jake? Is his gruffness reserved for his own colleagues, or only me—the airplane embarrassment?

There's been a lot more through-traffic by the women in the corner section than on a regular day. Their necks craned over the partitions as they passed—not even trying to be discreet.

I had to hold myself back from flicking their prying noses. Shoo, ladies. Let the man work in peace.

"Cool. Let's head back? I need to go to the gym." Jake pulls his laptop bag onto his shoulder and gives me a small sideways smile, which has my blood rushing, but at least I'm still standing. It's been touch and go today with his many smiles. Luckily, I sat safely in a chair most of the time.

I gather my thoughts and look around for Ash again. He's not been in today.

"Too bad you didn't get to talk to Ash. I mean Ashton. He's the project sponsor, and I'm sure he'd like to meet you."

"I'll come back ..." Jake's focus shifts to something behind me.

"Nor, I nearly missed you." I turn to see Ashton approaching with his arms wide, reaching out to shake Jake's hand. "You must be the new CTO, Jake Fielding? I'm Ashton Alexander. What a pleasure."

Jake nods. At first, he seems a bit taken aback. Presumably by Ashton's sudden and commanding presence. I wouldn't hold it against him. He squares his shoulders and grasps Ashton's hand firmly.

"Nice to meet you," he says with a smile that doesn't reach his eyes. Wonder what's going on behind them.

CHAPTER 24

JAKE

Nor? He calls her Nor? And she called him Ash. Didn't she *just* start working here? Does she know him? She kept looking around for him. It meant little to me until I saw him now. He's an inch taller than me. His eyes are like blue ice and I can't break myself away. I try to keep my expression as natural as possible while suffocating the roaring beast in me. Don't crush the client's hand. I release it and straighten out to make up for the missing inch.

"Did you get what you needed already? Nora's done a fantastic job with our workflows in only a few weeks, but we see room for improvement in the software."

"Absolutely. Thank you for sharing your team today. It's been of great help. I'll schedule in some time with you to get your views too."

"Perfect, our pleasure. Join us for drinks this week. It's on Friday this time, so will probably be a smaller group."

Humph, more of this guy, and we'll see him again at the client party too. I recognize the way he asks without asking, and one glance at Nora tells me she's into it. She flashes me a huge grin and nods.

I'm definitely not letting her go with this fucking whatchamacallim-Henry-Cavill-wannabe for drinks alone if I can help it. I put on a smile.

"Can't wait."

***

Nora's visible behind my computer screen. This glass office doesn't help to keep my focus, as every flurry of movement has me checking if it's her and her flowing green dress walking past.

I've spent the week learning how our tools are used, sitting next to her. It's been a constant test of my self-control and concentration. Heat radiates from her skin. Her sweet flowery scent hits me whenever she brushes her long curls off her shoulder. Her sparkling eyes bewitch me when she talks about these topics she knows so well.

I'm disappointed and relieved it's the weekend soon.

When I'm not with her, and let my focus drift, our conversations replay vividly in my mind. The little expressions and gestures she makes float past in a medley of Nora. The way her cheeks flush when our eyes meet in the morning. How she twirls a tendril around her finger while she waits for the program to load or wrinkles her nose when something on the screen isn't right. The way she bites her lip or sticks the tip of her tongue out when she's typing out intricate formulae for reports.

I go to the gym at lunchtime to decompress after morning meetings. Usually, talking for hours with my colleagues wears me down. I've been keeping to my old routine in this new job, but despite all the work talk, Nora doesn't tire me. I catch myself wanting to hurry back.

It's tempting to ask her to grab lunch together. But it's best we don't. It would feel too much like a date.

I've tried to keep our conversations professional, so I don't muddy the water after my slip-up the first day. I'm so curious about her though. What does she get up to in the evenings when I'm here in the empty office? I overheard her telling Sara her date on Monday was a dud, and it pleased me more than I dare to admit.

Today is another scorching day, and she was huffing when she arrived in the morning. She'd walked part way instead of going to the gym, she said. Sitting so close to her, every detail was visible. Small beads of sweat on her upper lip. On her chest. Her cheeks were red.

It was hard not to get distracted. I've imagined her like that too many times already—flushed, hot, messy hair—in a completely different scenario.

It's an act of pure willpower, not letting my mind go too far. As if I'm violating her in my fantasies if I do too much. I keep her face in focus. Her lips part. A sigh escapes them.

Gah. Stop.

I can't progress the investment memorandum when Nora occupies my mind.

I look up again and find her instantly.

She's been at her desk since our latest walk-through session. Did she have her lunch while I was at the gym today? The regular empty salad container isn't next to her, and I don't think she had her afternoon snack. A laugh escapes me. It's cute; her near religious, dark chocolate break.

When we sat on the train, she said she gets grumpy when she doesn't eat, which probably means she gets low blood sugar. Will Ashton sort food for his team? I need to help make sure she has something before we have drinks tonight.

Me: Shall we grab a bite on the way to Zyclon?

Nora: ...

The three dots appear. And stops. Then again;

Nora: ...

Jesus. I'll just walk over.

"Nora."

"Ah!" she shrieks and I'm so surprised I laugh, which makes her face contort into a strange grimace.

"Are you okay?" I ask.

She shakes her head, but then nods and relaxes her expression. "Yes," she breathes. "Uhm. Food sounds good."

"That's what I came to check on. Let's go."

She gives me a military salute and kicks her high heels off under the desk, stepping into a pair of sparkly flat shoes instead.

"Where to?"

***

I order us a large shared charcuterie and cheese board to a nod of agreement from Nora. We're huddled in a corner at the bar we're meeting the Zyclon team. I watch her put together mixes of cheeses, vegetables, and meats that make my inner French person scream silently.

"Are you not eating? Did we order something you can't eat?"

"I'll eat. I love cheese." Just making sure she has enough first before I dig in.

"Hmm." She narrows her eyes at me. "You're up to something," she says through a mouthful of bread, pointing at me with the crust in her hand.

"I noticed you hadn't eaten, and we're having drinks." I decide to tell the truth. She's not easily fooled.

"You don't have to help me, mister. Trust me to take care of myself." She lays a slice of Brie on top of a sun-dried tomato and an olive, and puts it in her smiling mouth.

"Good. And don't worry, it was completely selfish. I didn't want to see you grumpy." I hold back a laugh and take a sip of my water. She stops, cheese halfway up to her mouth.

"So you remember I said that?"

"Of course. Then you called *me* a grump, effectively."

"You are a bit." She raises her eyebrows at me.

"Not always." I flash her a wide grin and she coughs on her cheese.

***

After several rounds of cocktails, Nora and the remnants of Ashton's team sway on the couch to the music. I had one drink before I went back to my regular club soda, and retreated to a corner, where I'm pretending to enjoy the view of the city—not of Nora.

It's getting dark out here on the rooftop terrace. We're illuminated only by the overhead festoon lights and the golden hue from the bar inside. The sky is a deep pink, almost purple.

Nora's ability to connect with this diverse group has mesmerized me. She's been telling stories, clinking glasses, and even shimmying around with a couple of them in this small space. She makes them laugh. They seem at ease with her. And a few times she's been in quiet conversation, one on one, frowning and nodding. Ashton hasn't seemed flirtatious, thankfully. Maybe I read him wrong. In hindsight, I don't get my reaction to him. It was like when I saw Nora's name on Mark's phone. A primal response.

I lean back on the fence in the corner and catch Ashton's eye. He empties his drink and heads over.

"Good of you to join tonight."

"My pleasure. Nice to get to know you all." It eased my regular apprehension to work socials that it's a small team, and the ogling ladies from the other day aren't part of it.

Turns out Ashton's a Star Wars fan, traveler, and he's doing an advanced obstacle course in a few months which he casually invited me to join. I just might. He's cool. And making some friends wouldn't be the worst idea.

"Great team you've got," I add.

"I like to think so." He looks back to the area the team was gathered earlier. "Nora fits in. That's why she's an excellent consultant. They trust her. Tell her everything. And she shows them she listens."

He turns and talks toward the view, leaning his elbows on the railing.

"We've had many consultants from Upturns over the last two years and they never seemed to figure out where we go wrong. And they piss me off more than calm me down, blaming the team for making mistakes when it's the tool. I don't hire fools." He waves a large hand and straightens back up again.

"Hm."

"We considered changing providers recently. I never told Manuel in so many words. But it looks promising now. We'll stick around to see the improvements. It's a hell of a job implementing a new tool, so we'd hate to do it."

"Right." I'm absorbing what he's just said. There seems to be a lot more than expansion riding on a redevelopment.

"I've got to split. Seems most people have already."

Ashton pushes away from the fence. "See you next week. And think about that obstacle course, we could do with another strong teammate."

"Sure thing," I say and nod as he strides off.

I turn and take in the view of nighttime London; the Gherkin with its spiraled glass design below me, and the iconic Tower Bridge lit up in the distance.

A waft of sweet vanilla and flowers meets my nose before she arrives. Nora leans on the railing next to me.

"Magnificent, isn't it?"

"Hm," I say. A grunt of agreement.

She turns toward me and I realize I'm in a corner and can't step further away. Against my better judgment, I answer by turning to face her. Her long curls drape her shoulders. The soft fabric of her dress falls around her waist and hips perfectly.

"You're still here," she says, more a question than a statement.

"Yes."

"Were you waiting for me?" A smile plays on her lips.

"Have to make sure you get home safe. I wasn't sure how these drinks go."

"Mm-hmm." She smirks. Does she think I've been waiting for her for another reason? Do I want her to think that? No, of course not. I'm here to make sure she doesn't get hit on by our client.

"You're doing well with the team, I hear. Ashton's a big fan of yours."

I'm fishing.

She shrugs, looking up at me.

"You guys seem friendly," I continue, not doing a great job of being subtle. Her smile widens.

"We get along."

"Hm."

She inches closer. The warmth of her body is radiating. She leans in and angles her face up.

"Jealous?"

I huff, but don't look away. It's like I'm stuck in her gaze. Her pupils are dilated in the dark, and the reflection of the city's twinkling lights make her eyes sparkle even more than normal.

"I also get along with his *girlfriend*." Her eyes dart down to my mouth.

"Right," my voice is a raspy whisper. The air

between us crackles. I don't like where this is going, but can't seem to get out.

"I think we're alone now," she whispers, and her breath caresses my chin. It makes my body react. I have no control around her. As if she senses it, she glances down with a sly little smile and looks back up at me. I lean back. She's too close.

"You want me," she says in a low voice and the sweetness of minty mojito hits my nose. She graces my crotch with her hip, making me hard. Can she tell?

She bites her lower lip and leans in; her breasts an inch away from my chest as I tilt back to create space. It takes every ounce of willpower not to pull her toward me instead—not to rip that dress up and take her right here. Feel that warmth on me. Hear her moaning as I let my hands roam across that glorious shape.

I can't.

"It's not a good idea." It comes out as a deep growl. She's turning me into an animal. My brain works hard to overpower the primal urges. All I should do is go home, have a long shower and release this pressure. I glance sideways toward the bar to find a distraction and reason to move without being too rude. The two people left from the Zyclon team are now wrapped up in each other's arms—and faces. They're not paying attention to us. Nora follows my gaze and then turns back to me.

"Kiss me," she breathes, stretching up. Her pink lips look soft. Inviting.

I should get a fucking prize for this.

"Sorry, Nora, I won't." I put my hands on her arms and gently hint at her to move away.

"Nobody would know."

I would. *Sage* could. I wouldn't be able to stop at a kiss.

"You've had a few drinks. I'm sober. And I'm your senior. I'll get you an Uber now." I finally force myself into action and move around her, then I stop to maneuver my ridiculously hard cock into a less visible position.

Fucking hell.

"I don't care that you're my senior. I can see you want to." She smiles and glances down to emphasize her point.

"Despite what you seem to think, I can control myself." Except that once that keeps haunting me. "And *I* care."

"Okey-dokey." She waves a hand and starts walking toward the exit. Ugh, please don't tell me she'll be all cranky and upset.

As if she can hear my thoughts, she swivels and beams

at me. Thank God.

"You're right. It's for the best. I got naked with a man at my old job and it was awkward. I don't want it to be awkward at Upturns," she says with a grimace, pushing the button for the elevator that'll take us down and out. I'm hardly present as I step in. The words 'I got naked' echo in my mind and I need to compose myself. It's like I've become a teenager again. No control. Work, brain. What's not sexy? Biscuits. Knees. No, knees can be sexy. I bet Nora's knees are—I shake myself mentally. She's expecting a response, based on those big eyes glancing up at me.

"Oh yeah?" is all I say.

Nice one, Jake. If only the blood circulation could level out I might be able to sort out that Uber for her.

"Are you all right?"

"I'm fine." I take out my phone as we exit the building. "Let me get you that Uber."

"Have you not learned yet?"

I tilt my head to the side and frown. "Uhm."

"I do things myself." She holds up her phone, showing the little black car heading toward a dot on the map.

"When did you do that?"

"Just a moment ago, when your penis and brain were fighting over who gets to function." Her face breaks into a huge grin, green eyes sparkling, and my heart enters the competition.

Fuck.

CHAPTER 25

NORA

"Let me get this straight," Ajay says, turning toward me on the bench. "You hit on your CTO. Your Chief of Technology."

I drink my grapefruit sour beer, a newfound joy, and chuckle at his incredulity.

"It seems I did. And I could blame the alcohol. Or sugar. Fucking mojitos. But I think it was all me. I want him. Sue me." I take another sip but stop it short to add, "Although the way he stuck around like that, I thought he wanted something to happen. So I blame him a bit too."

"What's so bad about it, Ajay?" Dee asks. "He's not her boss. She's an adult. What's *bad* was when the Director of something-something—"

"Commercial and BD," I add, guessing what she's about to say.

"—BD whatever, hit on *her*. That's worse."

"I'm not saying it's bad. It's bad *ass*. You go, girl," he says the last part with an American twang—the complete opposite of his posh

Southwest London accent.

I was hoping this Sunday with Dee and Ajay would come with some advice, but so far Ajay is all jokes.

Dee hasn't told me about the family event he took her to yesterday, but I can only assume it went well as they're both here.

"I've shagged lots of people at work over the years, although I can't say any of them hit on me like that," he says and whistles. Dee punches his shoulder and he shrieks. "Before you, of course. And not in my own department. Yikes."

She pouts, but flashes him a smile and says, "I've slept with *lots* of people at work, too. And as I'm senior editor now, working my way up, I probably should've been more careful."

"Ew. I did *not* need to know that." He covers his eyes, and Dee and I glance at each other. Classic. He can dish it but he can't take it. "On that note. I'm heading to the gents. It's my round. What drinks would you like?"

I point at my near empty beer glass. He gives me a thumbs up.

"I'll have another mojito, please." Dee grins. "*Love* the sugar." She wrinkles her nose at me and my previous comment.

"Anything for you, dear." Ajay kisses her temple. He gets up and we sit quietly until he's behind the white concrete wall of the building.

Dee's across from me at a wooden table, the sun caressing us from on top of the sky.

The canal is covered in a carpet of duckweed, and little black birds float through it, picking at the garbage that has landed on top. The bright green layer perfectly complements the colorful graffitied wall on the other side, and the intensely blue sky above.

Another popping day.

"Who've you banged at work, then? That old wrinkly dude in the corner office?" I tease. There might be some eligible men at the publishing house, but I know the answer.

"Psh, I had to say that. Ajay doesn't need to know how special he is." A touch of pink spreads in her cheeks. Dee can count her 'special ones' on one hand.

I do hope he knows how significant he is.

"Do you mean it? Trying it on with someone at work is acceptable? Or were you taking the opposite side to Ajay for kicks?" I ask, angling my head.

"Hmm. If two consenting adults are involved, and the power balance is fair, then it's fine. Like with Jake, he's your senior, but as long as he can't affect your career ...?" She shrugs and smashes the mint leaves of her empty mojito with her straw. "But he said *no*, so I think you should leave it."

"He wants to, though. Seems like it, anyway." I groan. "*I* want to."

"Yeah. Suppose that's what the BD creep thinks about you. See how nice it is next time he corners you in a bar."

"Hah. Am I a creep?"

"Not yet." Dee laughs. "I'm your best friend and will always be honest. Unless Jake makes a move, I think you need to let it go."

"Bah. You're too wise for your thirty years." I scowl exaggeratedly at her, scrunching up my mouth, and she flashes me a knowing grin. I'm lucky to have someone who wants the best for me, and who cares enough to give it to me straight when I'm teetering on the edge of creep-hood.

The sun hits Ajay in the face as he returns from the bar, and he manages to whisk his pilot glasses out of the front of his shirt and onto his nose while balancing two pints of beer between his arm and chest. If I'd tried such a move, there'd be broken sunnies, shattered glass and an entirely beer-soaked dignity involved. His black hair glistens as his head moves and he flashes us his pearly whites. His physical appeal isn't lost on me. I understand how he keeps charming his way into my friend's pants. Sorry, arms. And heart.

Dee groans quietly. I try to determine why, and I'm guessing it's because he didn't buy what she asked for.

"Sorry, the wait for cocktails was inhumane. I got you a fruit beer. It's almost like a cocktail."

She musters a smile.

"What?" he asks, sensing something is off.

"Beer makes me … bloated," Dee says with a hint of a pout.

"Since when?" he asks, chuckling as if she's being funny.

"Since always?" Dee raises her eyebrows at him.

"You had beer yesterday."

"Yeah, I don't tell your dad when he offers me an open beer bottle that it makes me fart, do I?" Dee hides from him behind her hand and looks at me across the table. A mix of embarrassment and annoyance in her expression.

"Oh, that was you in the foyer? I thought it was the dog." He cackles loudly, and she scrunches up her mouth. I sense she's had it with this topic.

"How was the party, anyway?" I ask, trying to change the subject but grimace as I realize it's related to the same story.

"Not bad," Dee says cheerily. Phew. "And I didn't fart in the foyer, by the way." She punches Ajay lightly in his thigh. Her tiny fist must be a light tickle for him. He's not huge, but definitely strong. Tennis muscles. "Everyone was glad to meet Ajay's girlfriend, finally. Maybe next we'll go to see my parents in Lisbon." Her eyes sparkle as she looks at him. Beer debacle forgotten already. Ajay smiles at her absentmindedly and tilts his head to check a stain on the front of his shirt.

My phone vibrates on the table.

Preston: I'll try one last time. Do you want to grab dinner this week? Any time, I understand your new job is busy.

Why is he trying so hard? He didn't seem to like me all that much. Dinner sounds like pure torture if our first date was an appetizer.

"Dee? What do I do with this guy?"

"Just say no."

"Isn't that a bit harsh? Does he deserve another chance? He's very handsome."

"Christ." She gives me the classic Dee eye-roll again, but as always, while holding back a laugh. She knows I'm doing it a bit on purpose. "Well, invite him to ukulele night on Wednesday and Ajay and I can have a go at him for being such a pretentious knob on your first date."

I beam at her. "*This* is why we're best friends."

Me: Join for ukulele Wednesday at the Wellington pub? I'm learning! *thumbs up*

"All right, drink up ladies. We should make a move so we don't miss the main show," Ajay says and taps his fingers on the side of the table.

"Is it The Strokes you want to see so badly?" I ask, emptying my glass as ordered.

"Tribute band—don't be disappointed. Although, I've heard they're as good as the real deal." He shrugs.

Dee twirls into the park, bright and happy in her yellow romper, her long hair flowing around her shoulders. The sequin rainbow overalls I scored at a thrift shop on Brick Lane sparkle in the sun.

Sounds of the small one-day festival in Victoria Park surrounds us. Guitars and drums from the stage, people chattering, children squealing as they run. The sound of their feet hitting the pavement disappears as they cross from the path to the vast grass field.

Ajay volunteers to grab the next round again before the main band is on, letting us take our place in front of the small stage. I love a daytime park gig. Especially in East London. There's a lot of space. Room to dance. To breathe. Dee spins and flails her arms. It's not obvious how, but she makes everything look cool and carefree. I mimic her moves and try to relax into the music.

"Have you heard of the kitchen dance?" I shout across the guitar riffs.

"No?"

"Colette told me. Dance like no one is watching."

Dee gives me a thumbs up and seems to nail it already. She's free. I move around, letting my curls fly and my arms go where they want, and then I feel it.

That tingling.

Someone is watching.

I swerve, pretending it's a part of the dance, and scan the crowd.

He's here. I'm sure.

I keep dancing, but now it's impossible to pretend I'm carefree. Oh my god, there he is. He's not looking at me, though. Was he before?

He's with a stunning woman. For a moment I'm convinced he's on a date and my stomach aches. But she looks so much like him. It must be his sister.

Oh, I hope that's his sister.

"Dee. It's Jake." I grab her arm and point discreetly. "He's in a peach T-shirt and jeans."

"Jesus Daniel Christ. You weren't joking."

"No. I wasn't." My heart pounds hard.

I've not seen him wear color in the office. The peach complements his light golden skin and brown hair perfectly and makes him look soft. Warm. In a heart-stopping, pants-dropping kind of way. Oh gosh, look at how it hugs his broad back like that. I want to climb him and—

"Stop drooling. Let's go say hi." Dee pulls me along with a grin. In a daze, I follow and allow the excitement to take over. It's Jake out of his office habitat. He's been all work since day one. It seems he plays as well.

CHAPTER 26

JAKE

"Do you know her?" Sage asks, breaking my trance-like state. I can't take my eyes off Nora. Her glittering clothes and flowing curls caught my eye through the scattered crowd. She looks happy, dancing and jumping around. I was afraid she'd be here when Sage suggested we'd go to Hackney.

'*You can take the girl out of East London, but not East London out of the girl*' was her response when I asked why here. I'll give her a few more years in her pastel Primrose Hill house and we'll see about that.

"Who?" I turn to accept the cardboard bowl of paella she hands me.

"That girl you're ogling."

"No idea what you're talking about." I angle myself away, digging into my rice dish.

"You were smiling like an idiot. Do you like her?"

"I was smiling? What girl, anyway? Thanks

for the food." I take another bite. "Mmm, this is delicious," I say through a mouthful.

"She's gorgeous. Looks fun. I love those sequin overalls."

She *is* fun.

I try to coax Sage to turn away with me.

"Hmm." She bites on her fork. "You need some sparkly fun in your life. Let's talk to her." Her face lights up.

"Let it go, Sage." I give her what I think is my best angry stare.

"Oh-kaaay," she chirps and stuffs a forkful of paella into her mouth. "But she's coming over." Her words are muffled by food so it takes a second for them to sink in.

"She's wh—"

"Jake?" I hear the familiar voice behind me and freeze.

Fuck.

"Hey." I turn around and catch Sage's eye as I do. She's telling me off with her mind for pretending I don't know her. Will I get away from this conversation without her finding out we work tog—

"Dee, this is my boss man, Jake."

Fuckety-fuck.

I look at Sage when I say, "I'm not the boss. I'm not *her* boss," I emphasize. "Hi Dee, nice to meet you." I shake her hand.

"Likewise, Jake. I've heard lots about you."

Fuck's sake. Stop it.

"This is my sister, Sage. Sage, this is Nora and Dee." I gesture towards the girls, quietly praying this won't blow up in my face.

"Hey, *love* your overalls."

"Thanks!"

That smile. I'm blown away. Even without sequins, she'd be sparkling.

"So Jake's your 'boss man', is he?" Sage keeps her tone light, but I hear the dig at me.

"Not directly. But he's a chief and *I* am but his humble servant," Nora says theatrically with a curtsy, pretending to hold out a dress. She's making it worse. I need telepathy skills *now*.

I clear my throat and shuffle my feet, angling myself toward Sage. "Nora is advising me. She has many years of experience. She's a *senior* consultant." I keep eye contact with Sage. Her expression is hard to interpret. I'm certain she assumes the worst about me. But she keeps a polite tone for the innocent bystanders.

"That's great. Hope he's an outstanding leader and role model at your company."

"Absolutely. Almost to a fault." Nora's eyes flicker to me. Don't fucking go there.

Sage eyes me again, this time with obvious curiosity. I shrug it off and spy Ryan appearing with my gorgeous niece in his arms.

"My new favorite person," I say genuinely, but with added enthusiasm to be free from the work conversation. "Nora, Dee, meet Jackie."

I pass my paella to Sage and stretch out to

Ryan, who happily hands me the tiny thing. When I turn back to Nora and her friend, they look like they're about to burst. They must be loving her.

"Jackie? After you?" Nora asks. I kiss the little baby-face. Her skin is so soft. I didn't think I'd like babies until I met this one.

"Jacqueline Roshani. In honor of her favorite, albeit only, uncle, and our mom. Jackie for short," Sage responds. I steal a peek at Nora and her eyes are wide, looking at me. Her skin is flushed. Probably from dancing.

I grin at my sister. Having her daughter named after me proves she's truly forgiven me. She believes in me. That I can be an uncle to Jackie that she can look up to. A brother to be proud of. My heart swells and I want to squeeze her.

"Sage," I say, reaching over to pull her into a side-hug, cradling the baby bundle safely in my other arm.

"What's that sound?" Sage asks, as she accepts the hug, leaning into my embrace. "Nora, are you okay?"

Nora's slack-jawed. What's going on?

"Aaaaah." She squeaks. Sage and I exchange looks discreetly.

"She's probably dehydrated," Dee says and takes Nora's hand. "We'll go grab some water before the next band. Have to find my boyfriend as well. Nice to meet you all." Dee pulls her away and Nora waves with both hands and a sheepish smile. They disappear into the crowd.

"The baby effect," Ryan says from behind us.

"What's that?" I ask.

"She saw a cute baby. And Jackie's the cutest of them all. Who wouldn't go speechless at you, little munchkin?" He leans in and talks into Jackie's cheek.

"Hmm," Sage hums. Still staring after Nora. Does she not agree? I follow her gaze but can't see the colorful girls anymore.

"Be careful, Jake," Sage adds. "I think it was more than the baby she was looking at. Unless you like her? *Like*-like?"

"Nope. Stop it, Sage." I hand Jackie back to Ryan.

"What did she mean by 'to a fault'?" she asks with a crease forming between her eyebrows. Sometimes I wish she'd put the lawyer-side away. Nothing gets past her.

I sigh. "She flirted and I asked her to stop. I told you I'm not making the same mistakes again."

"Good. I think." Sage turns back to where Nora disappeared to.

"What do you mean?"

She meets my eye. There's a tenderness there.

"I wouldn't want to see you make other mistakes, either. You deserve someone in your life that makes you smile."

The Strokes tribute band takes the stage and

Ryan nudges us to get closer. I flash my sister a grin and wrap my arm around her shoulder as we walk.

"I've got you guys. Jackie. I'm not getting involved with anyone at work. No matter how fun, intelligent, and beautiful they are."

Sage narrows her eyes at me. Does she not believe me?

"What?"

"Nothing." She presses her lips together. "If you say so."

"I say so." But my stomach churns as I do.

CHAPTER 27

NORA

"It's harder than it looks," Preston says with a tired smile, and his voice tells me he hates it. We're one beer down and three songs in at Ukulele Wednesday and he's not able to follow the group. None of us are, but he's the only one who cares.

"Don't worry, Preston," Dee says softly and I chime in with sounds of agreement while sipping a fresh beer.

"It's normal to suck at things you've never tried," Ajay adds, strumming wildly on his four-string child sized guitar, which is what it looks like in his arms. The men have wooden rental ones, while Dee and I went all in when we found this event and have our brand new ukuleles in hand. Mine's a gorgeous royal blue, coincidentally matching today's pencil skirt, and hers is a shiny black.

"I don't suck at things. But this one is ridiculous." Preston frowns and tries again to form a claw-shaped E minor with his large hand while cursing under his breath.

I quickly found I couldn't do that one so decided to skip that and the rhythmic strumming until I've practiced at home. I have fun hitting the easier G, C, and F with clumsy hands and singing along.

I'm loving this.

When I'm not overthinking, not trying to be perfect—like Preston over there—it's fun.

After five more songs, and a near-death experience for Preston's ukulele, the two of us exit the pub onto the busy Strand sidewalk leaving Dee and Ajay to finish their drinks in peace. I'm happy to go home alone and hope Dee goes with Ajay tonight. I've heard enough of how strongly she agrees with his new bedroom skills.

The sky is a pale orange with a hint of pink—the late June sun is setting.

"Thanks for tonight," Preston says without emotion. His hair is disheveled, and it's like he's shrunk an inch. I feel bad for him now. It must be tough to strive for perfection like that all the time.

"Sorry you didn't have fun. Keep practicing, I guess." I laugh and he snorts in response, not meeting my eye. At least he's got some humor about it. I pull my ukulele bag further up on my shoulder and turn away to hint that I'm going *that* way.

Alone.

"I'm going this way," he says meekly, indicating behind him with a thumb. I remember that from our first date, which is why I've angled myself toward the next tube station instead of walking back with him.

"Okay. Bye, Preston." I give him a thin smile as I wave and saunter off toward Waterloo Bridge. I want to see my friend Big Ben in the sunset before heading home.

Well, Ben's a bell in the Elizabeth Tower, but nobody calls it that.

Up ahead there's a tall, broad figure I'm certain I recognize. The one that's been sitting next to me for the last three days, talking work and pretending I didn't hit on him last week. That we didn't meet on Sunday. When I asked how his family's doing and if they had fun, he answered 'fine'.

I've been trying to figure out what his various frowns, scowls, and other forehead creases mean. His eyes are very expressive, but most of the time they're dark and intense. I can feel them on the side of my face when I show him things on the screen. Occasionally, they almost twinkle. But I can't match it to what I said or did, I'm rambling on about my work.

Despite the emotion I sometimes glean behind his stern expressions, he's not interested in getting to know me. He's all about work. He's not had lunch with me once between our sessions. Is it because he needs a break from all my babbling? I've heard that before.

But now he's not in the office. He's right there. Will he talk to me about something else now he's outside those four walls and no colleagues around? Or is it me that's the problem?

"Jake?"

He turns around. I can't make out his expression from across the street, but he lifts a hand and waves, so I pick up my pace to catch up.

"Hi," I say breathlessly when I reach him. "What a fun coincidence running in to you. Have you been out?"

"No, just finished work."

Poor man. He's there when I arrive and there when I leave. He looks tired.

"Another long day."

He shrugs it off. "Where have you been?" He nods toward my ukulele.

"Ukulele Wednesday at the pub."

"Sounds fun. Was it another date? Sorry, none of my business." He holds up his hands. So he does care? Or just curious?

"It was, but as I'm here—alone—at nine o'clock, it was obviously not a great one. Well, *I* had fun playing. Can't speak for him, though."

He gives me a sideways smile. The tiredness I saw before is gone. God, he's beautiful.

"Why are you going this way from work? Aren't you in Camden?" I ask.

"No, I found a place in the Barbican. I can walk home. Where are you heading?"

"Temple station, it's down there." I point. "But I'm going to see the view from the bridge first."

"Any good?"

"Come check it out for yourself."

He hesitates.

"Don't worry, I'll behave." I grin at him.

"Fine," he grumbles, but the sides of his mouth twitch.

I skip ahead and look back at Jake. He's walking slowly, but covering a lot of ground with his long strides. When we pass the buildings at the foot of the bridge, he looks out over the Thames as it comes into view. Wrinkles form at the side of his eyes when he squints and smiles toward the sunset. I find myself staring at him much longer than I should before turning away. He must've noticed.

Despite Preston's mood, I'm elated and full of energy. The sight of the London Eye made orange by the setting sun on one side, and Big Ben illuminated in golden hues on the other, intensifies that feeling. The purple, pink, and orange hues of the sky reflect in the river and it fuels me.

I'm in London. I *live* here.

I twirl and dance farther up the bridge. It dawns on me what I'm doing and I stop to receive whatever comment Jake may have about it. He's looking out over the river and stops next to me. When he doesn't say anything about my silly dancing, I turn back to the view, standing out of reach. The air nearly buzzes between us, but I do my best to ignore it.

"When I was in university, we walked across this bridge often. Every time, I would stop to enjoy this view and remember where I was. What a privilege to be here."

"Why did you leave?"

"Job opportunity." I press my lips together. "I was only here for a year, but it was life altering. When I left, I think a part of me stayed behind and I couldn't slot back into the Norwegian puzzle." I'm talking toward the skyline. Musing loudly.

"Hm."

I swivel to see his face. He's furrowing his brow again, squinting into the sun. Wonder what he's thinking.

"Waterloo sunset," he says quietly, and turns to me with a grin. Frown gone.

"The Kinks." I smile back.

"You know it?"

"I love it."

He hums the next part of the song. I know the lyrics. Does he? I'm definitely in paradise here. Maybe all we need is this. London life. To me, that's what the song is about. Is he happy here too?

His humming trails off and we're quiet for a moment, taking in the spectacular colors playing on the skyline.

"I wouldn't have pegged you as an alternative

rock guy initially," I say. "Definitely didn't expect to see you in Vicky Park on Sunday."

"Seems like I'm full of surprises." He tries to hold back a smile, but the glimmer in his eyes betrays him.

"Seems like you are ... Has anyone ever experienced them all?" I study the side of his face. His eyes narrowed now, staring intently straight ahead.

"Not really," he mutters.

The sun is below the skyline, only an orange glow left as the final reminder of this gorgeous summer evening.

Has he never loved anyone? Has no one loved him? I've never loved or been loved either. Is it possible he's been as lonely as me? Or maybe he never wanted anyone. He never let anyone peel back the layers and explore what's going on underneath all those frowns.

Or did they, and found nothing?

No. I've seen how he smiles. Each time it takes me by surprise and makes me fizz with endorphins. There's more there. I saw how he was with his family.

"Has anyone ever tried?" I ask, my voice cracking.

He turns to me now, those intense dark eyes on mine, his jaw flexing.

"No."

Goosebumps travel up my spine. Is that what his sad face looks like? Is he the pained hero after all?

"Oh ..." My voice is barely audible.

I'm frozen, just looking back at him. I want to step closer; feel his heat, put my face into the crook of his neck, and breathe in his scent. But I promised him not to. I turn back to the view instead with a hum, not sure what to say next.

"Better get going," he says, checking his wristwatch.

"I'm not in a rush," I say quickly. "I can walk with you for a stretch and Uber home."

I want more.

He nods slowly. "Can I get you the Uber this time?"

"What do you think?" I give him a wry smile and start walking.

"Fine," he grumbles behind me.

CHAPTER 28

NORA

We walk back where we came from, strolling along the road. The odd car roars past, but it's quiet when we enter the pedestrian area. I steal a glance at him; he's looking up at the old buildings lining the street. Wonder what he's thinking now.

"How's Sri Lanka? Did you ever go?"

He turns to me before he looks back at where we're walking. "We went on vacation years ago. Mom wanted us to experience the food and see the diverse nature—rainforests, mountains, beaches ..."

"Oooh, how's the food? I've never tried Sri Lankan."

He chuckles softly, and it makes my heart flutter in a funny way.

"Aromatic, flavorful. Quite varied. Lots of coconut, chili, and rice-based dishes. There are a handful of restaurants here I've read should have decent Sri Lankan, although I've not tried them yet."

"Sounds amazing. Let me know what you find out, so I can try it. Do you cook it yourself?"

"I dabble."

His choice of words makes me smile. A fellow dabbler.

"Nice. Much more exciting than Norwegian cuisine, I'm certain." We're back where the cars roar and I have to speak up. Jake's deep voice carries easily over the noise.

"I quite enjoyed the simple flavors at the places I ate in Norway. Freshly grilled fish straight from the sea. Sometimes less is more."

A group of loud men exit a pub in front of us and we stroll quietly behind them for a stretch. They wave their arms animatedly as they laugh and break into a drinking song. We cut through a different route and find ourselves on a quiet street again.

"Did you grow up in Bergen?" Jake asks, angling his head in my direction. I keep peeking at him as we walk. Eager to see what expressions play on his face as we talk.

"Born, raised—pretty standard."

"What made you move to London initially?"

I let out a long breath, puffing out my cheeks. I know the answer to this in hindsight. "In the first years of university, I didn't put in the effort to make friends—the drawback of studying where you already have a life, maybe. Got increasingly isolated. My dad died right before I started as well, which didn't help."

"Oh man, I'm so sorry. What happened?"

"Pancreatic cancer. He was gone within months of diagnosis. It was … hard." The familiar knot appears behind my lungs, threatening to crawl up into my throat, but I don't let it.

"Fuck."

Sums it up.

"Thanks. It's been sad seeing my mom alone all these years. My big brother lives in Oslo. She puts on a brave face, but surely it's been lonely. Then she finally decided she'll travel the world. For as long as she wants."

"That's amazing. Good on her."

I balance on the edge of the pavement, focused on stepping in the middle of every second rock. "So back to how I ended up here. When a girl in my statistics class told me she applied for a course in Manchester, it hit me; there's a world of opportunities out there. So I followed her lead. Off I went to finish my master's and change my life." I wave my arms excitedly.

"Careful," Jake says and grabs me by the waist, moving me to walk on the other side of him. His touch lingers through my blouse.

"So old fashioned." I laugh, but I mean it. "I don't need anyone to take care of me."

"Well, you were making me nervous, so do *me* the favor of not balancing on the side of the road, please."

I salute him as I did once before. Although I'd never take anyone's orders, I can do him a favor.

"And then you made lots of friends?" he asks, continuing the conversation as if nothing happened.

"Yes. Especially Dee. She's my closest. Knows me better than I know myself, sometimes. Even from a different country, she noticed I wasn't living my best life and encouraged me to move back."

"It was bad? You mentioned on the train it felt relentless."

Jesus, does he remember *everything*?

"Not as bad as it sounds. But it could've become. I don't feel that here. Not now. Only endless possibilities. I'm so at home here."

Up ahead, the spire of one of the old church ruins is visible in between the tall office buildings.

"Are you familiar with the ruins of the city?"

"Can't say I am."

"Check this one out. It's easy to miss if you walk the way most people do here—laser focused or nose in phone."

The old bricks and overgrown plants are a stark contrast to the white modern buildings behind.

"This is quintessentially London. Something age-old in the middle of the brand new. There's another one down by Monument. Probably one of my favorite spots."

We walk in between the towering bushes. The whirlwind of the world moving on around it could've leveled this place a long time ago. It was old and unused. Overgrown with weeds.

But it's not anymore. The spire stands tall.

Someone noticed it and saw its worth. Its beauty. Brushed the dust off and made it an oasis in the big city.

"It's magnificent," he says in a low voice behind me and we stand quiet for a minute. The plants on one side and the remaining church wall muffle the sounds of the late evening traffic.

"Right, onward with the walk. Postman Park next?" I ask and swivel on my heel, nearly bumping into him.

He doesn't flinch.

We're closer than we've ever been. He breathes out just as I breathe in and I shudder. Goosebumps travel down my neck and arms. The air between us is charged and I'm pulled toward him.

The sensation of his touch on my waist haunts my skin, willing him to do it again. My lips tingle at the thought of pressing them against his. Aching for it.

He breathes out again and my heart pumps so fast and so hard I'm sure he can hear it. The heat moves downwards, making my legs shaky. How does he do this to me so easily? I've never been like this before.

Then he steps back and puts his hands in his

suit pockets. "What's Postman Park?"

"Can't you feel this connection between us?"

"Connection?" He angles himself away from me, rubbing his neck.

"It's like I'm supercharged whenever you're close. This physical attraction is insane. It's best we do something about it. Get it out of our systems." I shake my hands and feet as if it would help to get rid of the tingling. "Is it just me?"

Oh god, am I really the female Howard to him? Does he not feel it?

He looks down before he tilts his face toward me to meet my eye. "It's not a good idea."

"You keep saying that." I move to the bench next to us and sit down, hoping he'll follow suit.

It's dark, and it's late, but I want to keep talking. I need him to confirm it's not one-sided or I'm left confused. And embarrassed.

"What makes you think it's such a bad idea? I told you I don't care about work."

He clears his throat and sits down. That's a positive sign. He seems like he's contemplating spilling some locked up beans. I shift on the bench to face him, leaning an arm over the back of it.

"Did you have sex with someone at your old job and it got awkward?" I grin and wiggle my eyebrows to keep the tone light, sensing his unease.

"Something like that." He looks at his hands. Fidgeting with his cuticles. Was it worse? Why is he so nervous?

"Did it get more than awkward?"

The air is thick with apprehension in the seconds he takes to answer.

He grunts, still looking down. Seems it's twenty-questions game time for me. "Was she younger? I'm assuming it's a *she*."

"She was a junior engineer. Twenty-four," he answers more quickly. Warming up. The confirmation that there's something doesn't make me feel better. I hope it's nothing terrible. I want to like him.

"Ah. That's not so young, though. But you were the boss?"

Another grunt.

"Did you get into trouble? Did you break her heart, and she went crying to HR?"

CHAPTER 29

JAKE

A part of me wants to tell her everything. Be honest. It means the end of whatever this is. That's fine, though. It'll be easier to focus on work if I don't have this battle in my head anymore. I can put a stop to her flirting, but the words won't come out.

She's staring at me.

"Because, don't worry, I don't have those kinds of feelings for you. I don't think you're the type I'm looking for. This is only physical."

I turn to her, surprised at the jolt in my gut at this comment. Has she already decided she knows enough about me to not be into it? I should be pleased. It makes it easier for me to stay away.

"What *type* are you looking for?"

"I don't know exactly. But I promised myself no more 'handsome and heartless' men." She makes air quotes.

"You think I'm heartless?"

An icy feeling spreads in my stomach. What did I do to make her think that?

"No," she says and blows air out through pursed lips. "Disinterested, maybe." She grimaces. Sounds like I've been almost too successful in keeping her from realizing I *am* interested. More than interested.

"You've had your Scowlface thing going on. That's why you're in the 'hot but disinterested' category and not in the 'happily ever after'-bucket. No offense."

"Hm. Some offense."

What will she think of my past if she has this view of me already? I stand no chance.

Gah, Jake, you won't take the chance, anyway. Let it go.

"What's Scowlface?"

"You look at me like this." She knits her brow and presses her lips together.

"Hm. That's not been my intention." Maybe I need to check myself. I was trying not to smile too much, but can't recall intentionally *scowling* at her. "What does your happily ever after look like?"

She puts a hand to her chin and taps her lips. Her classic thinking face. "It'll be relaxing, and I'll feel free. Content. I want to be with someone clear and sure who doesn't make me worry about what's going on. No games. I think too much as it is."

"I like the sound of that, too."

"Yeah? Is there a wife and kids' section in your life plan?"

I huff. "No, I've only planned as far as the CTO role. It's my focus for the foreseeable future." Although, I've recently started musing about what that part of my life could look like.

"You have it, so what's next?"

I can't tell her about the investor meetings coming up, or my probation period. "I need to keep it. Do well. Better than well. I want to make a name for myself so I can take my pick at the next role. Help small, struggling companies. Have financial security and freedom."

"I like the sound of *that*. I quite enjoy this role, this consulting stuff."

And that's another reason we can't act on our attraction. If something ruins her reputation, her job ... I can't be the reason for that.

"So shall we take our pants off now?" she asks suddenly.

I laugh, a bark, tilting my head back. I rub my eyes with both hands to hide my smile so she doesn't think I've caved, and then run them through my hair.

"Aaah. I've never met anyone quite like you, Nora."

"Sure you have. They've just not shown you."

"Are you always like this—so direct and energetic?"

"Not at all." She shifts in her seat. "Some people take up more space, so I quiet down. Some make me feel silly. I can be too serious for some—you've not met philosophizer-Nora yet. And I'm too playful for others. I have many sides. Right now, I'm ... the way I like to be. I don't seem to worry about what I do around you."

She pulls on her curls.

"I'm trying hard to think what it is about you, but I can't pin it down." She hums, thinking again. "Are you yourself? Have I met the Jake you like to be? I've got a feeling you've put on an office-face. I'd like to learn what's behind all those frowns of yours."

She doesn't know it, but hearing her say that makes my stomach flip. She wants to get to know me?

Ah, shit. I need to tell her.

"Look, maybe I should—"

"Don't worry, Jake. I'm not flirting with you again. I've tried twice now, not counting the airplane lap dance, and that's my limit. I refuse to be your Howard."

"Howard?"

"Hah. Yeah. I don't want to be a creep like him."

I send her a quizzical look.

"He hit on me twice," she adds with a tilt of her head.

"He did what?" I'm surprised at how loud it comes out.

"It's okay." She angles her hands slightly toward me as if to calm me down. "Apparently, he does it with everyone. I'll tell him off if he tries again. Don't worry."

"If he does, I'll—"

"*You'll* do nothing. I can take care of myself. I only use him as an example, so you know. No creeps here."

A quiet moment passes as we stare at each other, and the word vomit comes before I can stop it.

"*I* didn't get into trouble. *She* did."

"Oh?"

I sigh and look up into the dark sky. "Heather. She was a junior engineer, and I was the head of the department. At HercuSoft that means I was her boss's boss, and I had no clue who she was. There were nearly two-hundred engineers in New York alone.

"It started at a work party. One of those big summer parties I couldn't get away from. She came on to me. I initially turned her down, not interested in having a work fling. But she was quite persistent."

I glance at Nora as I say this and catch her grimacing. She might take it as a jab, but so be it.

"She kept appearing on my floor in the office. She showed up where I bought my coffee in the morning. At the Christmas party, she caught me in the right mood, and I went home with her."

"Go on," Nora says quietly.

I can't decipher her tone. She's definitely going to keep me in her 'not her type' category after this.

"She knew what she wanted, and she went for it. I'm only human."

Tread carefully, Jake.

I fucked it up with Sage years ago when I dared indicate Heather had any fault in it.

"Mm-hmm. Then what?"

I glance at Nora. Her expression is open. She looks curious. Wonder what's going on behind those wide eyes.

"We hooked up once more in the new year and I disclosed it to HR. It wasn't against the rules to be in a relationship but they'd make sure I wasn't part of her performance reviews and that it was all consensual. I made it clear it was a thing of the past.

"Then, I told Heather we were through. Even after disclosing it, it made me uncomfortable. And I found out Sage knows Heather's sister —I wanted it to end. The whole thing was a mistake."

I rub my neck and sigh. The regret is heavy in my gut.

"Then one evening I was working late she came to see me. She—Uhm."

"She tried it on with you in the office?"

I chew the inside of my cheek, remembering the night.

"What, and you got caught?"

"Ah. Nearly. She tried to ..." I gesture toward my crotch.

"Give you a blow job?" Nora looks shocked.

I nod with a grimace. "I think she'd been drinking after work and came back, knowing I was there late. She was on her knees and I moved away. But someone saw. We had those semi-frosted walls."

I rub my forehead, the familiar gnawing in my stomach starts as I remember the fear I walked around with. The shame. Even though I hadn't done what the rumors said. Although, it was close.

Ugh, I need to be entirely honest.

"Before I stood up ... and for a moment ... I was about to let her have her way with me. She had her hands on my belt buckle before I heard a sound and stood up."

I let out a long breath. Nora's quiet. I don't dare look at her right now. Don't want to see what I feel about myself reflected in her eyes.

"Whoever saw it told someone else and at HercuSoft that means soon everyone would know. The story varied from me coming on her face to her chasing me around the office." I huff and shake my head. It was ridiculous that people believed any of it. "A lot of her colleagues had seen her flirt with me, then this story—it fueled the fire of a rumor about her trying to sleep her way up. It spread fast."

I rub the back of my neck.

"Jesus Christ. People are right shits. Such a horrible work environment! What happened to her? Did you help?" Nora asks, a hand on her cheek as if she's still in shock.

"I talked to HR. Told them I made the first move, and I'd called her that night. That she was innocent. I was sure I'd get fired, and it terrified me. But they said the rumors were already out there and they needed me more than her. We were in the middle of an expansion of a new product."

I shake my head again, knowing how unfair it is.

"It got worse no matter what I said. People questioned her recent promotion. Her achievements. Other managers were unwilling to work closely with her, even be alone with her; afraid of becoming the next rumor.

"After a few months of this, HR 'politely suggested' she resign. Gave her a cash package so she wouldn't cause a fuss. She was devastated. Her dream to work for HercuSoft was ruined because of me. Because I wasn't strong enough to say *no* that first time, like I should've."

I look up at Nora. The shame in my eyes must be visible even in this dim light.

"I ended up not applying for the CTO role I was preparing for. That top role rarely comes available. But I guess I deserved that, at least. They should've fired me on the spot."

I stop. Letting the quiet moment stretch out between us as I pick on my thumbnail.

Nora breathes out audibly, breaking the

silence. "I'll say two things. You might not like the sound of it, but ... I agree. You should've said *no*. The power dynamics were way off. No matter how persistent she was. Especially when it was just sex. I'm a fighter for *love*, but you can get pants-business from anyone, especially when you look like you, so why her?"

Damn. I knew she'd think worse of me after hearing it. And she's right. There's no excuse.

"What's the other thing?"

"Sounds like you're ruminating a lot. Punishing yourself by going over it again and again. You can't change the past."

Her tone is softer now. I dare a glance at her again. The thick curls hang down over her almost bare shoulders. Damn, she's a sight for sore eyes.

I sigh. My body feels like it's full of lead.

"I can make sure it doesn't happen again," I say.

She nods slowly, playing with a lock of her hair. "It's not the same at Upturns, by the way. Probably best not to grope your engineers, but the consultant team is under Manuel." She wiggles her eyebrows at me. "I respect if you're worried about your own career, but don't stay away from this sizzling thing here because you're trying to protect *me*." She stands up, pushing off the bench. "However ... I've already spent my two tries, so the ball is firmly in your court." She laughs and starts walking toward the street. "On that bombshell, I bid you *adios*. My Uber will be here any minute." She shakes her phone to show me and walks out of sight, leaving me speechless.

What? She still wants me? Well, physically, at least. And no one would bat an eye? That's perfect, isn't it?

Isn't it?

As the thought lingers, my chest tightens, telling me it's not true. My lungs scream for air and I take a deep breath. I want her. All of her. All the time. But I also want to give everything to this role. The investor meetings are approaching at warp speed and I'm working into the evening every day to stay on top of my plan.

"Aaah!" I let out a growl and lean my head in my hands. Don't lose focus now, Jake. Remember what Dad always says. Got to give it my all.

At least she promised not to make a move again, so I'll need to put my visors on and try not to notice her. Fuck, we still have a few more days of work together.

I'll at least avoid social gatherings. Ugh, except for the client party on Friday. I can do it. Just remember what's most important.

CHAPTER 30

NORA

The night of the big client party has arrived. The air is electric with the promise of an entertaining casino night. I step into the tall glass building alongside the consultant team. Sara is in a floor-length gold satin dress. The other ladies are in knee-length dresses, adorned with beaded tassels, and iconic flapper headbands. The men sport a mix of tuxedos, gangster vests, and sharp pin-striped suits. Perfect for the twenties-themed event.

"Now, remember," Sara says in a low voice while we wait for the elevators. "The clients don't want to talk work. They're here for the free champagne." She leans in and gestures for me to bend closer. "I'm most excited about the afterparty. Upturns only. It's the one party not to miss."

"Me too," I whisper.

"The rule is, before we get too drunk to still make a good impression on the clients, we ship out to Dave's place."

"In Chiswick?" I recall her story about the kitchen counter rendezvous. Wasn't that about Dave?

"No?" She angles her head at me as we exit the elevator into a gray marble hallway. "He's in Bethnal Green."

Woo, that's near my house.

"Got a penthouse apartment in a renovated building by the canal. It's amazing. We go on all night, so people crash there." She winks.

"Awesome. Let me know when we go." I beam at her. An afterparty with colleagues. Will Jake go? Could something happen?

After our talk on Wednesday, he's been smiling more at me, but keeping to himself in between sessions. There's been no recognition of our private conversation.

I'll stay true to my word and not make another move. He's probably only trying not to be a Scowlface, after I made him aware.

They've draped the room in black velvet, and there's swinging jazz in the background, adding to the speakeasy vibes.

Ashton arrives shortly after us, looking dapper in a black tux and a groomed stubble. Sara purrs next to me, and I hold back a laugh.

"Nora, Sara, nice to see you. Looking glamorous, both of you."

Sara mumbles something and waves a hand. I rarely see her lost for words.

"Great hair." He nods at me.

"Thanks! Had it done today. You've all seen enough of my messy bird's nest." I cup my waves, happy it's noticeable. "You clean up pretty well yourself. For once," I say and give him the classic smirk at his pretend-offense.

"I'll let that one slide, considering your boss is feeding me free champagne today." He greets the server appearing at our side with a tray of sparkling, golden liquid in tall, elegant flutes. We grab one each.

"Looks like I'm the first from Zyclon to arrive. I think I know some of these people, though." Ashton gestures with his glass to the room.

"I'm sure you do. That sparkly bunch around the roulette table are our consultants. That group by the blackjack table are other clients. There'll be more. It's still early."

"Ah. Yes. Any of your behind-the-scenes people here?"

"Developers? No. We hide those in the dungeons."

Sara cackles, and Ashton flashes me a half smile. I'll take it. It was a pretty lame joke.

"What about Jake? Hey, did he tell you I took him axe throwing last week?"

"No? Have you become friends? He should be here tonight." I look around for Jake again, slightly distracted by the thought of him throwing an axe. Muscular arms flexing. Him grunting as he throws it hard.

"Yeah, seems like we have." Ashton sips his champagne with an amused expression.

"Huh." What is this gnawing in my gut? Am I jealous? Jake's out and about making friends. I should be happy for him. Is he meeting women too? "Just the two of you?"

"Mm-hmm." He answers as he swallows his mouthful. "Celia doesn't do sports. She wants to set Jake up, though. So next time it'll be a double-date."

I choke on a sip and cough into my glass, but before I can say anything, Ashton points across the room.

"Ah, there's the big man. I'll go say hi. See you soon." Ashton shoots off to greet someone behind me. Adrenaline hits at the thought of seeing Jake. And in a tux to boot. Or is he doing the gangster look. I might need to hold on to something. I turn around.

Oh, he meant Manuel.

Sigh.

Additional servers sidle in through dark doors as if appearing out of nowhere, all dressed in black. The dimly lit room gives the appearance of champagne glasses floating around in thin air.

More people arrive in their best attire. It's turning out to be quite a glamorous event. I picked a soft, but tight, green dress with a portrait neckline, so it hangs on the edge of my shoulders. Perfect for my big wavy hair. Elegant and professional, yet sexy as hell. Hopefully a certain someone will think so, anyway. It's not twenties themed, but my dainty gloves and feather hairpin do the trick.

Trays upon trays of finger food glide through the growing crowd. I do the classic hors d'oeuvres dance—eyeing out the best, grabbing one at the start and another at the other side when the near-invisible server rounds the room. Mmm, pulled pork sliders. Need to go hunting for more of those.

I've yet to see Jake. Is he not coming?

While standing in a circle with some of the other consultants, enjoying a fresh glass of champagne, a hand grazes the back of my arm.

CHAPTER 31

JAKE

After finishing the first section of our tech strategy, and delaying as long as I could without causing a fuss with the boss, I arrive a couple of hours late. The party is in full swing. The room is crowded, and despite the velvet decor the loud chatter reverberates off the windows and dark marble pillars. I'm hoping to avoid Nora tonight. The feelings that bubbled up in me on Wednesday are … inconvenient. As proven by these last few days. It's so hard to focus when she's near, and I've only got three weeks before the investor meetings.

It's a sea of shiny suits and glittery dresses, but all I see is her.

Fucking hell.

That tightness from Wednesday hits me instantly. She looks sensational.

I stand here at the entrance, not wanting to make myself known to the room yet. I watch her chase the servers for food and chuckle to myself.

Even when she doesn't know it, she makes me smile.

Since I met her, the sight of her has made my body react in all kinds of ways. Racing heart. Obnoxious hard-ons.

Right now, I'm struggling to breathe.

And it's not because her hair is in waves, pinned up on one side, showing off her exceptional cheekbones and jawline. It's not because of the emerald-green dress that hugs her stunning figure. It's not because of the way it comes off her shoulders, showing her collarbones—however much it makes me want to peel that dress off and run my hands down her shape. Feel her skin under my fingertips.

It's because of what lies within. She's intelligent, easy to talk to, has a horrible sense of humor that annoyingly makes me laugh. She skips and dances when she walks, something that makes me strangely joyful. She's strong and stubborn, which drives me wild. And there's a tender side to her—something so fragile that I want to protect.

I take a deep breath to fill my needy lungs just as Howard approaches her.

Don't do what it looks like you're about to do, Howard.

He reaches out a hand and strokes the back of her upper arm. That fucking creep. He leans in. What is he saying?

A heat rises in me, stronger than ever. It's

more than the lizard brain reaction to Mark's message, more than when I thought Ashton was flirting. My hands are tingling. *Get your fucking hands off her*, I want to shout. It's not until I'm halfway across the room I realize I've started walking. Charging.

A few steps away, I stop, as her voice reaches me through the noise and I'm reminded of what she told me. She takes care of herself.

"... due respect, Howard—stop. It's a permanent, categorical *no*. Understood?" She waits for him to confirm. He nods, slowly, and she turns back to her conversation, leaving Howard dumbstruck. He pauses for a second, but then shuffles away.

My heart is thumping. Blood rushing in my ears.

I was about to—what? Yell at my colleague? I would've done it if she hadn't told him *no* like that. Her voice was low, but clear. No drama for Howard. She could've made it very uncomfortable for him.

I've never been a jealous man—hell, with some, I didn't care at all—but she's lit something in me. The mere thought of someone touching her makes my insides knot. I've never wanted anyone for myself like this. She has men chasing her, physically and on apps. It won't be long before I lose my window completely. Could it be worth the risk? She said nobody cares at Upturns. Howard looked like he made a move on her, right here, so maybe she's right?

Hm.

Yeah. Who am I kidding? I can't stay away from her. I ache for her. I want to kiss her so badly it hurts.

Casino night. Make my own luck, Nora said. Could she see more in me than a physical attraction—if I take a chance on it?

She hasn't seen me yet. I'm about to go up to her, but something flashes across her face, and she waves a hand at her group before rushing toward the hallway. Is she upset?

CHAPTER 32

NORA

Howard's got me so pissed off I need a moment. I leave my circle and am relieved to find the hallway empty. The photo booth stands unused by the elevators, allowing me a minute in peace. I don't want to show my anger in the busy ladies' room.

I stomp inside the booth to let out steam in private. How can he do that so fucking matter-of-factly, and right in front of everyone? It took all my willpower not to shriek at him. Tell him to fuck off. There's no way I'd show my fury. Then he'll know he's affected me.

'That dress should be on my bedroom floor.'

His breath is still in my ear. I wipe it furiously and then regret it, combing my waves back down with shaky hands.

"Nora?" a deep, familiar, and soothing voice calls out. The anger in me dissipates immediately.

"Jake?" I poke my head out from behind the

curtain of the booth.

It's him. He's in a dark vest, tie, and a white shirt with the sleeves rolled up. Muscular forearms on display.

Jesus Christ on a bike. He's breathtaking.

The vest accentuates his broad shoulders. The shirt hints at the power hiding under it. Add his chiseled jawline and a five o'clock shadow, and the whole package screams masculinity.

I grip the sides of the booth firmly and tighten my core so I don't melt into a puddle.

He's standing still, chest heaving. He's got that scowl on again, but it's not an angry one. It's the way he looked at me on the train, when I dreamed he wanted to devour me.

Is that what's been in his eyes when I've thought he's been Scowlface this whole time, or is it new?

Hopefully, he knows by now; I'll let him if he tries.

I flash him a grin, truly happy to see him. His expression softens, and he walks over.

"Are you okay? Did Howard make a move on you?"

"Oh, you saw … Yeah, he pissed me off. Needed to huff a little in private."

"Should I go?"

"No. Come in?"

He nudges me backwards and steps inside, closing the curtain behind him. My heart pounds so hard I'm sure he can hear it.

“I didn’t think you’d do it. Our feet are visible,” I squeak. It’s hard to talk when my body is in meltdown mode. He’s so close. It’s a party-sized booth, but it’s still the smallest space we’ve been in together. His intoxicating cedarwood scent fills me and I look up at his face to ground me before I take off.

“Thanks for the chat on Wednesday.” He scans my face and stops on my mouth.

“Oh.”

I carefully place a hand on his chest and gauge his reaction. Is that his heart pounding as hard as mine?

“Nice vest,” I whisper. The black fabric has an intricate woven pattern.

He runs a finger along my jawline and tilts my head up again, sending my nerves into a frenzy.

“You look ravishing.”

His breath on my lips makes my knees buckle and I instinctively shoot out a hand to stop myself from falling, accidentally hitting a button. The machine flashes a bright light.

“What?” We turn to look.

It flashes again. Jake puts his hand out towards wherever the camera might be.

“Shit.”

I laugh hard behind my hand, trying to stay quiet, and Jake stumbles out of the machine, looking around. The corridor is thankfully still empty, everyone engrossed in the casino. I smooth out my hair, fighting back laughter, while Jake chuckles nervously, rubbing his neck.

"Do you mind if I grab those?" he asks when the strip of photos pop out of the machine. "Wouldn't want them to get into the wrong hands."

"Can I have one? I won't show anyone."

He rips the top one off and hands it to me with a sideways smile. My contained laugh escapes when I see it. It's a profile shot of him looking flawless, his hand under my chin, and me, with wide-eyed surprise, arms out as I'm about to topple over. Brilliant move, Nora.

"Do you want to ...?" I gesture toward the booth.

"I don't know what came over me. That was too risky. Best not to push my luck." He smiles wistfully and we exit the hallway just as a group of clients enters to have their photo taken.

***

"What a view!" I lean on the brick railing of Dave's penthouse balcony. Sara, Jake and most of the company are scattered behind me in the vast apartment. The client party and the office party have merged into a loud, drunken Upturns affair in East London.

It's perfect.

After our near kiss, Jake's been nearby the whole evening—in my conversation circles, or lingering behind me, talking to others. I felt his eyes on me constantly. Wonder if he's been undressing me in his mind the way I've done him. That's what I want him to do.

Well, preferably not only in his mind.

"Hey," he says behind me. I turn around and he hands me a glass of something sparkling. "Saw you were empty-handed."

"Thanks." I clink my glass to his and beam at him. This is the first time we're alone since the booth episode. "How's your first work do?"

"Not bad. I've focused on the clients, mostly."

"I noticed. You and Ashton seem friendly?" I ask, repeating his words from last week. He laughs and nods.

"We get along." Two can play that game.

"I thought you'd been cooped up at work all week. I'm glad you get out and about as well."

"I *have* been cooped up at work. It's been full on. Probably will continue like that for quite some time, but I try to squeeze in a few things here and there." He sips his drink. "To be honest, both my sister and Ashton have that way of asking without asking, and it helps. I'm bad at carving out time for 'life', as Sage calls it."

Noted.

"What about you?" he asks. "Having fun?"

"A blast. Look at this crew. It's a madhouse." I turn and lean back on the railing, observing the mix of Friday casual and twenties glamor. Sara, in her golden gown, is already draped over Dave's jeans clad lap. They couldn't look more different, yet they seem to fit perfectly.

"Some madder than others. I'm glad that creep didn't try it on with anyone again." Jake nods toward the lounge, where Howard sways on the side of the couch.

Is that why Jake stayed close—to make sure 'that creep' didn't try again? I wouldn't be surprised. Jake seems to be a protective type. Overprotective, even. Normally, I'd be annoyed by that, but his presence is like a drug to me and he makes me feel wanted.

"Who wants Sambuca?" Sara shouts to a loud cheer. Jake and I look at each other and shrug before we peel off the balcony railing to gather around with the rest. Sara lines up a long row of shot glasses and pours the drink from one end to the other without stopping. To my surprise, Jake accepts a glass. So I do too.

And another.

There's music.

I'm dancing. Laughing.

Jake keeps his distance, but he's laughing too. It makes me so happy seeing him joyful like this. A genuine fuzzy feeling in my gut.

There's more champagne.

Who's singing so loudly? Is it me? I know the words!

Jake is all the way over there where he's been since we left the balcony. Even drunk me manages not to break my word. Not making a move. Probably for the best he isn't either. So many people around, it's not like we can do anything. Too risky, he said.

Oh, comfy chair is available. I'm just going to sit down here for a sec ...

***

Gah! My brain. The pain. The oh-so-familiar headache. The result of copious amounts of expensive champagne consumed at some ungodly hour. It's strangely similar to that of copious amounts of cheap white wine. Bah.

I groan silently and put a hand on my forehead to soothe my hurting head. I don't dare open my eyes. It won't be pleasant. What's going on with this sleeping arrangement? Am I sitting? My back and knees are aching. I'm curled up. My head is leaning back.

Oh god, I'm going to have to move.

Aaaah, poor neck!

My eyelids reluctantly peel off my dry eyeballs and allow the scenery to come into focus.

It's a large apartment. White and bright. I'm in the chair of a lavish brown tufted sofa group. The low morning sun shines in through the floor-to-ceiling windows behind me. It's dimmed by the thin white curtains blowing softly in the early July breeze, revealing an open window somewhere. I crane my neck an inch backward to peer out.

Wow, what a view.

The iconic gas towers are visible from here. Oh yeah, I remember that from last night.

Last night.

Jake!

The memories flood back from the boozy afterparty. I'd normally be filled with dread and anxiety at blurry memories, but I'm fuzzy and happy today. My memories are good.

Jake smiling. Jake laughing. Jake dancing.

Dancing? Yes, there are some definite memories of him doing some shimmying. I twirled around. No touching. We only danced. Other people danced too.

Hold on. There was some touching. He nearly kissed me at the client party. Are these memories real? They're too similar to my daydreams.

I sit up abruptly and stop myself from letting out a howl of pain. My body pops and cracks as I unfold myself from the chair and look around.

There he is. Right there on the couch. It's not a fantasy. I wasn't drunk in the photo booth, and the memory of his hand on my chin is visceral.

Dancing Jake must be real, too.

He stirs and I'm shocked into action. I need to check my face before he wakes up. I shuffle across the pale wood floor toward the bathroom and spy two shapes on the other couches. One is curled up on the ottoman. Sheesh, he'll hurt later.

In the bathroom mirror, I'm met by Alice Cooper. Blonde Alice Cooper. Yikes. I can't face Jake like this. He'll be terrified. My feather hairpin is gone. Ah, well. I drag my fingers through my still wavy hair.

I open all the drawers and cabinets and find something that looks like a cleanser. Score!

Hope he won't mind a face with no makeup. Much better than the alternative right now, though.

I stand in the doorway to the living room, looking at the sleeping Jake. He's stretched out on his back, still in his vest—tie gone—with an arm across his eyes. It's a magnificent sight. I want to crawl on top of him and stick my face into the open part of his shirt and breathe him in.

His arm moves down, and he turns to me. Eyes wide open. I jump back in fright, laughing nervously as I clutch at my chest.

"Jesus, Jake."

"Are you staring at me while I'm sleeping?" he asks, his voice raspy, a smile plays on his lips.

"No," I whisper, as the shape next to me lets out a snore. "You're obviously not sleeping," I add, and he chuckles silently. "Come, get up. We're right next door to Broadway Market. There's food."

***

I dance up ahead on the narrow path along the canal, grateful for my decision to stick some ballet flats in my purse yesterday. The photo I tucked in there last night is now safe in the zipped inner pocket instead. My stomach bubbles at the thought of it. My precious photo.

The hangover that threatened to form is gone in the thrill of what awaits around the corner. I've been here twice with Dee already, and it's become my favorite place to spend a Saturday morning in London.

I stop where the path meets the bridge and market street and turn to take in the heart stopping sight of Jake squinting in the sunlight. He flashes me the widest smile I've seen yet, and it almost floors me. I stretch out to lean on the signpost next to me before my legs give in, only to find the pole isn't next to me—I must have inched toward him without noticing. I nearly topple over but regain my balance just before he reaches me with his outstretched arms. Ready to save me, as always.

"Totally meant to do that," I say, laughing, brushing the hair out of my face. He chuckles in response, and his gaze meets mine. I disappear into his brown eyes, my body about to melt, but a sudden rush of people crossing the bridge keeps me solid and reminds me of the market buzzing around us.

"Come, I'm so excited to share this with you," I say, and a wistful look flashes across his face before he grins again. Another expression to decipher.

Broadway is a narrow street of shops. Each Saturday it's lined with stalls serving burgers, falafels, cheeses, desserts, vegetables, drinks, and things for your house and garden. It's busy, bustling and a treat for the senses. The smell of fried fish fills the air at one point, only to be swept aside by the scent of spicy curry. I hear clattering, chattering, sizzling, laughing, shouting, clinking, and the melodic sound of an acoustic guitar.

I turn around to steal a glimpse of Jake. He looks around with a smile playing on his lips. He catches me glancing at him and beams, making my blood rush again. Being here with him makes everything even more exciting than the other times. Sounds are crisper, smells stronger and colors brighter.

"You have to try this burger." I stop him at a yellow draped stall where scents of truffle, grilled cheese, and duck crackling dances in the surrounding air. The food sizzles loudly on the flat grill and a mustached man in a blue apron shouts in French above the sound to his co-worker.

We perch on a fence behind the stalls. "What do you think?" I ask, mouth full of goat cheese, truffle honey and pulled duck. Jake's face says it all. He's in heaven.

"Holy duck," he says with a smile, words muffled by the food. I laugh in response. That's what I said the first time I had it.

"Glad you liked it. Would've hated to ditch you already." I wrinkle my nose playfully.

He chuckles. "I love quality food. The French know their duck." He wipes his hands and mouth on a napkin. "What's for dessert?"

I gape at him.

"What?" he asks.

"Are you a mind reader?"

"That, and who goes to a market to eat only one thing?"

I blink. This moment needs to be recorded in my memory forever. A gorgeous man, in a brilliant market atmosphere, in my favorite city; saying exactly what I want to hear. This is too good.

A wave of unease crash over me and is gone again as fast as it came. What was that?

"Are you okay?" he asks, eyes tender.

"Yeah. Just tired." There was probably more to it, but I don't want to go there. "Let's grab some water from the offie." I jump up and start walking. Jake follows closely. "What's an offie?" He leans in toward my ear so I can hear him over the market noise. His breath is on the nape of my neck. It gives me chills.

He pulls me out of the busy main street and maneuvers me up against a shop window behind a stall. I catch my breath.

What's happening?

The touch of his hands on my wrist and waist makes my body tingle in anticipation and the hairs on my arms respond. He smiles, lets go of my wrist, and brushes my arm.

"You've got goosebumps," he says in a low, deep voice. It vibrates between us, sending shivers through me. Making my knees weak. It seems I've forgotten how to breathe. The bustle of the market is gone. My heart beats loudly in my ears.

He's so close. Like last night.

I can count his long eyelashes. He leans in closer and every inch of me is screaming for him to—

"Kiss me," he whispers, smiling.

CHAPTER 33

JAKE

Nora's eyes are wide, her pupils dilated even in the bright light. I'm waiting. My whole body is on fire, but I'm keeping still. Letting the hand I stroked down her arm linger near hers. The air between us crackles.

I know she'll do it.

She opens her mouth as if about to say something and bites her lower lip. The anticipation is almost unbearable.

"Kiss you?" she croaks, a smile tugging at the sides of her mouth. "Do you mean here?" She leans in and kisses the side of my neck, right above my shirt collar. Her lips are soft and warm on my sensitive skin and now it's my turn to get goosebumps. The blood rushes in me and my cock hardens instantly. This time, I'm not mortified. This time, it's right. She's right.

"Or do you mean here?" She moves to the other side, letting her tongue tickle me between her lips.

I groan silently in response to the sensation.

"Here?" She leans closer, stretches up and kisses my cheek. "Tell me where," she whispers onto my skin and I can't take it anymore. I wrap an arm around her back and pull her close. She lets out a small sigh at the move. I slide a hand into her thick mane and she leans into it, looking back up at me. Our lips an inch apart. I breathe her in and tug her hair gently for a better angle before I press my lips against hers.

The sensation in my body is intense. My heart pumps to keep me going, to keep me standing, leaving my brain empty. But that's okay—I don't have to think. This is what I was made for. Kissing Nora.

I'm soft at first, feeling my way. She wraps her arms around my neck and kisses me back. Her tongue is gentle, careful, but her hands move with deliberation—one into my hair, one caressing a shoulder, down the arm and up again. Her moans vibrate through me, making me harder. I kiss her more hungrily. All my fibers stand on end. Fully aware of every inch of us that's touching, and every inch that's not. The need to have more of her is growing. The untouched parts of me ache for contact with her. Even though she's holding on to me, flush against my front.

I let a hand slide down to her lower back, but a sudden shriek from the market reminds us we're in public. Nora pulls back, breathing hard, pushing stray hair out of her eye with a shaking hand.

"Jesus. Jake." She staggers slightly and laughs, touching her lips. "Uhm. I live nearby. Should we —"

"Yes," I say before either of us overthink this.

"Let's go." She beams and sets off through the market.

CHAPTER 34

NORA

Still dazed from the mind blowing kiss, I have to focus to make my feet move. I touch my lips again to check if it could have been real. No one has ever kissed me like that. I've never felt so wanted. Everything in me is tingling, dancing. I'm hot to the core, almost dizzy with euphoria. Those hands felt so right on my back. In my hair. Those lips ... I want more.

I turn to him and grin at the jaw dropping sight. Jake with tousled hair, the top three buttons of his shirt undone, and a vest that hugs him in a way that makes my knees wobble. And he's coming home with me now.

"It's right over there." I point across the field. He grabs me around the waist and kisses me again, breathing me in as he does; reigniting the intense sensation between my legs.

***

I open the door when we reach my house, and we

burst through it, laughing, kicking our shoes off and doing our best not to trip over.

I stretch up to kiss him again.

Now I've had a taste I can't get enough.

"Where to?" he whispers, breathless from our run across the field. Grabbing him by the belt, I drag him along with me past the kitchen and down the hallway to the bedroom. I'm shivering in excitement; aching to feel those hands everywhere.

The laughable number of dresses I tried on before the party yesterday cover the bed.

"These can go over here." I quickly pile them together, reach around, and hoist them onto my office chair. I scan the room for anything embarrassing. At least the bedsheets are clean.

Jake leans on the doorjamb, arms crossed and with a hint of a smile. He looks amused. I'd normally crack a joke right about now, but as I sit down on the edge of the bed, the rush from getting here slowly dissipates and blood flow returns to my brain. I'm nervous.

Holy shit, am I about to have sex with Jake?

His tall figure takes up most of my view as he steps up in front of me. The outline of his erection is visible in his dark suit pants. I stroke it as I stand up to kiss him, and he lets out a deep groan that sends shivers down my neck. His muscular arms wrap around me. Holding me close. His bulge is hard against my groin and the heat is back in my body.

"May I?" he asks into my ear, holding his hands on the zip at my back. I nod, humming, and lean into the crook of his neck, kissing the skin I can reach. This is what I imagined all those times. His scent makes me dizzy.

A warm finger strokes my back as he finds the zip and it almost shatters me.

"Hm," he says. It doesn't move. He tries again. Calmly, he stretches down and slides my dress up instead, but it won't come further than my hips. It doesn't need to—I pull him down on the bed with me before my knees buckle.

"I want to touch you," he whispers onto my cheek and slides down next to me. "Let me feel how wet you are for me." Mmm, does he talk dirty? His warm breath and lips on my skin are like a power surge, fueling the flame between my legs. It's so intense. Like the sparks from each time I've sat next to him, each near touch and shared look, are all coming together in one blazing inferno. When his large hand finds the inside of my thigh and he nudges my legs open, I'm about to come undone. I moan into our kiss, tugging his hair, and his hand slides further up. He traces the lace fabric of my underwear —tickling, teasing. I roll my hips toward him. I want to scream at him to touch me, but am also too aware of how desperate I sound, how I've flung myself at him again and again and now I'm about to beg him to make me come.

Stop it, brain, you have nothing to do here, go

relax.

His hand moves up along the side of the thin fabric and finds its way underneath, finally making contact with me and it's everything I need. I let out a loud sigh.

"Holy fuck," I breathe and laugh into our kiss.

"Mmm." His voice is so deep it vibrates as his tongue plays with mine. "You feel so good, so fucking wet," he murmurs through our kiss. I cling onto him, arching my back to have more of him.

"Oh god," I let out, my voice a mere whimper. His touch is just firm enough, moving up and down, circling—he seems to sense exactly which area is aching to be touched next. I'm about to fall apart. I moan and writhe; the sensation builds until one last move makes me shudder in his arms. I bury my face, crying out loudly into the collar of his shirt. He continues to touch me, making me convulse and kick my legs as the waves of pleasure course through me until he stops. I keep my face hidden; embarrassed. That was so quick. I was loud. This is the first time I've ever come like this in a man's arms. I'm suddenly so aware of myself.

"Are you hiding?" His voice is low in my ear.

"A little." I finally lift my head, but don't want him to see my face right away. "Woo, that was … great." I need to do something. I feel so exposed. I sit up and push him down, flashing him a wry smile and move down to find the belt buckle. He's rock solid and about to burst from his pants.

He lets out a nervous laugh. "Wait, don't you want to—" His massive erection springs free as I pull down his clothes. I caress it and he groans loudly instead of finishing his sentence. His hands come up to his head.

"Do you have a condom?" I ask and he sighs.

"No. I didn't have any plans ..." His voice is strained, and he rubs his hands down his face. "It's fi—"

"There are other ways." I straddle his legs as he's about to protest, and bend down, licking, teasing, making him writhe in pleasure. I wrap my lips around him and he lets out a loud sigh.

"Mmm," I hum. My voice tickles him. I let him hit the back of my throat and use both hands to cover the rest. The sounds coming from him are pure ecstasy. I love this part.

You're in my power now.

I look up and he peers down at me; I lick his length and his eyes darken. He puts his hands to his head and leans back.

"I'm close," he rasps with a laugh. His breathing quickens and I match the pace. With a final loud groan and heavy thrusts, he finishes and I take it all in. It's so satisfying to make him come like this. To know I can give him this. He's grasping his hair, staring into the ceiling.

"Fuck. You're amazing," he breathes and lets his arms drop. "Oh, fuck," he says again. This time, it sounds more upset than euphoric.

"What's up?"

He shakes his head, not answering. Laughing instead. "We're still clothed."

He props himself up, looking at me with hooded eyes and a sideways smile that makes my chest ache uncomfortably. His hair is messy in a ridiculously adorable way. Jake can't be adorable. He's hot—yes, Scowlface—yes. But not ruffled and cute. Damn, he's beautiful. He looks happy. And I'm ... terrified.

I inhale sharply. "I'm thirsty. Want a drink?"

"Are you okay?" he asks, with a slight frown on his brow this time.

"Absolutely." I spring up and pull down my dress. "Come, I'll make us a smoothie."

He gets up and closes his pants and belt, straightens his vest and shirt. I absorb the view, wondering if I'll see it again like this. The tall, broad shape, those muscular arms. So incredibly sexy. Damn, I didn't get to see him naked. Will there be a next time? Or was this us getting it out of our systems?

He runs a hand through his hair, and rubs his neck, looking at me. Still wearing that hint of a frown. Does he regret it?

"Are you about to throw me out on my ass?" he asks, attempting a smile.

Does he want me to?

"I'm not. Unless you want to go, that's fine. You must be tired from last night. I could do with a shower." I'm babbling and he makes a move toward me, like he's about to stop me. Maybe he'll kiss me and it'll be even more awkward because where do we go from there? What is this? Purely physical, I said.

I jump back and open the door before he gets closer, and he follows me to the kitchen.

"Sit." I mutter, pointing at the stool on the other side of the breakfast bar. "Water," I add. I can't seem to speak in full sentences. I turn on the tap, letting the sound fill the kitchen, and hand him a glass. "Here."

I get what's needed for smoothies, banging doors and rustling bags. Trying to give myself time to let my busy brain settle.

"What's going on? Talk to me," he says to my back as I throw frozen berries into the blender along with my flaxseed and pea protein mix. I turn it on and glance back at him, pointing at the machine that it's too loud. He sips his water and gives me a tight-lipped smile.

I fill up two glasses with the purple liquid and put a silicone straw in each.

"Here you go. Hangover cure. Lots of freshness. You'll love it."

He takes the glass but keeps his eyes on me. "Are you feeling better? Shall we go back? We didn't even get our clothes off." His eyes are wide and his forehead creased, but he's smiling. If I didn't know better, I'd say he looks worried. I'm freaking him out. I'm freaking myself out. "Do you *want* to?" he asks, staring me down.

"I do. I did. I mean. Yes. I'm just ..." I let out a long breath. How do I try to make sense of my thoughts? Let alone the rush of adrenaline he gives me. What's going on? "I don't think I've—"

The front door opens and Dee and Ajay enter, talking loudly with their hands full of paper bags that scrape and rustle as they shuffle down the narrow hallway.

"No, you're wrong. I'm telling you. He had pure talent, he got us the title without the—" Ajay's practically shouting as he turns to close the door and only shuts up when Dee punches him in the arm.

"Hello!" she chirps and stands frozen for a second, trying to send me a message with her eyes. We've yet to become telepathic, but I understand. She's practically screaming at me.

Oh my gooooood, what is he doing here? Did you have sex? How was it? Tell me everything! Everything!

"Hey, guys. We're just having a smoothie," I say. But my eyes are telling her:

No, we didn't exactly, and it's awkward as hell. Please save me. Stay!

"Do you want some? I can make more. Easy peasy." Come on, Dee. Read my mind. Ajay and Jake quietly follow our farcical exchange. Jake slurps his smoothie noisily.

"Nnn—" Dee starts. I'm nodding at her frantically behind Jake while he's distracted by her. "Nyes. Yes. That's exactly what I want," Dee says, keeping eye contact with me.

"All right," Ajay says loudly, looking at us pointedly. "That wasn't weird at all, ladies. Are we finished with this wide-eyed, nodding puppet show? Can I have some booze in my smoothie, please? And hold the berries, add some pineapple and some coconut cream?" He strides forward and reaches a hand out to Jake. "Ajay. Nice to meet you."

"Jake. Likewise."

My brain is trying hard to follow. "Ajay, did you just say you want a piña colada?"

"If you're offering. Why are you so dressed up on a Saturday afternoon?"

"Oh, we came from a work party, and afterparty. Our colleague lives nearby. Thought we'd come here and have a smoothie." I force a stiff grin and sip my fruity drink.

"Nice." Ajay comes into the kitchen and looks into the cupboards. "What do you do at Upturns, Jake?" He turns back with a bottle of rum and a can of coconut cream.

"I'm the CTO," Jake answers, and Ajay's face lights up.

"Oh right. Riiight." He looks back and forth between us and then at Dee, who's shaking her head frantically.

Jake clears his throat, obviously uncomfortable. "What do you do, Ajay?"

"I'm the head of digital at Floyd's. The bank."

"That sounds interesting. What does it

involve?"

Ajay lays into excruciating detail about his job, although Jake looks intrigued, nodding along, asking questions. I take the opportunity to check in with my racing mind.

Oh god, I'm so embarrassed. I'm embarrassed at being embarrassed and feel foolish about my reaction. I should've let him do whatever he was about to do afterwards. We could've been naked in a human pretzel shape in bed instead of talking about Ajay's management processes.

I feel odd and I can't put my finger on why. An unease similar to the wave I got earlier creeps over me. I've broken this already. Made it awkward.

Crap.

Where do we go from here?

CHAPTER 35

JAKE

As I listen to Ajay, I've got Nora in the corner of my eye. She's definitely not comfortable. She's staring blankly at something, chewing her lip. I shouldn't have let her go down on me like that, but once she had her hands on me, I couldn't get myself to stop it. But I should have. It became almost transactional. We even kept our clothes on. What happened?

Having her in my arms like that, her face in the nook of my neck. It was amazing. If only she'd stayed there instead of trying to repay me. Or why did she move on so fast? As I reflect on what happened I realize I'm lingering on her eyes and face, her sounds of pleasure and the warmth of her breath on my skin. Not the actions. My own pleasure. It's obvious.

I like her.

I *care* about her.

"The dream is to work for AbbleTech, of course," Ajay concludes with.

"Jake used to work there," Nora says, suddenly finding her words.

"Really? Why did you leave?"

"I was a software product manager. I felt a bit lost in the massive company. Got a Head of Dev role at a slightly smaller, but still fairly large firm. Do you want me to find a contact for you at AbbleTech?"

"That's okay. Thank you, though." Ajay smiles, mixing the final ingredients of his drink in the blender without turning it on. "What do you think of the smaller company in comparison?"

"It's so far been great."

"They tend to be quite laid-back." He raises his eyebrows and his eyes dart to Nora and back as he switches on the blender. With the ice cubes in there, it makes a hell of a noise.

I understand from his earlier comment that she must have mentioned me to him before. Knowing she's talked about me to her friends makes me wonder if she feels something more than the purely physical attraction. Or she would probably talk about that with her friends too, seeing as she so easily told me.

"Fancy a drink?" Ajay looks at me.

"No, thank you. I had enough yesterday."

"Today is a new day. But all good."

I wish I knew what to do next. I don't want to leave her being weird like that, but I don't want to be that lingering guy, either.

As if Dee senses the challenge, she grabs her

drink from Ajay and says, “Why don’t we enjoy these out back?”

Nora sends her a look that can kill, but Dee shrugs and tilts her head to me. They don’t think I can see all their glances and gestures? Nora’s awkward and doesn’t want to be left alone with me. Dee seems to disagree. I like her even better now.

“Nora,” I say once they’ve gone. “Talk to me. You’re obviously uncomfortable.”

“I’m okay. I think.” She sighs. “I’m terrible at real talks.”

“You’re normally a pretty decent conversationalist. We’ve had some real talks before, haven’t we? Why stop now?”

“I’ve no idea what to say—what I *want* to say. Can I have some time? We talked about just getting it out of our systems. Maybe this was it?” She sucks in her lower lip, biting it nervously.

My stomach sinks.

“For the record, I really hope not. But take your time. I’ll leave you to it.” I tap the countertop gently, suddenly unsure what to do with my hands, and slide down from the barstool. “See you Monday.”

I turn and stride to the hallway, put on my shoes as quickly as I can, and just as I let the door close behind me, hear a small voice,

“See you.”

My heart sits heavy in my chest now, weighing down on my stomach, making me feel sick. I need to talk to someone, make sense of it. But I can't tell Sage. She'll know it's Nora, a woman at work, and she'll be angry with me again. Her voice is in my head already. I'm setting a terrible example for her daughter, being the uncle who sleeps with employees. I can get what I need anywhere—why in the office?

But that's not true anymore. Because it's not only about sex. There's no question anymore. I like Nora. I want to be with her. It's what my body has been trying to tell me since that day on the plane.

I'll walk back to my apartment from here. It'll help me clear my mind. Think through what I did. I need to fix this.

The stretch of terraced houses carries me around the bend and onto a main street. My map app tells me it should lead me across the canal, past a park and down to another major road to follow.

I love how walkable London is. If I had the time, I would wander across the city.

Now I know the route, I let my mind drift as I stroll under leafy green trees, past brown apartment buildings and the occasional corner shop.

Seeing Nora last night was the highlight of my new life here so far. Her *joie de vivre*. Her smile —that bright, vibrant, heartwarming smile. Her laughter.

She's easy-going and seems to love amusing

others; dancing and singing, despite not knowing the words. Nora is entirely wonderful and charming. I sensed her glancing at me in between. Willing me to come closer. I kept my distance so I wouldn't do something in front of the team. It was too risky, what I did in the photo booth.

I stop for a moment to look out over the canal as I cross the bridge. Leaning on the red brick fence, I go through each step I took earlier to understand why Nora got so uncomfortable.

I can't recall having experienced this with anyone I've been with in the past. Maybe it was because I didn't care enough about them. Not like this, anyway. And they didn't care about me. There was nothing to be awkward about.

Hold on. Is that why? She cares about me too? No, she said she doesn't. That was only a few days ago. The words she spoke at the church ruins echo in my head. She doesn't have feelings for me so I don't have to worry. My chest clenches at the memory.

She seems happy in my company, though. Maybe she's scared she broke a friendship?

I continue walking, kicking nothing in particular on the ground.

She mentioned once she got awkward with someone at her old job when they got naked. Does she get self-conscious? She seemed flustered after she came; hiding in my nook like that. Was she embarrassed? And then she jumped on me. Why? To take control?

I get to the next major road; a bustling street with a flower market. The hard leather shoes are hurting my feet, so I crash down on a chair outside a bakery and order myself a large latte and a croissant. My mind has been ping-ponging between theories. Now what do I do? I don't want to leave it like this.

She's incredible, and I know I'll never meet anyone that makes me feel the way she does. This is the Jake I like. The one I am with her.

Just as a server arrives with the coffee, my phone vibrates in my pocket and I fish it out quickly to see Mom's face light up on the call screen.

"*Bonjour*, Jake."

"*Bonjour Maman, ça va*?" I ask.

"I'm good, Jake. Just calling to say hello. I was thinking of you. How are you? What are you doing on a Saturday?"

We speak in French to each other normally, and now it's particularly useful as she can talk without Dad overhearing. I can take this opportunity to air some thoughts and I don't need his input on how I'm getting distracted and wasting my time. Or maybe that's what I *should* be hearing. I'm definitely distracted, but I'm still doing my job. It just requires a bit more effort.

"I'm at a market, grabbing a coffee." I show her the street and my coffee. A slightly pathetic 'see, I have a life' gesture. Leaving out the part of how I got here.

"That's lovely. Glad to see you're enjoying yourself. Are you alone?"

I run a hand over my chin, thinking of how to ask for advice without giving away the details. I've never gone to her with girl problems before, but as a psychologist and a mom she's always been easy to talk to.

Still pondering if or how to ask, Mom jumps in before me. "Where's your mind, sweetheart? What did someone do to make you worry?" She points at her forehead and I understand immediately. Another frown. I let out a laugh and rub my worry crease away.

"Someone didn't do anything. That's part of the problem, perhaps. Hypothetically, what's your best advice when someone seems to need control? I'm not sure this is the right question." I sigh.

"Hypothetically?" Mom grins. "What do you mean by someone?"

"Just a person. A woman. Still hypothetical."

"Hmm. She could have trust issues, maybe anxiety, or she's feeling vulnerable, which can be quite scary for some and they counter it with trying to control the situation. Hard to say. It's a normal human emotion—not wanting to feel powerless."

"Hm."

"It's often difficult to understand *why* anyone reacts the way they do. But creating a safe and supportive environment can be helpful. Reduce a sense of uncertainty and ambiguity by being clear about what you're thinking and what you want." Her eyes twinkle as she speaks. "I'm happy to hear you've met someone you care about. I mean, hypothetically."

"Hm." I chew my cheek. Be clear about what I want. What *do* I want? What does Nora want? My last interactions with women flash across my eyes, reminding me of how shit things can get when I mess up. I don't want to mess up with Nora. We work together.

"You look concerned again, my darling boy."

"Yeah." I drag the word out. "Can I be that person you describe. Am I enough?"

I've been thinking about *me* taking a risk, because Nora seems so unfazed by it. But would I be worth it to her?

Mom's eyes shine. "What do you mean? You *are* that person. You're a caring, dedicated, and loving son and brother. You're stoic, but I see through it. Show her what's going on inside."

"Hm. It's the worst timing. I've got so much riding on me in my role. If I open up like that now, will I lose my focus? What if I make a mistake?"

Mom's expression hardens. "Your father has drilled it in hard. I don't always agree with him, you know. We would've been perfectly fine without his *chief* of engineering title. Without the years of travel." She waves a hand at the camera and shakes her head. "I won't go into that. Remember *why* you do what you do. You can do your job well and also open up your life to someone else. I'm sure of it."

[Sunday]
Me: Hey, I said I'll give you time, and I will, just wanted to message so you didn't think I didn't message :)

Nora: Thank you :)

[Tuesday]
Nora: I'm not avoiding you, I'm full on at Zyclon this week

Me: *thumbs up*

That's nice to know. Would she write that if she didn't care at all? Or is it an excuse? I drum my fingers on my desk.

Right. Work. Let's do this.

[Wednesday]
Me: ...

I want to tell her about the busker singing 'Waterloo Sunset' that I walked past this morning. But is it too much too soon?

Me: ...

Yeah, too much. Another time.

[Thursday]
Jake: Want to grab a drink?

Nora: I'm going tap dancing, wish me luck! I'll see you tomorrow :)

Jake: Have fun!

Tomorrow it is. My stomach flips at the thought of seeing her again. Fucking hell. When did I turn into a teenager again? I'm in an office surrounded by people who look to me for direction, advice, and expert opinions. Yet, here I sit. Nervous. Because a girl may or may not like me the way I like her. Today can't go fast enough. Tomorrow I'll find out.

CHAPTER 36

NORA

I slam the door a little harder than I intended, causing Dee to lean over on the couch to see me.

"You all right?" Dee asks, stuffing popcorn in her mouth.

"I hate tap dancing." I kick my shoes off and huff as I slump through the doors. Colette is snuggled up on the other side of the deep couch, munching her popcorn.

"No fun?" she asks through a mouthful.

"I can't do it. I'm like Preston on a ukulele. Can't follow the steps and can't stop focusing on me not knowing what I'm doing. I'm in over my head and it paralyzes me."

"Tap dancing makes you feel all that?" Dee asks, giving me a scrutinizing stare above the rim of her mug. What is she insinuating?

"Yes. I'm overthinking it, but I can't stop myself. I wish I could learn to let go and not get stuck in my head like that. Also, I have no rhythm." I throw my hands up and grimace.

What was I thinking, going *tap* dancing?

"Try a different dance?" Colette suggests. "Remember, you said you want to have fun?"

"We can go out dancing tomorrow? Do the kitchen dance you talked about at a nightclub without a care in the world?" Dee smiles reassuringly.

"I've got kayaking day and drinks with the team."

"Again?"

"Last week was with the clients. Well, we *did* have a company afterparty, but the kayaking is a team building thing."

"How many people fit in a kayak?"

"Two, tops." I see where she's going with this. "I guess the team building will be afterwards. We can bond over the riveting experience of paddling down the Thames."

"It'll be splendid, duck," Colette pipes up. "You'll see London from a different angle. It's quite lovely."

"Will you share a kayak with Jake?" Dee asks with big eyes.

I scrunch up my mouth. "I'm not sure." My stomach churns at the thought.

"Remind me again why you're being weird about him? He seems pretty great, to be honest."

"Yeah ... but he's just my Pedro. Mom reckons his type isn't meant to be tied down. I'm sure she's right. He said he's fully focused on his career now, anyway."

"Who's Pedro?" Colette asks.

I tell her the story of my parents and their break, how Pedro was my mom's lesson in passion and what she truly felt for my dad.

"I'll have to politely disagree," Colette says, and picks up her teacup from the side table. I tilt my head, waiting for more. "If you recall, my husband was my first ever date."

"How did you know it was right? You just met him, and weren't you only eighteen?"

"He made me comfortable. At ease. Maybe you and Dee have that. You can sit in silence and it's not awkward. But when you talk, sparks fly."

I laugh and catch Dee's eye. "Sounds about right."

"I had that with my husband early on. Along with the constant urge to rip his clothes off." She cackles. A bouncy, infectious laughter. "What I'm trying to say is," she adds, "We all have different journeys. Your mom had hers. You'll have yours. There's no rule about how many men you've known, or how long you've known them for. What matters is how he makes you feel. Are you at ease with him at all? Like you can be yourself without judgment?"

I think about Jake. Our chats, they flow easily, from my point of view, anyway. He doesn't say much, but he listens and doesn't seem to mind my ramblings. I relax with him. Dance, even. Eat my food without worrying. He warmed up lately, too. Stopped scowling at me, if that's what he was doing before. His tender eyes when I felt queasy at the market are vivid in my mind. The sheepish grin when he lay on the bed.

But I might be at ease with him because I feel *nothing*. There are no worries about what he thinks of me. Damn, I'm confusing myself.

"What type is he?" Dee asks.

"What do you mean?"

"You said your mom believes 'his type' isn't meant to be tied down."

What *type* is he? I rub my chin. "I initially pegged him as the kind who's so handsome he's probably quite arrogant and privileged. Maybe a womanizer." As I say it, I'm sure it's wrong, and I've known it for a while.

The way he carries the guilt for that junior engineer, he can't be. He's dedicated, adores his family, and he seems more shy than arrogant. And he only made a move on me after I asked him to. Repeatedly. Have I put him in a box he doesn't belong?

"I've only seen him twice," Dee says. "Once holding a baby and the next sitting on that barstool looking like a lost puppy, so I don't have that impression at all." Dee laughs the last words out. "Not at all," she repeats, shaking her head. I stare at my fingertips to avoid her piercing eyes.

The walls in me are cracking down. I've put all the flushes, goosebumps and racing hearts into a space they don't fit. They're swelling up inside me. Spilling over. I'm nauseated.

"Ugh," I groan.

"You okay there?" Colette asks.

"I'm a bit overwhelmed."

"Aaw, Nora," Dee says and puts a hand on my knee. I look at it absentmindedly.

"What's happening?" Colette whispers, leaning over to Dee.

"It seems Nora is falling in love for the first time." As I hear the words, the terrifying sensation from the weekend comes back. Cold chills on my neck, and an uneasiness sitting under my lungs, making it hard to breathe.

I push it back down. That's not it.

"No, absolutely not," I say, pressing the words out and taking a deep breath. "You're blowing it way out of proportion. It's just lust, and it's a lot of the same hormones. Easy to confuse. He's such a dish. How could I not lust for him? There's probably not a dry seat in the office." Colette coughs on a popcorn. "I'll see him tomorrow and get it all out of my system. Fully." I shake my hands theatrically to emphasize my point.

Dee sighs. "I thought you wanted to find someone. You've always done this. Come up with reasons not to give a man a chance, and maybe you did the right thing before, but this time I think you're scared. Why are you fighting this so hard?"

"I'm not fighting anything. This is what I need to get out of the way so I can focus on finding Mr. Right." I shrug. "What about you, anyway? You're not exactly proclaiming your love for Ajay, a man you've known for nearly ten years. Do you talk about it at all?" It's a low blow and I know it. But it works.

"I'm sure Ajay feels what I feel. He's not big with words, but he's *with* me."

"Darling, Nora. You need to open up. Let go of whatever fears are holding you back. Talk to him and you'll see," Colette says in her soft voice.

It's easier said than done.

Letting go of fears.

Talking.

Sometimes I hear the words I want to say in my head, but they refuse to come out of my mouth. Most of the time I regret what was said and ruminate on it for days. One thing is to semi-joke around with Jake about getting our pants off. That's just silly stuff. It's a completely different ballgame to talk about feelings.

He's seen a lot of me so far. What if he doesn't like me? It's proof I'm unlikeable. That I'll have to change to find love. Not be me. And that's devastating. It's best not to get too deep until I know.

Colette seems like one of those self-assured people who sees themselves clearly and can act accordingly. She met her husband and knew that was it. I've been fumbling my way through life, trying to figure shit out as I go along. I'll see how I feel when I meet him tomorrow. Maybe it'll be clearer once I'm near him again.

CHAPTER 37

JAKE

Standing on the pier below the London Eye with the sun in our eyes, all Upturns staff are gathered in front of tiny Rosie. She tries to make herself heard above the buzzing of people, traffic, and boats, her voice getting caught in the breeze so she has to shout.

"We'll kayak in pairs up to Tower Pier. We'll meet at the Vault on the south side by two p.m. for food and drinks. Now listen to the guide, please." Rosie waves to quiet down the cheers.

Seems the word 'drinks' sets them off each time.

The instructor lays into the rules of kayaking on the Thames in a monotonous baritone voice that could lull me to sleep. I glance at Nora and think for a second she's looking at me, but she seems to be miles away. A blank stare into nothing. She's in black and purple activewear that clings to her body as if it's been painted on. It's hard not to stare at her. It takes all my effort to tune back in to the instructor. "... you've got about two hours of slack tide and, from what Rosie said, another hour to walk across the bridge and enjoy the view. Have fun!"

I get close to Nora as everyone scrambles to find their kayaks and kayak partners. Sara lingers nearby, but she's shooting glances at Dave. She won't fight me.

"Hey," I say in a low voice next to Nora and catch a whiff of her sweet, flowery scent. Seeing her again confirms what I've been gnawing on this week. There's a fluttering in my stomach and my heart is racing. Fuck, my palms are sweating. She grins at me. Is she ... relieved?

"Share a kayak with me?" she asks before I'm able to get the words out. The awkwardness from Saturday is gone. Wonder what she's thinking.

We pick a red kayak and she's about to step into the back when the instructor stops her.

"*He* should take the rear. More power and weight in the back of the kayak means better control."

"Oh, yeah?" Nora doesn't budge and stares at the instructor. "I'm strong."

"Yes." The instructor doesn't budge either. "But he's much bigger than you. It's just science, love."

I do my best to hold back a laugh. She really seems to dislike not being in control, and I imagine being called 'love' in this context will annoy her even more.

"Fine." She huffs and scrambles into the front.

Finally, out on the water, we paddle quietly for a stretch, taking in the sounds of a busy city and the water lapping on the sides of our small vessel.

"Sorry about Saturday," she says softly, talking to the front of the kayak. I wait to see if she'll say more; to understand why she thinks she needs to apologize. "Look, it's our office." She points up at the concrete building visible to our left and sighs. "I got a bit flustered and confused. I thought I would be okay, being with you like that, getting it out of my system. But maybe—"

We're coming up to the double bridge.

Maybe what?

Does she feel the same as me?

"What did the instructor say about bridges?" she asks.

"You weren't paying attention?"

"No, I was distracted by a certain someone in an illegally sexy white T-shirt."

I chuckle and rub my chin with one hand, trying to tune into my memories from earlier. I had been distracted by her too. Did the instructor say anything about pillars?

Ah, it doesn't matter—I can think my way through here.

"Right, no worries," I say confidently.

"Do you know what to do?"

"Yeah. You need to paddle steadily, and I'll keep us on course. Trust me."

"I can see the currents near the pillars. We need to come out a bit."

"Yep. You're right. We're all good. Just sit still and keep paddling."

"You got us?" I can sense she wants to turn to look, to take the reins, but she doesn't. She sits still and paddles.

"I got us."

The current in the river is strong as I sink the paddle in behind me to use it as a keel and get us further toward the center. It's the right move and we're clear of the pillar. Once through to the other side, I remember she didn't finish her sentence before. She needed to get me out of the system, *'but maybe.'*

"Maybe what, by the way?" I ask and stare at the back of her head as if it would reveal something.

"Oh ... what was I saying? Uhm. Maybe it wasn't enough." She laughs a nervous laugh.

"Enough?"

"Yeah. We didn't even get naked." Her voice cracks on the last word.

"Very true." But what does she mean? I'll be out of her system once we do? She'll be finished with me. Bored of me?

I stare at the water flowing over my yellow paddle. From the bridge the river looks brown. Muddy, almost. It's clearer up close than I thought it would be.

Nora clears her throat. "Uhm. I've never ... I've

never come like that." She says the last part fast and rubs her temple. I bet she's blushing now, trying to hide even though I can't see her face.

"What do you mean?" I hold my breath, wanting to hear it again.

"I haven't come with a man. Never knew why, perhaps—sorry, you don't need the details, but no one made me ..." she mumbles incoherently. Talking to herself. I can barely hear her.

She's right. I don't want details.

But the thought that I'm the only one to make her scream out in pleasure has my blood rushing. My heart pounds in my ears.

I want to make her squirm like that, again and again. Now I wish we weren't in a fucking kayak. How do I get us out of here? I need to see her face. To touch her. To show her she's safe with me.

"No boyfriend ever made you—"

"Nope. Never had a proper boyfriend."

"I find it hard to believe—someone this fun, smart and beautiful." She turns her head and looks my way.

"I wasn't always ... beautiful."

"No?"

"Chubby, freckled and curly-haired Nora who went purple and sweaty in P.E. wasn't the most popular among the boys. I had lots of friends and was well-liked, but not in that way. The boy I had a crush on ... I remember the look on his face when the bottle spun and landed on me. He wanted to cry."

"Fucker."

She had low self-esteem? Wonder if she still has it, thinking of what she said when we sat at the ruins—how certain people make her feel silly. She said she's herself with me.

I get to see her the way she likes to be.

And she's incredible.

"Yeah, well." She shrugs, looking around at London from below. "We were kids. *I* wasn't any better. I nearly cried when I had to hold the smelly boy's hand at a group dance." She snorts, shaking her head. "What was child-Jake like?"

"Studious."

"Flock of girls following you around?"

"Nah, I was cute, I guess, my mom said, anyway. But tall and gangly. Bit of a geek. I was more interested in Star Wars and how the VCR worked than what the girls were up to."

Nora turns around as far as she can to catch my eye. "I love geeks. And Star Wars."

I cough-laugh in surprise and at how her choice of words makes my stomach flip.

"Really?"

"What about twenties-Jake?" She continues, probably taking my question as rhetorical.

"Studious," I answer again.

Nora laughs. "Still not interested in the girls?"

"Still a geek, but less gangly. I guess my twenties were my busiest years, socially. No girlfriend, though. Short-lived stuff."

"I see. A lot of euphemisms there." She turns

to the side again, eyeing me down. "You were a bit of a heartbreaker, I bet."

What is she saying? She thinks I was a player? I guess with what I've told her, why wouldn't she believe that. How do I convince her otherwise?

"I don't think so."

I can't tell her the few I dated didn't like me enough to stick around. I wasn't enough.

"Never found a good fit," I say instead.

"So ... have you ever been in love?" she talks to the front of the kayak again, her voice barely audible, like she's talking to herself.

I blink into the breeze. What do I say? Is that what I am now? I can't tell her that, though. It'll freak her out. I'm not even sure, myself. Isn't it a bit soon? I'm infatuated for sure. Never felt this way.

"I've never been in love before," I say.

"Me neither," she says quickly. "Wouldn't know it if it hit me in the gut."

Why is she saying this?

"Why's that?" I ask, to keep the conversation going.

"Never found a good fit." She chuckles. "God knows I tried. Well, I went on lots of dates but they never panned out."

"Hm. Can't say I tried very hard," I muse. "I focused on my career quite early on and started exercising almost religiously."

"Why? I'm not complaining. You look fabulous. But I hope you enjoy it too. That's why *I* exercise. I love to run, throw a kettle bell, shake my ass around to eighties pop." She does a shoulder shimmy, holding her paddle out, making the kayak wobble.

"I do enjoy it. It's my routine. Where I go to clear my head. I was very unhealthy as a student. Did a one-eighty on my lifestyle afterwards to be more awake and happier. I don't go hardcore anymore, I'm squishier now."

Nora turns again, looking me up and down. "I'll have to check that for myself."

I grin. I'd love that.

Her head turns sideways again, and I pause, pulse raising at the thought of her hands on me. She turns more and the kayak wobbles.

"What are you doing?" I laugh nervously.

"Trying to see your face. Which frown are you giving me and what's the answer it comes with?"

"Which frown? Do I have different ones?"

"I'm trying to get to know your various expressions. Forehead creases and eyebrow furrows abound. Not to mention those eyes. You say a lot with your eyes."

"What is this face saying, then?"

She twists her torso further and studies me. "It says '*fuck, yes,*'" she shouts and turns back to the front with a hearty laugh. I catch myself joining in. The joyful sound is infectious.

"Maybe we can ditch the office party and—"

"No." She cuts me off.

"No?"

"I mean, you shouldn't ditch it. It's a prime opportunity for you to get input from the team. Honest input. Hang out and be one of the guys. Be approachable."

"Hm." I think back to the night out with Zyclon and what Ashton said. She solves problems he wasn't even aware of because his team trusts her.

"You didn't do that in New York?"

"I find it draining, to be honest."

"Going out?"

"With certain people, yes. Colleagues, in particular."

"Are you shy?" Her paddle hits a small wave sending droplets into the air.

"No. It's not that I don't dare talk to people or that I struggle with it. I just don't want to. It's tiring. I'm an introvert."

Nora hums. "Does everyone tire you?"

She's worried she's one of them? "No. A handful of people energize me." She's staring at her paddle as she dips it in and out of the water. "You energize me," I add, it's almost a whisper but the twitch of her head in my direction must mean she heard it.

The busker singing by Tate Modern takes over the sound waves and we glide silently under the narrow Millennium Bridge.

"After Heather, it was pretty bad. I couldn't relax at all," I add to conclude.

"Scared of people hitting on you?" She turns

sideways again now, smirking.

"Exactly. Being pressed up into dark corners on rooftops, for example," I answer in a level tone, keeping my face serious despite the rush from the memory.

"You poor thing." The sarcasm is laid on thick. She paddles for a moment and swivels in her seat again. "Just focus on connecting with your team. No one will try it on with you."

"No one?"

"I promise. I'll be your anti wing woman. Ready for our last big bridge?" She points up ahead.

"Of course. What about you?"

"What about me? I'm following your lead." She paddles carefully at the same pace while I angle us on the center, safe and sound, under London Bridge. Majestic Tower Bridge and our destination are visible up ahead.

"No, I mean, are you planning on keeping your hands to yourself?"

She stops paddling and looks up at the Shard. Just over a month ago, I walked away from her at the station up there, sensing she'd be someone I couldn't stay away from. A distraction from my big career opportunity.

"Do you want me to?" she asks, her voice soft.

The best distraction I could ever imagine.

"No."

We paddle toward the massive old warship moored on the south side of the river. That means our pier is up ahead.

"Good, because I would struggle, especially now you told me you're squishy." I laugh and she turns to catch my eye, that sparkle in them takes my breath away. "Not in front of the team, though," she adds as she turns back. "I'll go home with you if you want. Don't make me ask again or I'll feel like a creep for sure."

I inhale sharply. "I'd love that."

Her head moves almost imperceptibly. I'm sure she's smiling.

"In the meantime, I'll socialize. Thanks, Nora," I say. She gives me a thumbs up without looking back. "We need to get to this pier here, by the way."

"Okay, you steer, I'll follow. And I apologize in advance for later."

"Why?"

"For my terrible singing voice. There's a karaoke bar near where we're going, and I have a compulsion to enter when I see one."

"Fuck, yes."

She swivels abruptly again, nearly sending us off course. "You sing?"

"Hell, no. But you performed for us all at the party last week and it was great." We're getting close to the pier and I paddle us downwards again so we get an extra minute.

"I have a vague memory of that. I had no idea I knew all the words to 'Take On Me.'"

"Your very own version of it, at least. A-ha

didn't sing 'it's no weather for the shaved and horny.'"

She throws her head back, laughing. "At least now I know what song to do at karaoke tonight if you can handle it again—with a microphone." I suck air in through my teeth and she turns with a mock offended laugh. "Hey! Be nice."

"I'll be very, *very* nice," I answer in a deep voice and she giggles, shaking off a wave of chills.

The song and its lyrics echo in my head. A-ha sing about pursuing love. Taking risks. That it's *not* better to be safe than sorry. I hope they're right.

CHAPTER 38

NORA

As I belt out the words of my countrymen a-ha's 'Take On Me', I can't take my eyes off Jake. When I saw him today, it was obvious there's something special about him. The way he looked at me and came straight to me—clear about what he wanted—was comforting.

Not terrifying.

Being out on the river with him was incredible. I'm impressed by myself, how much I said out loud of what I feel. It was easy to talk to the water, to him, holding my paddle. Not having to think about where to put my hands, or what my face looks like, or what he'd be doing next. He was just there, paddling us safely under the bridges. Listening.

Man, I love this song.

Jake doesn't seem to, though. Or it could be my singing. Either way, I can't fully decipher this particular scowl or stare—is he ready to devour me now or trying to block my voice out with sheer willpower? There's such a fierceness to his dark eyes.

I let my gaze dart over to the lyrics in between, so I don't sing my hilarious own version again.

When finished, I step off stage to a tumultuous applause and casually slide up next to Jake in the dark corner. My drink awaits on the high table next to him and as I lean past him to grab it, he whispers in my ear.

"I need to taste you."

Holy hell. It's the sexiest thing I've heard. The words and his breath on my skin sends shivers down my spine and sets me on fire instantly. The pants inferno is back; now my body knows what he can do, and it's ready immediately. I bite my lip to hold myself back from sighing out loud at the thought of his mouth on me.

"You leave first and I'll meet you in a couple of minutes?" I whisper behind my hand.

He nods with wide, black eyes. An intensity that could burn my clothes off right here.

***

We're in the back of a black cab. This time, I look at his large, attractive hand and instead of rambling to take my mind off it, I take it and place it high on my thigh. He glances at the taxi driver and I move it up higher, flashing him a wry grin when he looks at me with hooded eyes. He moves it down in between my legs, wriggling his fingers lightly on my warm, increasingly wet area. A moan escapes me and the driver clears his throat.

"None of that, please."

Jake slowly takes his hand back, but I don't want to break contact, so I put my hand on his. I let my fingers slide up his large palm and in between his fingers. Touching him is electrifying.

I look up and we lock eyes. Those deep dark wells I get lost in. The intensity of his stare reminds me of his expression before.

"You survived my singing."

"Survived? I loved it." His deep voice rumbles in the taxi seat. I flex my fingers again and he does the same.

"You looked like you were trying to set the place on fire with telekinesis."

He lets out a small laugh through his nose. "I take a lot from lyrics. It's a powerful tune."

"*Ta på meg,*" I whisper.

"Hm?"

"The direct translation of 'touch me' in Norwegian is 'take on me.'"

Jake slides his hand up mine, and ends with fingertips on fingertips. There's something incredibly sensual about the way he does it and the heat in me keeps growing.

When we arrive at the Barbican, outside Jake's apartment, we exit the car and I fling myself on him. His arms curl around my back, holding me in a firm embrace before he grazes my lips with his. He's smiling. It makes me giggle and I kiss his smile again.

"This way." He takes out the keys from his pocket and I follow him up one flight of stairs, not letting go of his hand. I'm scared if I let go, I'll wake up from this dream.

***

He peels my top off and throws it over the couch. He groans at the sight of my breasts, and kisses the skin above the black fabric, moving it aside to reveal a pink nipple that he takes in his mouth.

"Mmm," he hums. I let out a breath and curl a hand into his hair. He kisses his way up to my collarbone, along the sensitive skin of my neck and my jaw. I want to kiss him, but he moves past my mouth and down the other side. I laugh and nibble his shoulder.

He growls into my skin, sending vibrations through me. "Let me drive. You trust me, right?"

"I suppose," I say with a grin.

His rock-hard erection is clearly visible in his dark blue sweatpants, but he moves slowly. Taking his time. Tracing my shape with his warm hands.

"Sensational," he whispers.

I tug at his T-shirt and he lets me pull it up and over his head.

"Oh," I sigh at the sight and put my hand on his pecs, running them down his stomach. There's a light sprinkling of dark hair across his chest and down. A teasing path that tapers off into his pants. He's muscular, but soft to the touch. I made up a man in my wildest fantasies and he's sprung to life. "You're perfect," I whisper, moving my hands up again down the sides. Squeezing.

"What are you doing?" He laughs.

"Searching for the promised squishy bits. You exaggerated a little." I kiss the side of his stomach and up to a nipple, nibbling it, and he growls in response.

He guides me backwards toward the bedroom while kissing me. I go along, giggling. What will he do to me? He said he needs to taste me. Will I let him? My hands are shaking slightly as I caress his arms and shoulders, it's the familiar nervousness that creeps up in me. I only had one drink to avoid being drunk and numb, knowing what was in the cards for tonight.

His moves are deliberate. Certain. He knows what he wants to do. There's something about the way he is with me, the way he looks at me, that eases me.

We stand by the side of the bed; the anticipation thick in the air. He grabs the edge of my workout pants and pulls them down—my underwear along with them—and goes down on his knees in front of me.

Jesus. He's right there.

"Eek," I say and move a hand to cover myself.

"Don't you hide yourself from me."

He takes my hands away and kisses my front, flicking his tongue in between. Teasing me. Sending warmth throughout my naked body. Every inch of my skin wants him to continue touching me.

I let out a moan, and he pushes me gently down on the bed. After he pulls my pants fully off, he stands back. Those smoldering eyes are so intense I can feel them on me, like he just licked me again.

"I'm exposed," I say, and as if on autopilot, I move my hands to cover myself again, although this time I don't want to. It's a habit.

He gently grabs my hands and pins them to the sides.

I let him. It turns me on even more. His commanding approach is reassuring.

"Don't hide. I'll join you," he says, his breath teasing my face. I want to kiss him, but he steps back and pulls down his pants, letting his enormous erection free.

"Jesus Christ. I'm not sure you'll fit." I grin.

"Don't worry, I'll warm you up." His voice is strained as he strokes himself lightly in front of me.

"Kiss me first," I say. I want to feel his skin on mine.

He crawls up on the bed and leans down on me, letting his naked body press against mine. My senses are enhanced with the adrenaline that courses through me; my skin against his makes every cell vibrate. His lips on mine feel as natural as breathing. I bend my knee and rub my groin against his length.

"I want you inside me," I whisper into our kiss, so used to deflect from the pleasure I could get from a tongue down there. Stop, Nora. Relax. Trust him.

"Soon." It comes out raspy. He kisses his way down. His soft lips on my chin. My collarbone. My stomach. Leaving a trail of fire in his wake.

"You smell so good," he murmurs against my skin and I get goosebumps all over. Moving all the way down, he kisses the sensitive skin on the sides, and I catch my breath. He continues to kiss down the inside of my thighs, biting gently, turning me on—thoroughly.

"Tease," I breathe and arch my back.

"Mm-hmm," he answers, like a purr into my skin and I'm about to come apart already.

He straightens up and nudges my legs further open.

I can't quite believe I'm letting a man stare at me down there like that. But he looks at me with such reverence, such want. It's not awkward. *I'm* not awkward. He makes me feel sexy.

He groans at the sight of me and takes me in his mouth. Kissing me with the perfect pressure and suction. I gasp as the tingling sensation spreads in me, into my legs and up my body, making my breath ragged. His tongue moves as if it knows before I do where it should be. Up, down, hard, soft. Fluttering.

"Oh wow," I cry out involuntarily, to a chuckle from him. The pressure mounts in me as he moves. He's extraordinary.

I hope he likes it. Has it been many minutes? Is he comfortable down there?

Oh no, don't think.

"Look at me," he rasps. "Focus on me. I got you." He must have noticed a change in me. He can't be a mind reader for real, although I suspect it now.

"Are you comfortable? Sorry if I take long, I—"

"Shut up. Let me enjoy this. You taste amazing." He kisses me again, hooded eyes locked on mine. I do as he says and focus on the softness and warmth of his tongue and lips on me. That intense tickle grows. Like my blood is carbonated, and explodes into my legs and stomach with crashing waves with every move he makes. The pressure builds up. It's powerful. I arch my back to him, moaning, and grasp the sheets on either side of me.

"Jake," I breathe. "I'm close."

I can't contain it. It takes over; the most mind-blowing orgasm makes me shudder and writhe as he holds on to my thighs, giving me those last waves of pleasure before I fall flat. Finished. In ecstasy.

While I'm a panting starfish on his massive bed, he moves to the bedside table and finds a condom. I watch how the muscles in his thighs flex as he bends and take in every detail of his him as he stands in front of me, sliding it on.

"Are you ready for me?" he asks, his voice strained, rubbing his length.

I shiver. Am I?

CHAPTER 39

JAKE

I sink into her tight warmth, hearing her moan my name, and it's almost too much. She clenches and arches against me. It's fucking amazing. Not only because it's been so long, but because it's her.

My affection for her intensifies the physical sensation of her touch. Feeling her under me, under my hands, makes me realize just how much is going on in my chest and my mind on top of everywhere else. Sex has never been this all-consuming. Every sound of pleasure she makes is a heightens my already extreme experience. I grasp her hips, lifting her to meet me as I'm on my knees on the bed, her legs over my shoulders. My cock fills her up, and every time I thrust into her, she gasps.

She's gorgeous. The way her small breasts sway along with our movements makes me wild.

"Jesus Christ," she exclaims. She laughs and puts a hand over her face.

"Look at me," I say, my voice a hoarse whisper.

She moves her arm and locks eyes with me as I sink into her again and again. Spreading her thighs wider, I go deeper, and she mewls in pleasure.

I can hardly breathe at the tightness of her. Trying to hold the growing pressure back. It's no use.

"I won't last. You're fucking *exceptional*." I hardly get the words out as I strain against my body's imminent need for release. She bites her lip and gives me a wry smile.

"Come hard for me. Let me hear how I make you feel."

You don't have to ask me twice. I let go, thrusting faster, pressure releasing as she calls out at the last moves. I'm a shuddering mess. It takes all my effort to stay upright.

She didn't come there. I would know. But I'll make it happen next time.

I collapse next to her, turning toward her, and she rolls close. Skin on skin and her head on my biceps. We breathe together for a moment. This is perfect. She's my kind of perfect.

I kiss her forehead. Can I do that? It's oddly intimate. I don't think I've ever kissed anyone's forehead before. Her skin is warm under my hand as I let it slide up her hip, down the dip of her waist and around her back.

Her breathing slows down. She's asleep? Who falls asleep like that? Naked, and no covers? She must be exhausted from the long day. It's a good sign she feels safe enough to sleep here in my arms. I'm elated she'll be here when I wake up tomorrow. Hope I've made it clear how badly I want her. How good we are together. Taking this risk must be the best decision I've made.

CHAPTER 40

NORA

I wake up naked. Can't believe I fell asleep like that. I must have been more tired than I thought. A sense of regret and embarrassment creep up on me. But a heavy, exquisite beige arm is draped across my stomach on top of the quilt and I push the feeling away. It's a muscle memory from my past. My brain is so used to regret it's the first place it goes.

I will never regret *this.*

No matter what happens next.

Last night was out of this world. Jake is out of this world.

He's breathing slowly and deeply. I turn to look at the sleeping shape next to me. His hair is ruffled and his face is relaxed, half-squashed into the pillow. His mouth is soft. The beautiful Cupid's bow is prominent and inviting. I have a powerful urge to kiss it—and his dented chin, his cheekbone, the side of his eye that wrinkles when he shows me that heart-melting smile of his. I want to snuggle up into his arms and be the small spoon.

That unease hits my stomach again. A growing knot under my lungs. I'm queasy. Ugh.

Am I scared? Why? Is Dee right? Am I falling for him?

He's been very sweet. And so ... *right* for me. Last night, it's as if he sensed when I was weirding out and he squashed it before it festered. He understood my mind was racing and helped me focus. I thought I hated the lack of control, but on the contrary—the way he commanded the situation made me relax.

But he's not looking for a relationship—that's not part of his plan. Work is the focus for the foreseeable future, he said. We only did this to make our days in the office easier. This is just a huge detour on my winding road to finding the love of my life.

Sometimes it seems he likes me, though. He looks at me so intensely. It could simply be lust, of course. But he said I energize him.

He stirs, interrupting my spinning thoughts, and I jump back out from under his arm, rolling quietly out of the big white bed. I'm not ready to find out whether he wants to be the big spoon or if he prefers me to be gone. The potential is there as long as I don't open the door, as long as I don't question it. There's a solace in that.

After cleaning myself up, I wrap myself in a towel and stroll around the apartment, trying to learn more about him from his stuff. Not sure what's his and what's part of the fully furnished London rentals. The plants must be all Jake. I don't think apartments come with plants. I picture him watering them, plucking away dead leaves. The thought of him doing something so ordinary makes my heart flutter. He's not some nighttime sex vampire person who goes out after work to track women.

He's just a guy.

The books on the shelf next to the couch must be his. Star Wars novels. Graphic novels. Work related books. Still a geek.

I run my finger across the spines, imagining sitting on the couch with him—me with my romance book, him with one of these. My legs across his lap. Or we're watching a movie together and I'm snug in the nook of his arm. His strong, warm arm.

I shouldn't let my mind wander farther. It'll be hard to find my way back to reality.

His wooden desk is tidy, except for a pile of notebooks. The top one has charcoal art on the front. I peek inside it. Oh, it's a sketch book. He draws?

I pick it up and flick through.

Trees, flowers. He's talented. Is this Norway? Looks familiar. I skip further back and find drawings dated years ago of fruits and hands. Practicing shapes, by the looks of it.

"Good morning." I hear his voice before the

sound of his feet on the wooden floors and the familiar adrenaline rush kicks in. I close the book, turning around to see him.

"Morning." He's in gray sweatpants—only. They hang low on his hips; the strong v points down to what I know is below. What I know can fill me up and make me quiver in pleasure.

Holy hell, what a man.

I need to remind myself how to breathe again. "You sketch?" I squeeze out the words.

"I try," he says, running a hand through his bed-hair, giving me a pants-tingling view of his lightly flexing biceps.

"Can you draw me?" I ask after composing myself, flashing him a grin. Everyone's seen Titanic, right? "Draw me like one of your French girls," I add in a breathy voice.

"Hah. Those are grapes, actually." He points to the book and stops in front of me.

"Draw me like a French grape, then. You can focus on the round shapes." I let my towel fall and the front of his sweatpants bulge. It makes me smile. "Ever sketched with a hard-on?"

"I love fruit. But not like that." He laughs, coming closer. My phone buzzes loudly in my purse on the table by the door, but I leave it, letting him run his hands down my sides, kiss my neck and breathe me in. His lips graze my shoulder and I shiver. He cups my butt cheeks in his large hands.

"Mmm," he hums into my collarbone. He's got

me hot in an instant. My brilliant plan seems to be failing. It's not out of my system. He's very much in tune with my system. My system wants him inside it.

My phone buzzes again and again. It sounds like it's having a seizure.

"Sorry, Jake. It could be my mom." I wrap my towel around myself again and step over to reach my bag. Worry washes over me and when I lift the phone, I instantly get chills.

3 missed calls: **Dee**
4 new messages

I swipe it open.

Dee: it's over

Dee: Nora, can you answer?

Dee: Please come home

Dee: it's over

Me: I'll be right there!

I look up at Jake, tears pressing behind my eyes. "I have to go. It's Dee … I think Ajay has dumped her."

CHAPTER 41

NORA

I burst through the doors to find Dee face down on the couch. She lifts her head at the sound of my arrival; a bloodshot eye visible underneath the bush of her hair.

"Oh, Dee. What happened?" I rush over and kneel next to her, petting her tangled mane.

"He didn't say it back," she says into the pillow, her voice muffled.

"Oh, Dee," I say again. "That fucking shite," I mumble to myself.

"What?" she asks, lifting her head.

"Nothing. I'm not sure what to say. Do you want to talk about it?"

She sits up and pushes the hair out of her wet face. "I told him I love him this morning when we woke up. He looked so cute with his bed-hair and stupid pillow marks on his face."

I sit down next to her, letting her lean into the nook of my arm.

"I was furious at him when he didn't say

it back. Told him he's wasting my time again. When I asked what 'are we even doing here', he just fucking shrugged at me."

"Jesus."

"Yeah. I packed up my stuff, but then he stopped me and said he *cares* about me *a lot*."

"Oh?" I say in a high-pitched voice, hopeful there's a potential for a happy ending for her.

"But he said he's my second priority. That I'm too focused on my work and have this whole life completely independent of him. He said I don't seem to need him. Especially after I told him I'm saving for an apartment."

"That's amazing, Dee! That should be celebrated, not punished. And you just made senior editor, you've got lots to focus on to keep climbing. He's Head of department, he shouldn't talk."

"You know how he is."

"I guess. But it doesn't make it right. You shouldn't *need* him, anyway. What did you say then?"

"I told him he's selfish and old fashioned. And if he wants to be with me, he'll have to let go of that way of thinking. He needs to trust that he's enough for me without me clinging to his arm the whole time. And he'll have to *prove* it." Her chest rises as she takes a deep breath and looks down at her hands. "He said he can't get over it so easily. Maybe you don't care *enough*, I said ... and guess what he said next."

"Hell no."

"Mm-hmm." She nods, rubbing her head against my shoulder. "Maybe I don't," she whispers. It gives me chills and a lump forms in my throat. What a horrible thing to hear when you've just opened your heart up for someone. Someone you thought was yours.

"Do you think he's in denial?" I muse, tapping a finger on my chin.

"What do you mean?" She turns on the couch to look at me and I swivel around to face her.

"He loves you, but he doesn't grasp it himself. Could he be afraid?"

"Of what?"

"Being hurt? Change? That loving each other means a deeper commitment; the next step in the relationship." I talk fast, letting one thought string to the next, and they tumble out of my mouth. "Life will be different. When making decisions, he'll have to consider you too. And him you. That's daunting! He'll have much less control. And he might never be the same Ajay again. The one he's always known. Maybe he's scared he won't live up to your expectations of him. That he won't be enough for you. So he's pushing you away now instead."

"Are you still talking about Ajay?" Dee narrows her eyes at me.

"Of course?" I furrow my brow.

"Maybe you're onto something. I reacted pretty quickly. Could I have overwhelmed him?

I've always stepped carefully, knowing he's not a typical relationship guy. But I thought he'd grown out of that by now."

"Why don't you reach out and see if he wants to talk?"

"Yeah." She straightens up. "All right."

"I'm sure he'll say it."

"Potentially. But we'll see what he does about it. Action speaks louder than words."

Jake: Hi, how are you? How's Dee?

Me: Not great. She'll pull through, eventually. Always does

Jake: Poor Dee *broken heart emoji*

Jake: see you Monday?

Nora: No, I'll be in on Thursday, clients all week :(

Jake: Okay. Enjoy client sites. See you Thursday

Nora: *thumbs up*

Dee and I spend the day watching horror movies, as she wanted to watch men get their hearts ripped out. I suppose we all have different ways of coping. Just as the murderer jumps out from the woods, our doorbell rings and we scream in shock.

"Who the fuck!" Dee shouts.

I laugh and get up on shaky legs to check. Outside there's a paper bag with an UberEats label on it. I open it as I walk back inside.

"It's ice cream and chocolate. Who sent this?" There's no receipt on the bag. No note. It happens to be my favorite chocolate. Hm.

Dee's face lights up. "For me?"

My phone buzzes in my hand.

Jake: Chicken soup for the sick, but I think ice cream is better for the heartbroken. Hope Dee likes it

"Jake got you ice cream. And chocolate." I hold it up, not sure how to feel as my heart seems to be swelling into my stomach region, making me queasy. It's thoughtful and cute. Extremely cute. I picture him sitting on his couch, looking through the app. Does he know this is my chocolate or is it a coincidence? He must have looked up my address via his work laptop, there's no way he'd remember it from being here once.

He made an effort. I blink. Mind numb. Too many thoughts and emotions sent it into shutdown mode.

Dee looks slightly disappointed. She probably hoped it was from Ajay. But she smiles when I hand it to her.

"Tell him thanks. Sweet man."

Huh. Sweet man.

I immediately want to find something for him too. Something thoughtful that shows I've noticed him. While Dee spoons ice cream into her face next to me, I flick through various Google searches until I find the perfect thing. A drawing session. A date, perhaps? Would he go with me on a proper date?

Dee's head is in my lap and I've been absentmindedly twirling my fingers in her long locks.

"Whoops. I've got my hand stuck in your hair."

"What?"

"Your tangled, cute mess."

She hums. "It's time it came off. Come with me to the hairdresser tomorrow? I'm going to get a bob." She turns on my lap and looks up at me. Her eyes are shiny, she's been silently crying.

"Of course. A bob will look epic." I stroke the hair off her forehead. "You all right there, Dee?"

"Ajay responded." She holds her phone up. It's been in her hand since she sent him a message earlier. "I haven't read it yet."

"When you're ready."

She opens it, and her eyes widen. "He wants to meet on Thursday."

I bend down to see the screen. "That's a long time to wait. Why Thursday?"

Her thumbs move quickly on the screen as she types a response.

"Says he has a work trip and something to sort out, but he really wants to see me after work."

"It'll come around soon enough." I tell myself as well. That's when I'll see Jake again too. It feels far away. "What are you hoping for?"

"Honestly? I want him to crawl on his knees and tell me he loves me. I want him begging me to take him back."

"Then I hope that too." I pat her head again. She pulls on the long locks and sticks her lower lip out. This is the style she's always had.

And Ajay's the man she's been off and on with for almost as long. He better come through this time.

***

"Hey," I say to my mom's face on my phone screen. Dee is finally asleep and I'm snug in my bed. "Where are you now?"

"I'm in San Francisco. I'm curled up on the couch, waiting for Karl to disappear." She grimaces.

"Karl?"

"The fog. How's London?"

I laugh absentmindedly, scratching my chin while contemplating what to tell her about Jake.

"You look like you're about to burst." She sits up, her gray hair swaying. "Tell me, what's happening? Did you go out with your American?"

"Sort of."

"And?"

I groan and rub my eyes with my free hand. "A part of me is certain it's only physical and I'm crushing a bit because he's gorgeous."

I grimace, knowing it sounds silly. It *is* silly. He's more than his looks. So much more, I don't dare let my mind go there for fear of sinking so deep I can't get out.

"But the other part of me daydreams about him and bought tickets to a life drawing class for next Thursday and wants to invite him on a proper date." I grin sheepishly. My internal battle leaves me insecure and anxious.

"Go for it. Don't wait around for him to ask you out if you want to be with him."

"Do you not think he's a non-relationship type, after all?"

"You'll know best. Don't take everything I say literally." She waves a hand.

"I wish he'd tell me how he feels. I can't guess. It'd help settle this emotional war raging in my head."

"Can you *ask* him?"

"I don't think so. I can't put him on the spot like that. What if it scares him away?" I wonder out loud, thinking of Ajay. "I'll see how it pans out organically."

My mom nods and gives me a weary smile. She's been traveling for over two months, and it seems to be catching up to her.

"Nora-kitten ... is it too soon to come to London early next week? I could do with a stretch of sleeping in a quiet room. Do you have space for me?"

"Absolutely. You can sleep in here, or I'm sure Colette has a spare room."

"Thank you. I'll book my flights. The coming week suits?"

"That's fine. Anytime." I look at her closely. "Are you okay, Mom?"

"Yes, yes. But it's been hectic."

My phone buzzes in my hands. A Messenger

notification pops up on my screen and a wave of nausea with it. I ignored him the first time and now he's back.

Martin: Hey, not sure you saw my last message. I'm in London in a week and a half. Grab a drink? I'll be all alone and lonely

CHAPTER 42

JAKE

"Thanks for this, Jake. It's coming together well," Manuel says from behind his desk, leaning back in his large, black office chair. He's reviewed the draft of the technology strategy over the weekend. "Howard's set up the first meeting with the American company on Monday, two weeks from now. And there's a video call with the Canadian potential. I can't recall the time."

Manuel shakes his head and rubs his temple. Does he look a bit worn? Is he worried about something?

I nod slowly, studying him. "That's great. Let's iron out any kinks before that. Need to make sure all the sections align." An idea springs to mind that might help relieve his concerns. "I can have a friend review it. He does this for a living."

"If you think that's a good idea. What's his name? Would I know of him?"

"Mark Becker. He developed a fitness tech app that he sold a few years back. Longevity, I think it was called." I forgot to look into that, actually. Making another mental note to check it out.

"It rings a bell." Manuel scratches his chin. "He'll have to sign an NDA like the investors." He clicks in on his computer as if to find one straight away. "Damn, I'd forgotten to ask our lawyer about that and now we're squeezed for time. He's always swamped, so it's probably too late to get him to do it." He scratches his eyebrow, staring at the screen with wide eyes. "I need a secretary or someone to remind me of things these days."

"My sister is an IP lawyer. I'm sure she can help. Would you want her to review them?"

"That's excellent. Yes, thank you." He leans back again and breathes out.

"Right, if that's—" I'm about to make a move to get up, but Manuel interrupts.

"I've been mulling something over since you told me what Ashton said." He plays with a pen on the desk. Spinning it on top of his notebook.

"What's that?" I shift in my chair.

"He's not impressed with our consulting services. That includes excellent people, like Sara. The bar is too high. It costs us thousands to train them and they're becoming increasingly hard to keep. Leith has just resigned to become a project manager." He throws up a hand, loosely holding the pen between his fingers as he does.

"What are you saying?"

My mind goes to Nora. She loves this job.

"We should phase out the current version of

the Upturns Suite instead of keeping it. Then we can reduce the team to a handful of finance experts, like Nora." He gestures to me with his pen and draws doodles absentmindedly.

Phew.

But it means a rewrite of the strategy. Adding another scenario.

"Interesting. You've run the numbers for this?" I ask.

Manuel nods and gives me a thumbs up.

"I'll update the product strategy this week and get Mark to review," I conclude.

Manuel nods. "I'll send over my estimates so you can see exactly what I'm thinking." He leans forward and clicks into his computer. "Thanks, Jake. Sorry, I appreciate it's a last-minute change. From what I've seen of your dedication—if anyone can pull it together in time, it's you."

"Great. Thanks." I put my hands on the sides of my chair again, but wait until I'm sure Manuel's finished talking this time.

"Done. I've sent you my scribbles. Hope they make sense. Glad I didn't stay out on Friday after all. I had a very productive weekend."

"Special times, I guess. Or do you always work Saturdays?"

"Meh." Manuel shrugs. I take that as a yes. "How was karaoke? Did you enjoy your first big team outing?" he asks.

"Ah, yes, I got to know the team better, which was great. They seem to love it here. I'll make sure to keep it that way." I smile at him, and he gives me a thin line in response.

What is he thinking?

"That's good." He rubs his chin and sighs.

"Something wrong?" I ask. My heart rate picks up as if I'm about to get told off.

He lets out another sigh and slaps his hand down on the table. "Howard."

I mentally sigh in relief.

"Rosie received another complaint about him this morning," Manuel continues. "That's the third time in a year. God knows how many episodes haven't been reported."

"Wow. That's ... not good."

"No. What's worse is—" He blows air out before he continues. "I wasn't sure how to broach this, but here it goes. Howard saw you getting into a taxi with a woman on Friday."

I keep my face straight, but my heart is pounding. Shit. Shit. Shit.

"Sorry, Jake, it's none of my business what you do outside the office, and I try not to meddle with the staff. But you're the *CTO*. It's different."

I bite my cheek hard, hoping the panic isn't showing on my face. Manuel holds my gaze, his face serious, but riddled with concern rather than anger.

"Howard thinks it's someone from Upturns and uses it as an excuse—there's no policy and no harm in trying."

"There *is* a harm in 'trying' multiple times on

several people." I make air quotation marks to emphasize. "But don't worry about me. I won't be a liability."

Fuck. What do I mean by that? My stomach churns at the thought of what I might have to do.

Hope he doesn't ask again. I don't want to lie about who I was with.

Fuckety-fuck.

Nora was wrong. They *do* care.

The *CEO* cares.

I took a risk. Again. And it's blowing up. Again. I rub my sweaty palms on my pants discreetly. How do I fix it?

"Good. Glad we're on the same page."

My heart plummets into my stomach as I nod slowly, holding Manuel's stare. Damn. Does he know more than he lets on?

"We need to present ourselves as a professional, ethical leadership team. I can't have scandals with investors looking into us. Howard makes me nervous. What do I do with him?"

I clear my throat, willing my body to come out of panic mode. "Give him an official warning, I suppose. Make sure he knows it's not okay to harass anyone."

"Not sure I want that in the system right now, in case it comes up later. I'll talk to him." He bites his lip nervously. "But suppose he's right. Should we have a clear policy about it? Make it prohibited?"

"Oh, we don't have to get too corporate

about it. I think there are some blossoming relationships in the teams and it'd be sad to make that punishable."

"You mean Sara and Dave?"

I raise my eyebrows at him. He knows about them.

"Don't look surprised. I keep my ear to the ground. And Howard tells me everything. He's a bit of a gossip. Probably to take the spotlight off himself."

I feel nauseated at the idea of office rumors making Nora's life difficult. And mine. I'm still on probation, and Manuel has made it abundantly clear what he expects from me now.

"Classic whataboutism. It's a distraction tactic," I say, keeping my voice steady despite my inner turmoil.

"Yes, I'm familiar. My two teenage daughters are experts." Manuel rolls his eyes and chuckles.

What do I do? Will he be okay with us being in a relationship down the line? Will *she*?

"There's a difference between finding a relationship with a colleague and using work as your personal playground, though. Howard treads on the edge of the law. You don't need to punish everyone to deal with him. People might get scared off from the office socials. You'd have to stop people getting drunk to start with."

"No, you're right. It's a downward spiral."

"One of the team's favorite aspects of this company is the social side. Several of them told me on Friday. Said they were glad I joined them out."

Nora was right about that. And I'm surprised at how much I enjoyed myself.

"Yeah, our previous CTO was a bit stuck up. Never connected with the team. We lost a few good developers under him because he didn't notice them. I'm glad I can trust you to steer the crew and the ship in the right direction."

"Absolutely, sir."

Swiveling on my chair back in my own office, I open Nora's Instagram on my phone. I need to see her face.

The punch in the gut reaction my body has to her smile and those green eyes leaves no room for doubt.

I've fallen hard.

Has she? She seemed comfortable this time. That's a good sign, isn't it? She didn't snuggle up, though. What would've happened if Dee hadn't called?

I'll talk to her on Thursday. If she tells me she wants me, I'll have the conversation with Manuel. Fight for it.

CHAPTER 43

NORA

My stomach hurts from massive, violent butterflies. The thought of seeing Jake has my body short-circuiting. I'm both elated and terrified. What if he brushes me off?

At Zyclon yesterday, Ash told me he'd invited Jake out for a double-date next weekend. And he'd turned it down, saying he's not dating right now. He's got too much work on. Was it an excuse to Ash, or does it apply to me as well?

I stare at my screen, watching the spinning cursor of our analysis tool. Loading ... slowly. A dark shape appears in the corner of my eye and a whiff of his cedarwood scent reaches me before he does. My body tingles in anticipation as I turn to see him.

He smiles at me, but there's a wrinkle on his forehead I think I can identify by now. Is he worried about something?

"Hi," I breathe and get up. I need a certain level of privacy to shake my butterflies away, and gesture for him to join me in the kitchen. With shaky hands, I grab a mug from the cabinet. Fucking adrenaline. He sets me on fire standing there in his gray blazer and white V-neck tee. It should be illegal looking this handsome in an office.

He hasn't said a word yet. He turns to close the door. Is he chewing his cheek?

Uh-oh.

That's not the cheerful face of someone happy to see the other. He's going to tell me we're done, isn't he? That it wasn't a good idea, just as he suspected.

Yep, that's what his face says. That's his sad face.

Oh, crap.

I'd thought the words but I wasn't ready for it. I actually thought he liked me. Stupid daydreamer.

I turn away, blinking frantically to avoid the sudden burning sensation behind my eyes and press the button for a coffee. The machine hisses and splutters into the Big Ben mug. The ridiculous novelty mug calms me. My man Big Ben.

I'm here. London. Waterloo sunsets abound.

That's all I need. Right?

I turn to face him with my bravest smile.

"How are you?" I ask.

"I'm ... okay. You?"

"Hunky-dory." I keep smiling. It feels stiff.

Does he notice?

"Can we talk later? At the coffee shop?"

"You don't have to take me anywhere to turn me down. We're both busy enough as it is."

"What?"

"I'm true to my word. Thanks for letting me get you out of my system. That's it." I brush my hands off in an exaggerated gesture.

"Really? Like that?" His eyes are dark and his jaw muscles are flexing hard. I can't determine what he's thinking now. Is he upset I said it first? If he wants me, he'll argue, won't he?

"That's what we said, right? To get rid of the crackling electricity or whatever?" I turn to get my coffee, blinking hard again when he can't see. "Look, no more tension." I hold out a shaky hand as if to prove a point. "I promise I won't follow you around like that other girl." A laugh escapes me. A hard, fake laugh.

"Right. If that's what you want. I have to go. Sage is on her way."

He turns and exits the kitchen. I take a deep breath and get back to my blinking. Don't cry in the office. What did he mean, if that's what *I* want? He would've said something if I was wrong, right?

Gah, I hate this pain in my stomach. It's a huge rock pressing up against my lungs and I take another breath to check if I'm even able to, before heading back to my desk.

***

"Hey. It's Nora, right? I'm Jake's sister. We met a few weeks ago."

It's Sage. She's in a black jumpsuit I could kill for. Holding a takeaway coffee and a green Birkin bag in her hands. Even *I* recognize a Birkin.

Wow, she looks like she could own this place.

"Hi, Sage," I say after getting over the initial shock of her presence. "Of course, I remember. How's little Jackie?"

She lights up. "Good, thanks."

"Going for lunch with Jake?" I ask, trying not to show any emotion at the mention of his name.

"No, I'm doing some work with him, actually. He told me to wait in the reception, but I saw you in the reflection and wanted to say 'hi.'"

"Oh. That's nice of you." I continue smiling at her, not knowing what to say next.

"Are you involved in what Jake's working on?"

"The assessment?"

"Hmm. Okay. No. Oh, there he is."

I turn automatically and indeed, there he is. He waves at Sage and points at the kitchen. When he catches my eye, he gives me a tug at the sides of his mouth. My lungs nearly collapse as it hits me; I'll not be kissing those lips again. I inhale sharply and turn back to my computer.

"Are you okay, Nora?"

"Oh. Yes." I blink, staring at my screen.

"What's wrong?" Her voice is gentle, and I

make the mistake of looking up at her. She has his eyes. The same big, brown eyes. I scrunch up my face to not make a sound. Warm tears flow down my cheeks.

"Bloody hell. Nora." Sage comes around to the side of my chair and kneels as I try to hide my face.

"Oh my god. I'm so embarrassed. Sorry. It's probably my period or something. Hah. I have to check." I mumble into my hands and get up, leaving her standing by my desk. Jake is still in the kitchen—the hissing of the silly old machine reaches me as I rush past.

CHAPTER 44

JAKE

I sit across from Sage in the boardroom and she looks at me as if I've just stabbed her favorite purse.

"What's going on?" I ask as I connect the screen to the laptop and navigate to the documents we're about to review.

"Nora," Sage says in a deeper voice than normal. The sound of her name makes my heart skip a beat. Why is she saying it like that?

"What about Nora? You were talking to her?"

"Mm-hmm." Sage swivels her coffee cup and takes a sip.

"And?" I'm genuinely curious.

What the hell could have been said within two minutes that makes her look at me like that? She can't know anything, can she?

"You're such an asshole," she whispers it sharply, as if shouting without shouting, leaning forward in her chair. I look at her, searching her face for more.

"Please elaborate." I stop what I'm doing and lean my arms on the table in front of me.

"You *fucked* her, didn't you?" she whisper-shouts again, staring me down.

"Excuse me?" I ask, louder than intended. How the fuck did that come up in the moment she stood there?

"You're not denying it, then. She was drooling all over you at the festival, and today she's bawling her eyes out when she sees you. It doesn't take a bloody scientist to figure that one out."

"She was what?"

"Crying. She saw you, went all red-faced, and then cried. Surely it's not a coincidence. I'm not stupid. Why did you have to go and do that again?"

"She *cried*?" My stomach sinks. I replay the scene in the kitchen. Didn't she say that was it? Why did she say that if she didn't mean it? I realize I'm gaping and run a hand over my mouth. A stinging behind my eyes surprises me and I clear my throat.

"Jake," she says more softly. "Talk to me."

"It's not the same, Sage."

"Because she has feelings for you, and Heather didn't?"

My eyes cut to hers.

"What do you mean, she has feelings for me? You talked to her for two minutes."

"I wasn't born yesterday. That look in her eyes.

She's got all the feels, Jake."

"Fuck," I breathe, rubbing my forehead. My skin is prickling. My lungs are shrinking. I need to talk to Nora properly.

"So do you, by the looks of it."

When I look up, Sage is smiling.

"Why do you say that?" I raise my eyebrows at her.

"Did you love Heather?"

I pick at the side of my laptop. "No. Heather was a mistake."

"And Nora?"

"Nora ... she's anything but a mistake. Despite the trouble I might get into again. I was going to talk to her about it, but she told me she wasn't interested."

"In those words?"

I think for a moment. Did she? "Not exactly, no. But she said I'm out of her system."

"Something tells me that's not the case. Talk to her after this, be one hundred per cent honest. What did you say to her before she said that?"

"I asked to talk. Then she said I didn't have to take her out to ... *turn her down.*" I put my head in my hands. And what had my face been doing? Did she read into my expressions again? I must have looked fraught with worry, thinking about what Manuel said. "I didn't say anything useful. Argh, I did it again. Fucking bad decisions."

"Only if you don't fix it. Remember what Dad always says: if there's something you want in life, you need to give it all you got."

"I thought that was about work."

She shrugs and tilts her head. "I like to apply it to where it suits me."

"Why are you being supportive? I thought you'd be livid with me."

"That was before I learned my little brother's all fuzzy with feelings." She makes a gesture toward me as if petting an invisible dog. "You can work out the legal stuff, I'm sure they're not too bad here. Love doesn't just fall into your lap normally. I hope you work for it now you've found it."

I laugh as her choice of words conjure up the memory from the plane.

"What's funny?"

"Nora fell into my lap."

Sage rolls her eyes at me. "It's a figure of speech. You're both working here." She waves a hand.

"No, she literally fell into my lap. On the plane here from Norway. We had a moment, so to speak. Took the train in together, too. And then I saw her here when I started."

Sage gasps and puts a hand to her mouth.

"What?"

"How romantic." She beams at me.

"Is it? You and your love stories." I huff, but can't help but smile.

"Yes. Now let's get through this dull stuff so you can go make your own love story happen."

My stomach flips as she says it. Love story? I put it aside for now. The blinking cursor on my screen reminds me why we're here.

"You love this boring shit," I say finally. I click into our documents and see her rolling her eyes at me in my periphery. I try to focus despite the tingling sensation at the idea of holding Nora, kissing her happy face after I tell her how I feel.

"Maybe a little. You're using these for the investors only?"

"And Mark. You work with him, don't you?"

"I review his contracts. Is he a potential investor?"

"No, he's helping me out, making sure it's tight. How would he be able to invest in this? We're talking tens of millions."

Sage shrugs. I search her face for more, but she's got her lawyer mask on.

When I come back out from the meeting room, Nora's not at her desk. Her things are gone.

"Sean, where did Nora go?"

He looks up from his corner desk. "She said she's not well. She took the rest of the day off. Anything I can help with instead?"

"No worries, I can get it later."

Stomach churning, I walk to my office. If it was any other day, I'd go find her. Talk to her face to face. But the pressure is on having to rewrite the strategy and get it to Mark in time for him to review it before the investor meeting. God, I hope I don't have to make any big changes. It's rare I stress, but my adrenaline is coursing hard trying to get all my ducks in a row.

I call Nora once I'm behind my closed office door. It's not even ringing. Is she on the subway?

Me: Can we talk? I don't like texting like this, but it's the only option right now. I think there was a misunderstanding when we spoke earlier

Two hours later ...

Nora: Did Sage say something? Don't worry about me, I was just sad about my mom. I'm concerned about her

Me: Is she okay?

Nora: She says so, but she's coming here soon and I think something is wrong

Me: Sorry to hear. So it wasn't related to what we talked about in the kitchen?

Nora: No, I told you not to worry. I'm okay. Are you?

No. I'm very much not okay.

My hands shake, holding the phone. People rush past my office, going about their day as if it's just a normal fucking day.

Damned Sage and her romantic ideas.

Why did she make me think Nora actually has feelings for me when she said she doesn't? It made my heart soar and now it's crashed back down. Why did I let myself get so worked up? It seemed like she liked me.

I rub my forehead and angle myself toward my screen so no one walking past can see the agony on my face.

The idea of being with Nora, of sharing my

life with her, had me feeling euphoric. I never thought I needed anyone like that until I met her.

It's clear now that something is missing in my life. In me. My chest feels hollow, and it's hard to breathe.

I can't tell her that in a text, but I don't want to lie. Chewing my cheek and squeezing my eyes shut, I take a deep breath and put away my phone without answering.

At least now I have no reason to be derailed from the investor meetings. I can give it my all. Whatever they need.

CHAPTER 45

NORA

Jake hadn't answered my last message before I went to sleep last night, and I don't dare to check yet. It's been all week. I can't believe I lied to him like that. It's true that I'm worried about Mom, but it's not why I cried. What's wrong with me? Why couldn't I say what was on my mind?

I guess it made it easier for him, anyway. Now I've turned myself down for him, and don't have to hear those words come out of his beautiful mouth. That he doesn't want me like that.

I study the small photo in my hand that I've kept safe in my bedside drawer—until it moved in under my pillow this week. My skin tingles at the memory. Of Jake's hand on my chin and breath on my lips. Two days before this I told him I only wanted something physical. That I didn't have feelings for him. What an idiot I am.

The birds in the bush outside scream at the world and the orange Friday morning sun sneaks in through the slit between the window frame and the blinds.

It's early.

Do I have to go to work today? I should. Need to prove to Jake I'm nothing to worry about. It would be horrible if he walked around with even more guilt because of me. It's not *his* fault I was emotionally confused then. And crushed now.

It hits me; I fell asleep in a quiet house. No door slammed. No crying from the room next door.

Did Dee get in last night?

Could she have stayed at Ajay's? That would be a good sign. I roll over and grab my phone from the bedside table to check. Two new messages. Neither is from Jake.

Mom: I'm on my way already. Got a special price on standby tickets. Should I come to your home or office? Arriving eleven at Heathrow.

Me: Come to my house. I'll book you a taxi.

That settles it then. I'll go in for a few hours and leave early—limited exposure. Probably for the best.

Nice one, Mom.

Dee: How did it go with Jake? I'll be home early today. Have a surprise :)

Me: OMG! I'll be early too!

***

I power walk home from the overground station —I'd run, but it's not ideal in a pencil skirt. Mom has arrived and Dee is home. Right now, I'm not sure what I'm more excited about; to see Mom or hear what Dee has to share?

Luckily, I didn't see Jake in the office today, so I managed to concentrate and get everything I needed out of the way to spend a few days with my mom next week.

As I open the door, the sound of happy chatter rings out from the kitchen and I run in.

"Mom!" I beam at her, arms out.

She puts down her steaming cup of tea and gets up from the chair to give me a big hug. Dee is here, wearing the same dress as last night—a telltale sign. Colette smiles at me over the rim of her cup.

"What a wonderful surprise to have you here already." I squeeze Mom so hard she squeals and laughs.

"Good to see you," she says in Norwegian into my curls. I let go of her after another squeeze and she makes a deal of turning to Dee with a wave of her arm. I shoot my friend a quizzical look.

What's this all about?

Dee answers with a sheepish smile.

Then she lifts her left hand and a glittering, shining, blinding piece of jewelry sits on her ring finger. When she moves her hand, the ring sparkles in the kitchen light.

"What!" I run to her to see and take her hand in mine.

It's an engagement ring!

As engagement-ringy as engagement rings could ever be.

It has small diamonds along the band meeting the big square rock, also in a frame of small diamonds. It's breathtaking. I'm gaping. Its magnificence distracts me from what it means for a moment. It takes another second for my brain to switch on and I'm able to say something.

My mouth is dry.

"Ajay *proposed*?" I croak.

Dee nods, her new short bob swaying along her jawline.

"Last night. He took me up to the top of the Shard."

Magnificent view of the city she loves. Not a bad choice.

"Of course he knows someone, so we got to go past the queue. Got a private area." She gestures for us all to move to the couch as she continues talking.

I hold her tiny hand. I don't want to let go.

"He said he's been a fool. That he should be inspired by me instead of scared. He said he knew it the second I left that day, that he doesn't want to be without me."

She beams, as wide as her face allows.

"The bartender showed up with champagne and, when I turned back, Ajay was on one knee, the London skyline behind him, this sparkly beauty in a box in front of me." We all look at the ring again.

"He even called my parents to get their consent." She makes a grimace at this that I can't place; is she moved or annoyed?

"That's a good thing?" Mom asks with genuine curiosity.

"Oh yeah. I mean, it's old fashioned, but it means he's serious."

"Wow, this is amazing, Dee!"

"I know," she says, putting her hands to her face as if in shock. "My parents are coming over to meet his parents first, which is a huge deal." She makes big eyes at me. "It's in two weeks. He's booked a table at some fancy restaurant I can't even pronounce to impress them. Can you come?"

"Of course! But are your parents coming from Delhi on such short notice?"

"No, they're in Portugal. I told you." She shrugs and laugh. "It's still pretty short notice. I suppose he's quite persuasive."

"That's ... great!" I hug her so she doesn't see my face. This is moving fast. Is Ajay coming through, finally?

CHAPTER 46

JAKE

"Jake," Manuel says, his voice sounds panicked on the other end of the phone. "I made a mistake. We're meeting the Canadians the coming Wednesday. You need to send them the memorandum right away."

"Right away? Are you sure? Mark hasn't reviewed it yet." I put my coffee down on the kitchen counter a little too hard, spilling onto my sweatpants. Fuck.

"You, Howard and I have read it. It's good."

"Okay, let me know when they've signed the new NDAs and I'll send it."

"Still share it with your friend. I looked him up. What a great resource." Manuel speaks fast. It seems stress brings out some of his Spanish language traits. "I've booked a conference room at the Hilton for us to prep next week. We need to be ready."

Damn. I was hoping we'd meet the private equity company first. I've looked into this Canadian firm. It's like HercuSoft. Will they approve of our investment requirements? Manuel wants to stay in control. Keep the team. But I saw how HercuSoft did their acquisitions. Complete absorption. Which means layoffs. Relocations.

"Are you sure about this, Manuel? Have you read their history?"

"I'm aware of the negotiations we may need to enter."

I leave it at that for now. His tone says he's not interested in discussing it.

There are still three other potential investors. One of them must find Manuel's requirements acceptable.

I look out over my apartment, the view of the city through the floor-to-ceiling windows. I hope they won't relocate me. Despite having spent a lot of my time in the office, I've fallen for London.

And some.

My laptop is open next to me, Nora's face smiles at me from her Instagram grid. Working from home today was meant to help me not get distracted by her in the office. Yet here I am. Doing some light cyberstalking. The newest picture is of her and her mom in what I assume is her garden. I check Dee's page to see if she's shared something with Nora. She got engaged to Ajay. That's a surprise.

I accidentally double click it and the heart icon flashes up. Whoops. Ah well, it's not Nora's photo.

I open my phone instead, looking at the latest messages with Nora. Should I ask about her? If her mom is well?

Grinding my teeth, I put it away again. Sage said I need to tell her what I feel in case I'm wrong and she's right. That Nora was deflecting. I'll do it once I'm certain about the investors. Why start something when I don't know what'll happen next?

CHAPTER 47

NORA

Viktor Wynd's Museum of Curiosities and Absinthe Bar greets us with its quirky first impression of taxidermy and animal skeletons in the window. Dee added it as a stop on our canal-side walk in East London that we're taking my mom on.

"Why would Ajay want to play tennis instead of joining us here?" Colette asks, peering inside, her voice thick with sarcasm.

"Hey, don't knock it—got many other options on a Sunday, do you?" Dee sends her a wry smile.

"No. This'll have to do." Colette steps up and opens the door. "All my friends are dead." She takes one look at our shocked faces and laughs so hard I think for a second she might fall over. She enters, cackling, and the rest of us follow her into the ground floor bar section.

After relaxing at home for a couple of days, my mom seems to have regained her energy. She's been adamant nothing is wrong with her, so I try to put my worries aside.

It's dark and wonderfully weird in the basement museum, and my mom loves it, too. She notices all sorts of little details.

There's a jar full of Rolling Stones' used condoms, a book about how to poo while on a date, a magician taxidermy mouse, Ronald McDonald in a wind-up car, and an alien in a jar.

"Oooh, look at this!" She crouches down to inspect the world's longest standing erection. And then moves abruptly to the other side, like a child in a toy shop. "Oh gosh, finger jam. It looks like real fingers." She turns to us with her hands covering her mouth and a mock look of horror on her face.

I'm getting to know Mom better by watching her discover things. Did Dad ever see her like this? A wave of sadness about my mom traveling around alone hits me. She's unnoticed. Unwitnessed.

The familiar squeeze of my stomach at the thought of ending up alone makes a fleeting appearance. Dee shows up on my side and leans her head on my shoulder.

"I'm nervous," she whispers.

Mom runs around pointing at things for Colette to look at. Shrieking and laughing in between.

"That's okay," I whisper back. "It's normal, don't you think? A lot happening quite fast."

I'm nervous too. She'll move in with him only

after they're married, so we still have some time to live together, but selfishly, it feels too soon.

"Yeah ... Hey, I didn't get to hear about Jake. I guess it's not good news." She glances up at me and I suck in my lower lip to hide the quiver. "Oh, Nora," she says quietly so the others can't hear, grabbing my hand.

"I'll be all right."

"It's okay not to be okay for a bit too."

"I don't even know why I react like this. It's just a silly crush."

There's giggling coming from the corner where my mom and Colette stoop over something. Another mummified penis, by the sounds of it.

"You *say* that ... What exactly did *he* say, though?" she asks more directly, this time.

"Hmm." I try to recall his words, but what fills my mind is his pained expression. The worry crease between his eyebrows. "He looked upset. Asked if we could talk elsewhere."

"And did you?"

"No, I told him what he wanted to hear without having to waste any more time. That he's out of my system. I don't want him to think I'll cause him any trouble. You should've seen him when he told me about that other girl."

"But what did he *say*?"

"He said 'really? Okay, if that's what you want.' Or something like that."

"Hmm."

"What? He would've spoken up if he wanted anything more, don't you think?"

"Maybe."

"Don't give me hope where there is none," I whisper, not even sure she can hear me. She's got her phone in her hand now, slowly inching away from me. Texting.

Sigh. Only a few hours since she saw him last and she can't leave Ajay alone. It's good to see she's absorbed in him, so in love, despite being nervous.

***

As we walk along the canal down toward Mile End and the end of our day, my mom hooks her arm in mine. Dee and Colette trot along behind us.

"Thanks for lending me your bed, kitten," she says in Norwegian, as the others are outside of earshot.

"No problem. Colette said she'll have her guest room ready for your last few nights. Don't let her give you too much booze in the evenings."

She squeezes my arm and laughs. "Of course I will. Two old ladies will do whatever they want."

"You're not old, Mom."

"Not the point."

"I guess. Drink away. At least you're not alone up there."

"I'm not afraid of being alone."

"You don't get lonely on your travels?" I turn

to see her expression. It's calm; a small smile playing on her lips, as she studies the canal boats we walk past. "There's no one to see things with you. No one who sees you."

"Oh, Nora, you're sweet." She sighs. "If a tree falls in the forest, it makes a sound even though no one hears it."

I stare at her. When did she become a philosopher?

"I'm living my best life. I don't need someone to be with me to enjoy it. Coincidentally, I'm with people when I travel, just not the same person all the time." She angles her head to catch my eye. "I'm happy. I make myself happy. Always did. Your father *enhanced* my life—mostly. But I didn't depend on him, or anyone else, to be the main source of my happiness." She pats me reassuringly on the cheek.

"You're not an island, Mom." I can do philosophy too.

"That's not what I said. I'm self-reliant *and* enjoy community. It's the beautiful contrast of human existence. We are social beings who crave independence."

"What was in your absinthe?"

Maybe there's something to it. Have I sought another person for so long, I didn't consider looking to myself for love and validation? For happiness? I am happy, I realize. Except for the gaping hole Jake left in me. Am I capable of filling it myself?

"*You* are self-reliant. You took yourself through university after your father's death, moved to London—twice—to shake things up when you felt stuck. You reach out for support when you need it. Give yourself some credit. London seems to do you good, though. You're more yourself than last time I saw you. More vibrant. Despite your recent disappointment with Jake."

"You're probably right. I'll be fine." The words come out of my mouth, but my heart still aches at the mention of Jake, and I want to change the subject. "So, there's nothing wrong with your health?"

"My health? No. Nothing, honey. Except I seem to require quality hotels and restful sleep. I'll need to take a break from my travel and do Asia next year. I'll go to Oslo and annoy your brother for a while." She laughs.

"That's it? You need better beds?"

"Yep. That's it."

I tilt my head back, letting out a hearty laugh, thick with relief.

"Let's pop in here?" Colette pipes up from behind us. "I think you'll like this place, Mari." She picks up her pace and grabs my mom by the arm, guiding her up the path toward the old house just off the canal-side.

"This pub was here when I was young. It's hardly changed in the last thirty-odd years. Still has its Cockney vibe," Colette says in a low voice.

It's dark and quiet in here, compared to the sunny afternoon outside.

It has a certain charm with its heavy red velvet curtains, sticky blue carpet, and dimmed lighting.

We used to come here as students when the other bars were too busy, but we didn't appreciate it for what it was back then.

"I already prefer this place to those loud brick wall places with wooden chairs," Mom says, sipping her beer and making a face. "Although this beer is flat."

"And they won't excuse it." Colette laughs, gesturing toward the old man behind the bar. "You get what you get with this place. I hope it stays like this. Simply because people expect them to upgrade the furniture or have a bigger selection of beer, like the other pubs around here, it doesn't mean they have to. There's still enough people who come here. Shouldn't have to change a single thing."

"I like that." Dee talks to her glass, drawing circles in the dew on the side. "They need to appreciate the customers who love it as it is."

"Exactly. They shouldn't have to change or settle for anything less. You should check out their Thursday jazz night. I'd take you myself but my daughter set me up with a bridge group." Colette grimaces as if it's the last thing she wants to do.

"Oh, I'm leaving Wednesday," Mom says with a

pout.

"Let's go together next time." Colette pats her hand on the table. "You're back in December, right?"

"Absolutely, Nora is taking me to the Ritz!" She grins at me.

"I've got tickets to life drawing class this Thursday, I just remembered. Was going to invite Jake …" I look up at Dee. "Sure you can't come?"

"I've got a work thing," Dee presses her lips together and turns her mouth down.

I'll have to find someone else to join me. I don't want to go alone.

Me: Hi, join me for a life drawing class this Thursday?

Sara: I'd love to but have dinner plans!

Hmph. Getting desperate now, none of the wider group can join. What about my trusted old app? Ugh, definitely not Preston. Oh, this guy …?

Me: Hi Mark, this is a bit out of the blue but you seemed nice from your profile, despite ghosting me, I mean. Haha. Wanna join me for a life drawing class by Monument this Thursday? Already have the tickets, just need the company :)

Mark: Hi, sorry about the ghosting. Can I ask why you're inviting me of all people?

Me: You can ask. But you might not like the answer! I have tickets and the person I wanted to invite doesn't want to date me, and weirdly everyone's busy, so I've desperately turned to Crosspath. Regretting it now! Never mind :)

Mark: Sorry. Hope you find someone

It seems I'll have to turn to the last person I want to after all. Again. Like on the night I saw him last, he's annoyingly there when others aren't.

Me: Hi Martin ...

CHAPTER 48

JAKE

Manuel rubs his temples. The air in the taxi is stale and heavy with exhaust fumes, making me nauseous. The investor meeting adds to my queasiness, and Manuel has so far failed to ease my concerns.

"That wasn't what you hoped for, I gather," I say, studying his reaction. He lets his hands fall onto his thighs with a smack.

"Not exactly."

"Can't we just turn them down? It's the complete opposite of your requirements and you won't even have a majority share. Most people would lose their jobs. You don't want that. Right?"

They'll definitely lay me off. Why would they want two CTOs?

"It wouldn't be sudden. That kind of merger would take several months and we'd give them plenty of notice. They'd be all right. It's just the dev team. And IT. Maybe Rosie." He rubs his temples again before he looks up, forcing a smile. "I'll argue your case. I didn't know they'd bought up that AI software development company they talked about. What a career-maker it would be to be part of that."

"Yes, that was interesting news indeed." I'm familiar with the company they've acquired. They were recently ranked top third in the world in AI business tech. "Thanks, Manuel. Worth a shot, I guess."

The idea makes my blood rush. It's as if my old self invented a role based on my career dreams. AI innovation backed by deep pockets. A 'career-maker'.

What about my new self? I've warmed up to the small company vibes. To London.

Tiny baby Jackie.

Nora.

I know she didn't tell me the truth last week. She likes me. There's a chance there.

But do I let a chance of love determine what I do next? What the hell will my dad say? He'll be fraught.

It's more likely I'll be fired, anyway.

"Manuel. Are you sure? They'll swallow the company whole. It's the end of Upturns. We can't accept this."

Manuel leans his head in his hands.

"The other investors fell through. Howard called yesterday. They've canceled. Not the right requirements for them either."

"So we wait. We'll redevelop on the side with the people we have. It'll be slower but we can make it work."

"I can't sleep, Jake. All it takes is *one* of the bigger clients to get rid of us and we go negative. We don't have enough consultants or support for them."

"We'll make it work. I was thinking—"

"My wife is ill. Uterine cancer." Manuel looks down, blinking furiously.

"Oh, fuck," I breathe, "I'm sorry." I put a careful hand on his slumped shoulders.

"I want to spend time with her. Be there for our daughters. The doctors are optimistic, but she'll need multiple surgeries. It's such a wake-up call." He rubs his eyes with a hand, breathing out heavily and I take my hand back as he straightens up. "Sorry. I can't lose everything. And my mental health is wearing thin worrying about it constantly. This sale. I need it. I need it now."

"All right." I sigh. "I'll do what I can to help make it happen."

CHAPTER 49

NORA

I arrive at the restaurant and spot Martin by the bar, talking to a giggling bartender. Classic Martin. I knew he wouldn't actually be lonely tonight. Again, I'm the one leaning on him to avoid being alone.

My phone buzzes in my purse, and I fish it out to check before approaching him.

Sara: Howard getting drunk talking shit to Dave, stay tuned

I sigh, putting it away. Why should I care?

"Hey," I say breathlessly as I slide up next to Martin. "Nice to see you." I don't mean it, I realize. Seeing him stirs up old emotions of feeling ridiculous. Scrutinized. Constantly reviewed and critiqued. It gnaws in my gut.

"You too. You look good." He grins, but I'm never sure if he's simply laughing inwardly at some joke I don't get. I brush a hand over my hair to check. Seems fine.

"Thanks? The same, I think. Shall we get a

table?"

We order pizza to keep it simple and I get a much-needed crisp white wine.

"What's been going on for you?" he asks with raised eyebrows, sipping his beer. "Any men on the horizon, finally?"

"Uhm. I thought there was, but …" I look around, hoping he can't see the sadness in my eyes. The pizza arrives and we each grab a slice. The melted mozzarella strings as I lift mine and it's a mess. Jesus. Martin will have a ball laughing at me trying to eat this. I use cutlery instead to avoid a scene.

"Any action?" he asks halfway through his slice.

"Excuse me?" My eyes cut to his.

"You know …" He wiggles his eyebrows at me. "Or I can take you home tonight. I've learned a new trick or two."

I'm gaping. "Is that why you messaged me? For a booty call?"

"Isn't that what we always were to each other? Friends with benefits?" He continues on his pizza with a small shrug.

"We're not friends, Martin," I say flatly.

"No?" He smirks. I want to flick it off his face.

"You can't stand most of the things I do. I talk too much, embarrass you, dance weirdly, eat too fast, have frizzy hair, and what else …?" The knife and fork are screeching on the plate as I'm cutting too hard. I put the cutlery down and sip my wine instead.

"You're a bit neurotic."

"That too?" I ask, incredulously. I'm aware I can be, but I'm still appalled he says it out loud like that.

"But I still enjoy hanging out with you. Despite all those things," he says, beaming.

The word echoes in my head.

Despite. Despite.

He's not changed. And I'm a version of myself that I can't stand when I'm with him. Bitter. Prickly.

Standing up abruptly, my chair scratches loudly on the floor. Martin glances up at me over his beer. I grab my purse and fling it over my shoulder.

"I'm going by myself."

I'd rather be alone than with someone who makes me feel this way, even if he's not doing it intentionally.

"Jesus, Nora. Don't take it so seriously."

"Sorry, Martin. I shouldn't have come. This was a bad idea. I'm sure you'll find something to entertain you."

"Calm down," he says, and grabs another slice of pizza. "I'm never lonely."

I stride out of the restaurant and feel a ton lighter. Being alone wins.

***

Arriving at the class right on time, I plop down

at the first available easel. I'm not used to doing things by myself like this. Does anyone notice? Who else came here alone? Maybe this was silly. I was supposed to come here with Jake. This class was for sharing an experience with him.

The urge to leave grips me, and I'm about to get up just as the instructor closes the door and welcomes everyone.

Fine, I'll stay.

It's a group of at least twenty, each behind a wooden easel. The instructor, a gray, bespectacled man in an oversized linen shirt, glides around the room to greet people and hand out kits to the ones who ordered them. His shirt billows behind him when he moves.

"Your kits." He passes me two tote bags after checking my booking.

"I only need one," I say in a low voice.

"Didn't you pay for *two*, darling?" He asks with a louder than necessary voice. Ugh, who cares, I answer with a normal voice.

"Yes, but I'm *alone*. I only need *one*."

He raises his eyebrows at me and looks as if he's about to say something. He shrugs and moves on.

I noisily unwrap the beginner's kit—a pack of charcoal pencils, eraser, and two rolled up sheets of A3 paper. While I pin them to the easel, a man steps up on the middle stool and takes his robe off. He's like a bronze statue come to life and I've got the full frontal.

It does nothing to me.

I look around. Everyone's focused and the sound of pencil on paper fills the room. Maybe it wouldn't be normal to be titillated by the model, anyway. But I'm pretty sure I'm broken for other men indefinitely.

I have no idea what I'm doing, but I try my best. Somehow, this man in front of me turns into Jake on my paper.

He's all I think of.

Huh, I'm not so bad at this. It's quite enjoyable. My mind is focused on Jake, but in an easy way. Not the soul numbing stomach ache kind of way that I'm almost used to by now.

A tingle forms at the base of my neck. *Is he here?* I shake my head at myself. Why the hell would he be? I'm thinking so hard about him, it's as if he's appeared near me. He fills me completely as I let it all flow out onto the paper.

The instructor moves quietly around, commenting on people's drawings.

"Interesting. Very interesting." His voice is naturally loud and cuts across the scratching of the group's working hands. I can't help but peek out from behind my easel to see where he's standing. He rubs his chin, looking at someone's drawing. I can't see it nor the artist. Then he catches my eye and freezes. I move back into hiding, embarrassed at being caught staring.

I do my best to shape the lips and eyes based on the vivid image in my head. Adding the two-day stubble I find so sexy.

I think this could become my new hobby. I focus intently on what I'm doing; thoughts aren't flying through my mind uncontrollably. It's relieving. Satisfying.

"Hmm." The instructor hums at my side. "Huh. Interesting. Nice work on the shading here. You're a beginner?"

I nod.

"Very impressive. You've captured some intriguing details. Stunning resemblance." He points around the face I've drawn. "If you learn and practice the techniques, you can be extremely good at this." Then he pointedly eyes me up and down, nods and moves on.

Was he being sarcastic? My drawing looks nothing like the model. I send Preston a thought. This time, I think he's right. I'll learn more, and I'll enjoy it even more. I can draw.

My phone buzzes for the umpteenth time, and I steal a moment to check it.

Sara: Howard says Jake was seen with a woman after work drinks last Friday and Manuel is mad :O

Sara: Howard loves rumors that aren't about himself so not sure if true

Sara: was it you???

Holy shit.

Holy fucking shit.

I blink at the screen. Reading the messages again and again.

Manuel is mad.

Is this why Jake looked upset last week? I didn't let him talk. I should've let him talk. Fuck!

I squeeze my eyes shut. It's hard to focus now. How long has it been? Can I leave? I need to call Jake.

The instructor speaks up as if on cue, telling the room we're wrapping up, and I force myself to calm down. Taking a deep breath, I tune back in to the room. I'll call him in a few minutes once we're done here.

Deep breaths.

"I invite you to walk around and look at everyone's interpretations before you pack up. Not to critique, but to be inspired by different styles and techniques. Move this way, please."

The group circles slowly. Painfully so. I try to take in what I'm looking at and can't help be amazed at how different these drawings are. Some are more abstract and dark, some very detailed. There's whispering up ahead and I glance at the source. The people in front keep looking back at me. What the fuck? I bet I have a charcoal pencil beard. I check my fingers first. No, I'm clean. I keep moving and the next drawing makes me gasp.

It looks a bit like me.

Adrenaline hits instantly and I'm shaking.

It *is* me.

My curly hair, my eyes, my face.

My breasts, artistically covered by my arms

and flowing hair. I look wistful and am staring directly back at me from the page.

I look around. Only half-conscious of the people waiting behind me.

Who drew this?

My eyes land on him across the room and my stomach plunges. I haven't seen him in a week and now he's here. More beautiful than ever. And maybe he *does* want me after all. He's standing by my easel. Dragging a hand over his mouth and chin as if he can't believe what he's seeing.

Then he looks up, catching my eye and what I feel is reflected in his expression.

Longing, relief, euphoria.

I stride across the room and don't care about anything or anyone around me. He drops his hand from his face and I fling myself into his open arms, wrapping mine around his neck as I plant a kiss on his gorgeous, smiling lips.

He kisses me back softly. We giggle as I lean my forehead against his and breathe him in. Then he tucks an arm around my back and one into my hair. As our lips part as they meet again, and our kiss deepens, I close my eyes—letting the emotion wash over me.

Pure bliss. This is where I belong.

The sound of people *oooh-ing* and *aaaw-ing* becomes impossible to ignore and we break free. His broad smile and sparkling eyes are the most wonderful sight of my life. I beam at him and he kisses me again.

"Let's get out of here," he whispers and grabs my hand, sending the familiar powerful surge through me, making my heart race and setting my core on fire.

CHAPTER 50

JAKE

"Come, it's this way," she says, squeezing my hand, pulling me along. The streets are busy with pub patrons spilling onto the sidewalk, enjoying the onset of dusk and the lingering heat of a sunny day.

"Look." She points up ahead between tall office towers, and as we round the bend, I see what she means. It must be the other church ruins she told me about before.

"The gate's closed. Oh, it says it's not open after seven." She turns to me with a sad face.

"That's perfect. It means there's no one else here." I push the gate to check. "It's open." I pull her along with me under the ancient arch.

"Naughty!" She laughs.

"Wow," I exclaim. "This place is phenomenal." When we enter the ruins, it's as if the outside world disappears. The atmosphere has changed. There's a sense of tranquility that comes with the tall trees and climbing vines embracing the old stone walls around and above us. Work and worries momentarily erased from my mind. It's only us in this space.

"I love this place." Nora spins around. Her dress flows out as she does, giving me a glimpse of her strong, exquisite legs.

She stops in front of me, and I embrace her immediately, leaning my forehead onto hers.

"How's your mom?" I ask in a raspy whisper.

"She's good, gone to stay with my brother for a while. Thanks for asking." She presses her lips together in a thin smile.

I stay quiet for a beat, thinking of where to start. She told me she wants to be with someone who makes her relaxed, someone who doesn't make her worry what's going on. No games. No ambiguity.

"Dee messaged me," I say first. "On Sunday. She said you were upset and that you probably hadn't told me."

In fact, Dee told me Nora pretended to be okay so I didn't have to feel guilty about her. Classic Nora, she said.

"How did she get your number?"

"She messaged on Instagram."

"Oh. Yeah, I wasn't upset because I was concerned about my mom."

I close my eyes and breathe in as she says this. I'm so annoyed with myself that I didn't get that she was playing strong for me.

"I *was* worried about her, though." She adds

quickly.

"I would've come to see you straight away. Tell you what I wanted to tell you last week."

She weaves her fingers through mine. "Is it about the rumor? You with a woman? I'm sorry I got you into trouble. It's all my fault. Is Manuel angry?" She talks into the crook of my neck, sending small vibrations into my body.

"How did you know?" I pull back to see her face, not letting go of her hands.

"Sara messaged me today. Howard's talking at the pub."

"That maniac."

She furrows her brow, looking up at me. "I'm sorry I lied. I thought I was doing you a favor. You looked so pained. I was certain you were there to say we were finished." I stroke her upper arms, looking at her intently.

"I'm sorry too. That I made you worry like that. But please don't assume with me. Just ask. Or listen. Because I'll tell you if there's anything."

"Noted." She presses her lips together again, a hint of red in her cheeks. She's embarrassed she didn't get it right. Is she always this hard on herself?

"Where were you all week? Why wait till today?" She picks at my shirt collar, talking to my chin.

"There's some stuff going on at work."

"What you're working on with Sage?"

I give her the simple version. "Yes."

"Can you share?" Her eyes are big with curiosity.

I sigh loudly. "It's unclear what'll happen. You can't tell anyone this, but … we're looking for investors."

"Oh?"

I nod. "We met with one company yesterday who are interested, but they might …"

Do I tell her? I'm not allowed to. She can't know others might lose their jobs.

"Ugh. They might let me go." I let my arms drop. Getting a role there for me is so far-fetched it's not worth mentioning.

Nora gasps.

"We're meeting them again next week, and I'll know for sure. In the meantime, I'll continue as normal."

"Oh, Jake …" she whispers, and puts her arms around me. I wrap mine around her. The ache in my stomach from worrying about work dissolves now I'm with her. Even saying it out loud didn't cause my insides to churn.

"I wanted to see you today. I'm so glad Mark told me you messaged him about this class. And glad you came alone. When I heard you say those words—it was clear I'd finally get my chance to tell you how I feel."

"I was going to invite you, you know. Carved out some time for life together."

"Thank you."

Life together. I like the sound of that.

She tilts her head and narrows her eyes at me. “How the hell do you know Mark?”

“Oh. He’s a friend. It’s my fault he didn’t respond to you when you matched, by the way. Sorry, not sorry.” I grimace.

She laughs incredulously. “What? That’s insane. What are the odds?”

I shrug and give her a sideways smile. It’s not what’s on my mind right now. Her expression relaxes. Letting it go.

“So I’m not out of your system?” I whisper. Leaning closer. Pulling her body flush against mine.

“Not in any way,” she whispers. “You seem to have gotten stuck there.” She angles her face upwards.

My pulse races and I grin. This is an incredible feeling. Being here with her. Have her look at me like this.

“Tell me, then,” she says.

“Tell you what?”

“How you feel.”

I cup her face in my hands and take in all the details of it. One tall lamppost shines in over the ruins, lighting her up in front of me. My heart is pounding. Can she feel it?

“I’m falling for you.”

She inhales sharply, a ragged breath.

“I’m falling for you too,” she whispers, and her gaze darts to my mouth.

My stomach flips at these words, and I meet

her lips as she stretches up to kiss me. It's soft at first. We wrap our arms around each other. Then it grows hungrier. I've been hardening since she brushed against my neck, her breasts pressed up against me. But now I'm rock solid. I crave her so badly every inch of me is vibrating. Wanting. She grabs my hand and guides it down to her inner thigh.

"Touch me," she whispers. Her breath on my face fuels the fire in me even more. I let my hand slide up her smooth skin and find the edge of her underwear. Teasing her, grazing against the front before I slip two fingers in through the side of the lace fabric to feel her properly. She's soaking for me. I groan onto her cheek as she bites my earlobe.

"More," she breathes into my ear.

I do as she says and circle her with my now wet fingers. She moans in my ear, holding on tight, as I slide them down and into her tight warmth. She moans and bites my neck. I bend my fingers in a 'come-hither' gesture, rubbing her clit from the inside, and she gasps. With a hand in her hair, I tug her back lightly to see the pleasure on her face.

"Holy hell, that's good," she breathes, a smile pulling at the sides of her parted lips, as I play with her.

"Thought you'd like that," I whisper "I can't wait to explore you fully."

I love how she feels on my fingers. Warm.

Wet. Velvety. Her reactions to my moves are obvious, and I relish being able to please her. My cock strains in my suit pants and I press myself against her hip.

"I need you. Here." My voice is low and deep, close to her lips, and she mewls in response.

"Yes. Right here."

CHAPTER 51

NORA

He's got me so hot I see nothing but him. I wouldn't notice or care if a row of people stood peering through the windows of the surrounding ruins. I need him inside me. Around me. All over.

There's a bench along the wall behind a bushy section that I nudge him toward, kissing him hungrily. I push him down on it and he looks up at me with wild eyes and a broad smile. Standing in front of him, I lift my dress and hook my thumbs into the sides of my underwear, pulling them down and off. Raising my flowing dress to give him a glimpse of what he's about to get, he groans loudly. With swift movements, he opens his buckle and pants, pushing them down enough to allow his gorgeous cock to burst out, and my core vibrates in anticipation.

"Please tell me you have a condom," I say, and he flicks one out of his back pocket and puts it on, no questions asked.

I straddle him and sink down on his length, slowly, relishing how he fills me up. I grind my front against him and pleasure fizzes through me. It's all-consuming. My mind is blank and full at the same time. My body exists only where I'm fused with him. All I can feel is him inside me, in front of me, where his hands leave warm trails on my sides as he caresses my shape, and his lips as I angle my head down to kiss him.

I keep moving, focusing on the tingle in my core, the growing intensity of it. He grabs my hips and moves me further onto him, as deep as he can. He groans and I latch onto his shoulders as I move with more vigor.

"Jake," I breathe into his mouth as I move up and down his rock-hard length, letting my front rub against him. "Jake, I think I'm going to come. You're making me come."

He growls, not able to form words, it seems.

"Holy shit," I let out. It's impossible to be quiet. Together we grind, moan and thrust as the waves of pleasure crash over me. With every move and every touch, I come apart entirely. I shudder and buck at the same time as he pushes through his final thrusts, groaning loudly into my chest. Laughing.

"Fucking hell," he says, his voice muffled by my dress. I can hear the smile in his voice. "If nobody heard us, I'm amazed."

He laughs again and looks up at me, a lock of hair across his forehead.

I move it with a careful finger. Taking in the details of his achingly beautiful face. His eyes are big, full of emotion and energy.

"You're quite remarkable, Jake."

He lets out a small laugh. "And you. You're exceptional."

I kiss his lips gently and whisper, "What happens next?"

"I suggest you come off me before we make a mess. And then we go home to mine and do it again and again." His low, rumbling voice sends vibrations through me.

"I like that." I laugh and carefully step off him and find my underwear again.

Sitting down next to him, pulling his arm around me, I allow my body to relax and the sensation of the orgasm to settle. It's still tingling. My blood is rushing. Heart thumping.

"This place is magical," Jake whispers. It truly is. It's like stepping into a world separate from the big city. A portal to another dimension, where we can exist for a moment in peace.

Or to have a calming lunch break, which is how I found it.

"But what happens next?" he continues. "I'm going to be as transparent with you as possible, but I can't tell you more about the investors." He sighs and threads his fingers through mine. "I want you to be mine. You already have me, if you want me."

I breathe in sharply. My heart hammers in my

chest. Is this real?

"But we'd have to keep it secret at work until the deal is signed, at least. Manuel worries about appearing unethical."

"Yes," I say. We stare at each other for a long moment. "I'm yours."

"Then I can handle whatever happens next."

***

[Thursday]
Me: Staying at Jake's tonight! He says he's mine!

Dee: WOW!

[Monday]
Jake: Hello

Me: Hello

Jake: I know it's only been half an hour, but I miss you

Me: I miss you too.

Me: How am I going to do any work with you and your delicious lips so close. Eight hours feels like ages

Jake: Plans tonight? Want to watch a movie?

Me: By watching a movie, do you mean cuddling up on the couch pretending to pay attention to the movie for twenty minutes and then get naked? If so, I'd love to.

Jake: Mind reader

[Tuesday]
Me: Hey, I'm staying at Jake's again :)

Dee: Enjoy! Remember to hydrate, haha. Also, don't lose track of days, I need you next to me on Friday.

Me: I'll see you and Ajay tomorrow for ukulele night, Jake's joining!

Dee: Sweet! I can't wait to see him holding a tiny ukulele

[Thursday]
Me: Good luck today, I found the key on my desk

Jake: Thank you, I'll see you tonight, make yourself at home while you wait

Dee: Tell Jake he's a bumhole for making everyone play 'Gangnam Style' last night. It's been stuck in my head all day

Me: Will do. He'll be happy to hear his evil plan worked *wink*

Dee: *rude hand gesture*

***

The birds chirp cheerily outside Jake's balcony door and the soft light of an early morning sun peeks in through the blinds. A deliciously heavy arm is draped across my stomach and I turn my head to see Jake's sleeping face.

My Jake.

I've woken up like this nearly every day this past week and I'm in heaven. I slide up to him and wrap his arm tightly around me. His skin is warm and I wriggle even closer. He hums and his nose and lips appear at the nape of my neck, giving me goosebumps.

He grows hard against my lower back and I open my legs, letting him in between them. Grinding gently in response, he teases me with his erection at my wet opening. No words necessary. I move his hand to my already swollen and intensely sensitive front, and he abides. He circles me, moves up and down, just perfectly, and soon he's got me shuddering and kicking my legs.

This week has been magical. I want to wake up like this every day.

He turns away, and I hear the familiar sound of a condom wrapper being opened, before he's back as my big spoon. I arch my back to tell him I'm ready and he carefully inches his large length inside me. We move slowly, quietly. Letting our bodies wake up. His powerful yet soft arm is up around me, caressing a breast and I grasp onto his thigh, willing him deeper. His kisses on my neck become fiercer, our breathing heavier. He nearly growls as he flips me onto my knees to a gasp from me, thrusting hard and deep from behind, circling my still tingling front until we're both a quivering mess.

I cuddle up into his arms again. The sun is brighter now.

Jake's phone buzzes on the bedside table, and he reaches over to see who it is. He sits up and clears his throat. We still haven't said a word.

He hasn't said anything about the meeting yesterday yet either. When he opened the door and found me here last night, he wrapped his arms around me and said 'I need you' and the rest of the evening went by in a blur of skin and moans. It felt right to not press it, and instead relish his warm embrace.

"Manuel. Good morning," he says, his voice raspy. "No, no. Just woke up." He sits up. I hear him carefully pulling the condom off, and he keeps talking while walking around. Buck naked. His muscular body is an absolutely magnificent shape. Those broad shoulders and toned forearms.

All mine.

As he turns, I enjoy the fantastic view of his well-shaped butt. I want to bite it.

He swivels back and I expect a sideways smile, as he must sense I'm completely objectifying him, but it's the crease on his forehead that greets me instead.

"Okay. Of course. I'll see you soon," he says, rubbing his neck.

The knot appears under my lungs. When he didn't say anything last night, I thought it was bad news, but I didn't dare to ask. I pushed it away. Stuck my head in the sand. What could be happening that has him so worried? Is it about what he said last week or something worse? What could be worse than losing your new job?

"Sorry, Nora. I've got to go."

"Are you okay, Jake?"

"I'll tell you everything once I can. Promise."

"I trust you."

"Can I see you again tonight?"

"I've got Dee's engagement dinner tonight and tomorrow is parent sightseeing palooza they've invited me along to. Maid of honor duties already. What about Sunday?"

"I have a thing Sunday." He chews his thumbnail. Something's else is going on. His eyes meet mine and widen into the tender expression he's given me before and it makes the knot worse. "I'm worrying you."

"Yes."

"I'm sorry." He rubs his forehead and chews his cheek as he opens his wardrobe and pulls out a suit and underwear, which he puts on while I wait for more. I sense he wants to say more. He continues to dress, looking increasingly distraught.

"Jake …" I move to the edge of the bed, quilt wrapped around me. "I understand you can't tell me. Don't be upset."

He lets out a long breath, pulling on a white shirt. It's time for me to dress as well.

Standing in my jumpsuit and my hair in a classic messy bun, I'm scared to leave, as I have a strange feeling in my gut. An instinct. Something is very wrong. It's too upsetting to linger on, so I focus on Jake's hands. His beautiful hands, tying a maroon tie to go with his navy suit. He must be going to a meeting. He doesn't normally wear a tie in the office. What's going on that he can't tell me now?

He turns to me, his full lips hidden in a thin line, and throws his suit jacket on. It fits perfectly around his shoulders. Absolutely perfect.

"What's wrong?" I whisper, and warm tears stream down my cheeks. Jake rushes to me as I wipe my face with clumsy hands. "Jesus. I'm sorry. That was surprising."

"Nora," he breathes and kisses my curly head. "I'm sorry I've made you sad. Ah, fuck..." He sits down on the edge of the bed and I press in between his legs, raking my fingers through his hair as he leans his forehead on my stomach. "They want me in Canada."

"Who?"

He sighs loudly and faces me. Eyes shiny with sadness and the worst kind of frown. The crease between his eyebrows.

"Investors. They want me to be the CTO for a new branch. Specializing in AI for businesses."

I keep my hands in his hair, trying to understand what he says.

"In Canada?"

"Toronto. I shouldn't be telling you this. It's not settled. I don't have to take it, but then I'll be out of a job. I have to choose."

What he's telling me is sinking in. He'll have to leave me. When I finally found him. Anger bubbles up in me at the unfairness of it. But I know it's not his fault. I squeeze my eyes shut and rub them with the balls of my hands.

"Fuck. That fucking sucks," I whisper, squashing my eyes with my hands so I can't see his face. His scent fills my nose. I hold my breath and walk away, feeling the warmth of his hands fall away from my waistline.

Of course he'll go. We've only just begun. I can't expect him to choose me. He told me he's focused on his CTO role and career. Now he's got an even bigger one. The weight he added to his words; '*specializing in AI.*' It means a lot to him.

"Nora ..." He gets up and walks to me. "It's not decided yet. I'm meeting Manuel and the lawyer now to prepare. We're flying out Sunday morning for a few days of negotiations. That's what Manuel called about now. We need to prepare."

"Do you already know what you want to do?" I ask, my voice shaking.

He chews his cheek and his worry crease is back. It tells me what I need to know. He wants the job but also wants me and it pains him to have to choose.

"I want to be with you," he says. I'm waiting for the 'but'.

"But ..." I help him along.

"It's a big decision. Big opportunity. I'd be a fool not to consider it. It's that or I'll be without a job. My dad would—" He shakes his head.

"It's huge, Jake. I can't let you give up your dream job for me. That's too much pressure. What if you regret it? What if I'm not enough in the end?" I squeeze my eyes shut, trying not to spiral further. "It's okay. You know what I always told you about me," I say in a falsely calm tone.

"Which part? You do things yourself? You don't need anyone? You'll be fine?" He quotes me and slumps. This must be the saddest I've seen him yet.

"Exactly." I straighten up. "I'll be fine. You do

what you need to do. I can't be in the way of your biggest career opportunity."

I give him my bravest smile as I shatter on the inside.

CHAPTER 52

NORA

The restaurant is a fairy-tale place invented in my dreams. Tree vines climb each pillar lining the sides of the small room and into the ceiling, covering it in white flowers. Fairy lights wink at me as I step under the blossoming branches toward the floor-to-ceiling fireplace at the far end. It's awe-striking. Perfect for a special occasion such as this. We'll even be able to hear each other talk.

It takes a moment to let my eyes adjust and notice the people sitting in the corner, waving at me and laughing. It's Dee and her parents.

After drinks and appetizers, Ajay gets up with a nervous clearing of his throat. He doesn't seem the type to get flustered, but maybe the occasion is getting to him. Seeing the parents get along. His future wife.

Oh my god!

Dee is *engaged*. I'm freaking out a little. I take a long sip of my wine as Ajay kicks off.

"Dee. Deepa. My gorgeous fiancée. I've been looking forward to this, as giving a speech is the only time I'll get to talk for more than a minute without you contradicting me." The parents chuckle, and Dee sticks her tongue out at him. "We've known each other for many years, but it wasn't until you forced my eyes open I realized you're *it*. You are, as your name means, the light. My light. The sunshine in my life that brings out a rainbow on gray days."

I cringe and involuntarily snort, earning a slap on my thigh from Dee. Her eyes are glued to her fiancé, but her hands are under the table. Ajay continues, unperturbed. Dee's fidgeting, but her expression is calm.

"I'm the luckiest man I know. Except my father perhaps, because Mom—your cooking is ... Chef's kiss." He kisses the tips of his pinched fingers and lifts his hand as his parents giggle, looking up at their son with eyes full of adoration. Dee flinches. I know why. She doesn't cook. Anything. And if she does, it's the same way I do my dance tutorials. With a lot of cursing.

"We're so grateful to have you here as we unite our families. Thank you for coming on such short notice, Mr. and Mrs. Ladhani. We have been bursting to tell you this fantastic news."

There's murmuring around the table. Everyone looks at Dee. *I* look at Dee.

What's going on?

Is she pregnant?

Has she been drinking or is it fake bubbles in her glass? I peer into her glass theatrically and she waves me away as Ajay starts up again.

"I've been offered the role as director of digital services at AbbleTech. We're moving to the States!"

What?

I swivel in my chair to see Dee move her mouth into a smile, but her eyes are screaming at me. I'm screaming back.

What are you doing, Dee?

We sit through several long speeches as each of the parents share their well wishes; increasingly intoxicated and decreasingly intelligible. Ajay and Dee hold hands on the table. The knuckles on her hand gripping the glass are almost white.

***

Without being able to pin Dee down by herself at the restaurant, the Uber ride home with her parents is painful. I can't ask her anything. I keep trying to catch Dee's eyes, but they're fixed on her hands. She has to tell me what's going on. Is she leaving?

"It's late, time for bed for me," I hint when we're in the hallway. Dee stays in my room when her parents are in hers. She refused to let them get a hotel room in the city, saying she wouldn't see them enough on their brief trip.

Finally in bed, I turn to face Dee. Her eyes are wide, staring blankly at me.

"How long have you known?" I whisper.

"Since this morning." Her voice is thick. "It came as quite the shock, you could say." She huffs. "I said I'd think about it. I'm mad at him for not telling me when he proposed that he'd interviewed with them. That's where he'd been that week. He claims he thought it was a long-shot. And when he got the call today he was so shocked he accepted it outright."

I'm raging on the inside, not sure what's showing on my face. Willing my stomach to settle and the knot to subside, I hope it helps relax my frown as well. I can't believe this is happening. To both of us! But she's going with him?

"He announced it. Does it mean you said *yes*?" I ask in a small voice. She sighs.

Oh no.

"He's ecstatic. His dream job. Said he really wanted to tell his dad."

"But did you say *yes*?"

"I told him *maybe*. He took it as a *yes*, it seems. I feel a bit trapped now." She bites her lip and her gaze drifts down. I've not seen her so resigned before.

"You can change your mind, Dee." I add a bit more volume to my voice this time.

"I love him. Should I not give it a chance?"

Her eyes are big. I sense she's trying to tell me something. Does she want me to argue the case for her or support her in moving? I don't want her to go and I'm fighting with my selfish self.

"Where is it?" I ask, not sure which side to argue yet.

"Cupertino."

"Never heard of it."

"It's in California. I had to Google it. It's got vineyards and nature hikes. I'll become a fit alcoholic."

"Not too unlike here," I say, mustering a smile. She laughs and squeezes her eyes shut, scrunching up her mouth.

"Boo."

What would I want her to say to me if I contemplated going with Jake?

Huh. *If*? Should I consider it? My mind hasn't dared go down that road yet. I won't now. This is about her.

"Dee. I have to ask, because you seem unsure. What about London? Your career? You worked so hard to become senior editor and you're killing it. This is where your connections are, your future clients. Is there a major publishing house in Cupertino?"

"That's why I don't want to go. I've carved this path for myself. And it's been hard. I love what I do. I love London."

"And you're saving for your own apartment."

"Imagine that. My very own apartment in

London."

"Your favorite city."

Her eyes are shiny and when she blinks, tears drip down across the bridge of her nose and onto the pillow. I wrap an arm around her and lean my cheek gently onto hers.

"Would you go, Nora? You're the romantic of us," she asks from under my curls, her voice muffled. I move back again with a giggle.

"Sorry. Wasn't trying to smother you. Figuratively or literally." I sigh, thinking for a second. Hypothetical scenario. "I want to say *no*. London is so much for me. And our friends here. Well, I mean you, mainly, but it's a quickly growing list. But the *romantic* in me wants to say that if Ajay brings all the color to your existence, the way he said you do to his. If he lights up your life and makes you feel more like yourself when you're with him than without. Then it doesn't matter where you are. Cupertino, London, Sydney, wherever? Home is where the heart is, they say, for a reason."

I think about Jake. He not only brings color to my existence, he makes everything more intense. More real. He brings a sense of buoyancy. By being the way he is, and letting me be the way I am, he makes me lighter. It's not been long, but I've been through enough ups and downs in my life to know what I feel for him is real. It's deep.

Dee blinks her tears away and rubs her nose,

sniffling.

"I'm sure he'd be able to work from London later," I add, trying to be in both camps.

"Right. Yeah ... I'll think about it some more." She turns toward the wall and curls up into the fetal position with a long sigh. The thought of Dee *and* Jake leaving sinks into my body like a rock. My stomach churns and it's as if I'm spinning. As if I'm standing on the edge of a cliff, looking down. Will I be able to catch myself if I fall? If I end up alone again? Deep in my gut, I know I'll be okay, sort of. Whatever happens. Like Mom said, I should give myself some credit. I'm self-reliant.

I'll be fine.

CHAPTER 53

JAKE

Waiting for them to answer, I rest my forehead on the table in front of my laptop. They might be out on a Saturday afternoon. As soon as I think it, I hear the familiar bleep of an answered call and lift my head. The small selfie-window in the corner reveals I look about as bad as I feel. My hair sticks up and my eyes are bloodshot from rubbing them, thinking hard.

"My goodness, Jake, what's happened?" Mom's hands fly to her face in shock. My father's face is still, a crease forming between his eyebrows.

"I need some advice." I breathe out loudly.

"Is it Nora?" Mom asks.

"How do you know about—" I know the answer before I finish the sentence. I close my eyes in exasperation. "Sage."

"Your sister doesn't think you tell us enough. You know, she calls us every day."

"Well, there wasn't much to tell until recently, so she's ahead of the game there. She has a baby. I have nothing to call you about *every* day." I moan, not in the mood for a guilt trip.

"What do you need advice about?" Dad asks, jaw working hard.

"I know you always told me I needed to give it my all. Work hard and stay secure."

"Mm-hmm." The crease deepens.

"Well … now I'm going to have to choose." I know what I want, but based on my history of decision-making, I'll feel better if one person could assure me it's the right thing to do. Mainly I want *him* to tell me that. I want him not to be disappointed in me. Or to look at me as if he thinks I'll walk into a bus lane any minute. Which is kind of how he's looking at me right now.

I rake a hand through my hair to appear less of a mess.

"CTO for a—" I stop myself to add, "Mom, not a word to Sage, okay? I'm telling you something I shouldn't."

She nods and mimes a zipped mouth.

"So … CTO for an AI software company based in Canada. Or *temporarily* jobless, but close to you, baby Jackie and … Nora. In love." I let out a small laugh and run my hands down my face. When did I turn into a cheesy romantic?

"Oh, Jake," Mom breathes and moves her hands over her mouth, looking over at my dad.

"Why do you look so sad, Jake? Is this a hard choice for you? Do you want this job?" he asks, narrowing his eyes at the screen.

I take a deep breath. Here goes nothing.

"No. For a moment, I thought I did. The techie in me did. I want to stay here. But I'm torn because I don't want you to be disappointed in me. For not listening to you. For not giving work my all. You've been telling me to do that for years."

Dad's jaw flexes and his eyes are fixed on the camera, looking right at me.

"Mm-hmm. So you know what I'd say," he answers in a level tone.

I do. That's what I was afraid of.

"An AI company?" he asks.

Mom turns to him, "Robert, remember—"

My dad holds up a hand to stop her, gesturing for me to answer his question.

"Yes. Similar to what I did for HercuSoft, but AI-powered. But it doesn't matter, Dad. My place is here. And I enjoy working for a small company. I'll find another one. There are tons of them."

"The AI role sounds like it would set you up well for the future, though. How long have you known this girl?"

I rub my eyes again. Dammit.

"Would she come with you?" he continues.

"Robert Fielding, that's enough." Mom slams a hand on the table. I drop my hands and look at my parents, although they're blurry and little stars dance across my vision after rubbing too hard. Mom has never raised her voice to my dad in front of me before.

"I told you after Paris. You were too hard on him. Has it completely escaped you what we talked about? Tell him." She points at me. Dad's jaw muscles are working hard, his eyes unblinking.

"Tell him what you told me," she says again, staring at the side of his face. "Robert."

He sighs loudly and slumps, and my mom's expression relaxes.

"Sorry, Roshani. Jake." He pinches the bridge of his nose and groans. "I worked sixty—sometimes seventy—hours a week, and I've always told myself it was because I had to. I had to be the best so I could stay secure. Not lose my job. Not end up like my brother."

"I know, Dad."

"But it was a sacrifice. I missed your mom. I missed you." He waves a hand toward the screen and sighs. "Those hours, days, weeks—however long it adds up to—are gone. I used to stay up to watch you children sleep. I didn't get to see you enough during the day."

He squeezes my mom's hand and turns to see her face.

"Your mom reminded me how I felt in the beginning. Before you. Back when I traveled alone. When I'd been gone for three months and came home and her hair was longer, and it made me cry because it was a visible reminder of the time I'd missed with her. But I was too stubborn to change my ways. Change my belief that I was doing the right thing. So I kept it up." He rubs his brow and takes a deep breath. "I've been pushing you too hard. And I promised I wouldn't push you again if the conversation came up. And here we are."

"Here we are," I repeat, taken aback. Heart pounding.

"But I'm going to have to break that promise, son."

"What?" I freeze, confused. My mom stares at the side of his face with narrow eyes.

"I expect great things from you. You're the best at everything you do. So I'll push you once more."

I hold my breath, waiting for his next words. My heart soars in expectation. Is he okay with my decision?

"If you're going to choose her. Give it your all. Be the best partner you can be. And make her feel loved for who she is—every single day." He emphasizes the last three words. "Can you give her this? And as important—will she give you this, Jake? Is she enough for you to give up this opportunity?"

His question hangs in the air and I stare at the screen as my heart crashes back down again, settling like a rock in my stomach. Nora asked that same question. But it's not her I'm worried about. Am *I* enough?

CHAPTER 54

NORA

I wake up Sunday morning to Dee staring at me with wide eyes and her lips pressed together in a thin line. My body aches after a hectic family Saturday spent with their parents and Colette, seeing the major sights of London.

"I can't move, Nora."

"Me neither. I'm broken from all that walking. How are the old people so fit?"

"No. I can't move to the States. I can't marry Ajay," she whispers. She hasn't blinked yet. The words sink in slowly.

"Wow."

"Yes."

"What made you change your mind?" I whisper back, as if talking loudly would force the day to start and Dee will have to take this into the world. But when we're quiet, it's just us, and time stands still.

"Many things. What you said, for one."

Shit, what did I say?

"Does he bring all the colors to my existence the way he said I do to his?" She puts a hand over her eyes and rubs gently, as if to stop tears from forming. "No."

I press my lips together and scrunch up my brow in a sad face. Not sure what to say.

"There are too many red flags. He didn't tell me about the potential move when he proposed. Then he didn't ask me before he accepted the role. He doesn't notice little things. Like, he wouldn't know for shit what my favorite chocolate is, like Jake does with you."

"Huh?"

"I saw it. He sent the ice cream and your favorite chocolate. I know it seems insignificant, but he sees you. Ajay doesn't see me. He didn't even know I don't drink beer. Even the old wrinkly guy in the corner office at work knows I don't drink beer, for crying out loud." She's whisper shouting now and sits up. Making it real.

"You have a point. Some points."

"I'm more excited about going to work on Monday than seeing Ajay again because, at work, people value my input to their decisions. That says a lot. I'd rather go for a walk along the canal by myself than hang out at his house because I find it more rewarding. What have I been doing with him all this time?" She puts her face in her hands and starts shaking.

"Oh, Dee." I lean over to embrace her, but she tilts her head back. She's ... laughing?

"It's ridiculous. I've been so focused on *him*. What he wants. What he needs. Treading carefully so I don't scare him. And then going along with this *farce* because he realized he's more afraid of being alone than being with the wrong person. He doesn't care about me enough. If he did, he wouldn't let me give up my career when he knows it means so much to me." She jumps out of bed and twirls. "I feel free! Now that I'm saying it out loud. I can't believe I considered changing myself, changing my life, for *him*. I'm free!"

I laugh and jump out of bed with her.

"And our tourist parents taking us on East London walks and sightseeing have reminded me."

She picks something out of a bag from yesterday. It's a T-shirt she bought at the market with a painted 'I heart' and the iconic city skyline.

"What?"

"*London* is the love of my life. London lets me be exactly the version of me that *I* love." She twirls again.

I know that feeling.

I hug her when she stops and a waft of cedarwood hits my nose, making my head spin and my heart pound like it's about to escape my chest.

"Why do you smell like that?" I ask.

"Like what?" She sniffs her armpits.

I sniff her and find it's the T-shirt.

"It must be from the bag," she says, laughing. "My dad bought handmade soap bars at the market yesterday. Cedarwood, something or other, man stuff."

"Yeah," I breathe it in again. "I love it."

Everything Dee said about London and Ajay echoes in my head and I realize what I need to do.

It'll be heartbreaking, but I know now.

"Dee. I need to go."

"Where?"

"To the airport. I hope I'm not too late."

"To find Jake? Isn't that a bit dramatic? Can't you just call him?"

"Not to say what I want to say. I need to see him."

"All right, let's find his flight. Why don't you text him?"

I chew my thumbnail. "Yes, that's probably the easiest approach. You do it, I'm too nervous."

Dee grabs my phone. "What are you going to tell him, Nora? What's happened?"

"Uhm. I can't tell you the details yet. I'm so sorry for stealing your moment right now. You have a lot to process. But this is something I need to do." I grab onto her arm, nearly shaking her.

"It's okay. I'll probably be spending the day sucking up to the parents before telling them, anyway." She's already texted him from my phone, holding it up for me to see. "Oh, he's responding." We watch the three little dots. "His flight is at twelve-forty and he's asking why. What to write? Why don't you go to his place?"

"No, I don't want him to feel pressured or in a rush to leave for his flight. Uhm. Tell him to wait by the check-in. I don't dare do it rom-com style and hope to catch him there on time by a fluke. London traffic and all."

"Yeah, best not." She wrinkles her nose at me and nods.

***

I run into the check-in area and find the right desk. I'm super early. It's not even open yet. My body is vibrating from the rush of hurrying over.

With a completely irrational fear of being too late when I had over two hours to get here, I'm now suffering from anti-climax issues. I imagined I'd run in and see him and use my adrenaline-fueled momentum to say what I wanted to say, like in a movie. And he'd smile and embrace me and kiss my forehead, saying—

"Nora?"

I swivel.

"Jake," I breathe, adrenaline rushing through me again in an instant, and I have to lean on the pillar next to me so I don't fold over. A rumbling stomach reminds me I forgot to eat breakfast as well.

"Why are you here?" He moves slowly toward me, rolling his suitcase. "I mean. You texted me to meet you, but you didn't say why."

"I did it again."

"You did what?" He stops a few paces away from me.

"Pretended to be all cool. But I'm not. I don't want to be *fine*, Jake."

He shakes his head. "What do you mean?"

"Alone—I'd be fine. Eventually. But I don't want to be fine," I repeat. "I want to be ecstatic. I want to be with you, Jake."

"And me you." He takes one step closer, searching my face. "I'm not taking the job."

I blink.

"I can't have you turn down that role for me. I'll come with you."

He cocks his head. "Seriously?"

"Yes. I mean, I need to figure out the details. Visa and work stuff."

He chuckles softly and I continue, "This is worth taking a chance on. We make our own luck, remember? Can't wait around for a miracle and miss life with you."

"Am I enough for you? What about London?"

"Enough? You're everything, Jake. More than I ever imagined a man could be."

He nods, eyes fierce, his jaw working.

Before he can say anything, I move closer. I grab his free hand and let my fingers intertwine with his.

"I spent most of my adult life looking for love. But I never gave anyone a chance because I couldn't picture life with them without changing myself to make it work. It became too much of an unknown and I was afraid.

"It's not like that with you. When I think of us together, it's already familiar. Because I'm exactly me when I'm with you. It's incredibly freeing. I know this is right. Do you feel the same? It doesn't matter where we are or what we do, as long as I have you."

I laugh nervously caressing his fingers in mine. Jake rubs his eyes with the other hand and shakes his head.

"Are you okay? Say something."

He drops his hand, giving me that wide smile that lights up my world. "You have no idea what it means to hear you say this. And yes, I feel the same. I'm the best version of me when we're together," Jake says, his voice cracking.

He finally pulls me close and wraps me in his arms. "You have me. I told you, I'm yours. I've been yours since we met." He leans his forehead on mine and whispers, "I'm not taking the job. I was going to tell you, but I wanted to do it face to face."

"You decided? Are you sure? What if you regret it?" I lean back to see his face. There's no trace of worry on it.

"I won't. There isn't a doubt in my mind about what I want. The concern you saw in me on Friday was all about my Dad. I just didn't realize at the time.

"I want you. And I want London, baby Jackie,

my sister, my parents. I want to work for a small company where I can go to lunch and karaoke with the team, and go out with friends after work. Have *time* for life. For us. I'll lose this job, but I'll find another."

"Wow," I breathe.

"Yeah. Meeting you, moving here … it's opened my eyes to what matters." He traces a finger along my jawline the way he did in the photo booth that night, tilting my head up. My pulse races and I hug my arms tightly around his torso so I don't fall over.

"I can't believe you'd leave for me. You love London," he whispers and his breath caresses my face.

"Well, it turns out, I—" I interrupt myself meeting his lips and a powerful sensation spreads in me. I pull him closer, letting our kiss grow hungrier until he pulls away, looking dazed.

"Hah. I need to be careful, Manuel is on his way."

"Do you still have to go to Toronto today?" I whisper and bite my lip.

"Yeah, I have to help with the investors. It'll only be a few days."

Jake's phone rings and he fishes it out of his pocket, looking surprised at whatever he sees on the screen.

"I've got to take this."

I nod in response.

Two shapes reminiscent of Manuel and Howard appear in the distance behind Jake. Trying to avoid them seeing me here, I wave goodbye and sneak behind the pillar and away toward the next row of desks. I hate to leave him like that, but at least I'll see him again later in the week. This conversation won't sink in until I do.

He's been mine since we met, he said.

And now I see I've been his too. I was scared to realize it, afraid of letting go—losing control. But I've learned, I can be his without losing myself; not depending on him for happiness but allowing him to enhance my life.

I've found where I belong. I'm not a puzzle piece searching for *one* fit. I'm a colorful shape in life's mosaic, wonderful on its own but more vivid when surrounded by the right pieces.

***

"Hmm." I tap my chin, thinking. "I can't decide. I'll just take all three," I say to the burly Cornish pasty cart guy and accept the greasy, brown paper bags from him. I can't wait to dig in. This rumbling stomach is screaming for buttery, crusty pasty.

"Glad to see you got me one."

I turn on the spot.

"Jake! What happened?"

"Nothing short of a miracle." He grins and I step closer to him. "It was Mark who called. I couldn't believe what he was saying. He wants to invest. On Manuel's terms."

"He what? Why did he call *now*?"

Jake laughs and shakes his head. "He said a little birdy told him he had to hurry up and call us. He was originally going to wait until tomorrow, but luckily it seems I have a very meddling family. I've left it with Manuel and Howard now." He gestures behind him. "Don't worry, they're not coming this way," he adds, takes my free hand in his and kisses it.

"Wow. You look a bit shocked still."

"Yeah, I am." He runs the other hand over his mouth. "I didn't realize Mark could invest."

"You didn't know he's got the funds?"

"He sold his company a few years ago, but I never knew for how much."

"Did he tell you now?"

"No. I didn't ask. It doesn't matter."

"What happens next?" I ask, moving flush up against his front.

"Well," he says, leaning his forehead on mine and I catch my breath. "I notice you've bought three pasties which must mean you're famished, so we're going to get on the Gatwick Express and eat so you don't get grumpy." I pull back and laugh, heart soaring at that bright smile that's all mine to kiss. "This time I'll let you sit on my lap. No need to pretend you're falling over."

"Hah, you wish," I say, but I most definitely will. I put an arm around his waist and hold on tight, wanting as much contact as possible as we stroll toward the elevator.

"Then we're going to go home, and I'm going to ..." He leans down into my curls and whispers the next part. His breath is in my ear, sending goosebumps down my back and sparking the fire in me as always.

As we stand on the platform waiting for the train to carry us back to the city and into our new life together, he pulls me in and wraps his arms tightly around me. The warmth from his embrace and the familiar cedarwood scent fill me. My heart swells and I blink back tears. Happy tears.

"Hey, what were you about to say before? It turns out...?" he asks the top of my head.

I pull back to see his face. My heart lunges in my chest as I'm about to say the words that have been ready to burst out of me.

"It turns out ... I love you more."

He beams at me, and he lights up my world in the way only he can.

"I hoped that's what it was." He kisses my forehead before leaning down to whisper, "I love you, Nora." His lips find mine again and we disappear into our own world until the train rumbles into the station.

While it squeals to a halt and we wait for it to stop, he hugs me tight, swaying gently, and whispers a song I know very well.

"I am in paradise ..."

EPILOGUE

Three Months Later...

NORA

"That's amazing, Dee!" I jump up and hug her, trying not to spill my beer. She reaches up to return the embrace from the wooden chair that teeters threateningly on the soft grass.

"I don't dare celebrate fully yet," she says into my curls. "It's a long process. I'll scream with joy when I have the keys in my hand."

"When do you think you'll move?" I ask and sit down next to her again. Dee's distracted by a group of men gathered in front of us, but peels her eyes off them and turns to me.

"It'll take a while. After Christmas, probably. So we have a few more months of cocktails and popcorn with Colette."

"Yeah," I say, giving her a wistful smile. I've done my best to savor evenings with Dee, and let Jake find his feet in London independently, but most of the week I'm wrapped in his arms in bed. Or curled up next to him on the couch. Or in restaurants exploring cuisine from around the world. Sri Lankan is easily my new favorite.

Life's good.

"Will you move in with Jake?"

"Absolutely." I'm ready for anything and everything with Jake. There are no doubts. We fit together better than I'd ever dreamed. Living with him will be easy. Another familiar. I'd move in with him sooner if I didn't have Dee and Colette. I know I'll miss our time together at home, so I appreciate every moment we have there.

"Good. That guy has been ready to move in and make you his wife since he sat in our kitchen the first time."

Wife. The word gives me goosebumps. The good kind. I laugh and nudge her gently with my elbow.

"I thought I was the romantic of us."

"You are. I'm stating facts."

The sun shines down on us from a clear sky, keeping us warm in the October chill. Dee's attention is again on the event unfolding in front of us.

"They're doing this voluntarily?" she asks.

"Mm-hmm," I answer while sipping my beer. I lean my elbows on my knees and look out at the steady stream of muddy people.

"On purpose?" Dee turns to me.

I laugh. "Yep. Look, those guys just finished and they're smiling."

"Yeah. Probably because they survived." Dee stands up to peer over the metal fence that separates us from the last few obstacles of the course Jake, Ash, Mark, and some of Ash's friends are doing.

"That guy has been lying there for a while. Do you think he's okay?"

I laugh. Dee has been cringing hard at each of the teams that have come through the hanging electric threads. There's at least one person from each group that shrieks and topples over. I find Dee's reactions more entertaining. It looks thrilling to me. I want to do it next year.

"I don't want to see Jake fall like that," Dee says and looks back at me.

"Me neither, to be honest. Let's walk up to the frozen lake area instead."

"Okay, sounds marginally better. This is supposed to be fun, is it?"

I take her question as rhetorical and scan the river of people running through the vast obstacle course, searching for Jake. I know his shape so well, and I spot him by the edge of the pond. His shorts and T-shirt cling to his body after going through the water, and suddenly I find it difficult to stand without wobbling. My magnificent man.

I want to shout it.

He's mine! He loves me!

Jake waves and points toward the final part. They're finishing up.

Moments later, I kiss his wet, muddy grin after

he escapes the 'electric eel' obstacle unscathed. "Hope that was as fun as it looks." I laugh. "No sarcasm, by the way."

"It was a blast! Exhilarating! We should do it together next year," Jake says, rubbing his hands together. "Cold, though. I don't want to get you wet or I'd hug you. I'll get changed."

"We'll be in the beer tent," I gesture with a thumb behind me. "Hey," I lower my voice. "We've been waiting for Celia, is she not coming?"

Jake leans down to speak into my ear, and the hand hovering near my spine makes me tingle.

"Ash is upset about something, been going hard on the course today."

He pulls back and presses his lips together. I respond with a sad grimace. "Poor Ash."

"He probably doesn't want to talk about it in front of everyone. We'll have to find out what happened later."

Jake shivers despite the sunshine on his wet skin.

"Of course. Go get dried up." I kiss his soft lips. They're as warm as they look.

***

JAKE

I exit the changing room, flanked by Ash and Mark. The cold fall breeze greets us with a whiff of mud and sweat as a group of contestants passes by. But the fresh air takes over again, reminding us of the splendid green surroundings of the vast Winchester farmland.

"Thanks for inviting us, Ash. That was fucking fantastic," I say, blood still rushing from the obstacles. Mark hums in agreement.

"My pleasure. Sorry if I was a bit off." Ash kicks at the grass while we make our way toward the tent to find the others.

"Everything okay?"

"We're working through it. Celia and I."

I pat his shoulder. "I'm here if you want to talk. Not that I can give much advice, but I can listen."

"You're doing all right." Ash juts his chin toward the tent where Nora is currently showing Dee her latest tap dance moves, making bits of grass fly.

I chuckle.

It's been inspiring watching her try to learn. Although she still struggles, she's improving. Having fun is the main point.

"Can't argue with that part," I say, not digging further into his issues with Celia until he raises it again.

"Glad Manuel didn't give you too much grief."

"Yes, and thankfully, our investor didn't make a fuss." I lean past Ash and grin at Mark.

"As long as it's serious, I don't mind relationships in the office." He shrugs and quickly adds, "And consensual and power-balance and all that, of course."

"Oh, it's serious," I say, automatically picking up the pace to get to Nora faster.

"Yeah?"

"Yeah." She looks up and meets my eye, giving me that bright smile I love so much. "I'm gonna marry that girl one day."

***

Another Two Months Later...

NORA

"*God jul*," I say and clink Mom, Colette, and Jake's glasses with mine. "Merry Christmas."

"*God jul*," they respond in unison, Jake doing his best Norwegian accent. Colette says '*goo yewl*', which isn't far off.

Mom has had hearts in her eyes since she met Jake yesterday. This afternoon it's been particularly bad; or good, depending on how you look at it. A goofy smile has been plastered on her face all day, and everything she says is with abnormal cheerfulness.

Jake's a charming, helpful, and delightful man, Mom pointed out after dinner last night—which he made for us. He also did the dishes, and Mom stood next to him, babbling and giggling, while drying what he handed her. I'm not surprised she likes him, of course. I love him so much my heart nearly swells out of my chest several times a day, but I'm not sure what he said or did this morning to bring out this exaggerated glee.

It could be the surroundings. She's a Christmas fanatic, after all.

I put my champagne down, enjoying how the light from the chandelier above reflects in the drink, making golden stars dance on the white tablecloth.

"I'm loving this, Nora. Thank you so much for taking me here." Mom looks around and sighs loudly before turning back to the three-tier silver serving tower in front of us. "But I don't understand these tiny cucumber sandwiches." She picks one up and bites it with raised eyebrows and a shrug.

I let out a laugh through my nose and grab one of the decorated mince pies instead. Sweet and spiced dried fruits fill my mouth when I bite into the delectable treat.

Afternoon tea at the Ritz is entirely what I dreamed it would be, and a little more. The pleasant scent of freshly baked scones hangs in the air. There's a cozy ambiance of chatter, cutlery clattering on plates, and soft piano music.

The hum of voices is muffled by the large Christmas trees standing in each corner—perfectly decorated with gold baubles and huge red velvet bows. The room itself is a Christmas decoration, with its gold-patterned walls and multiple crystal chandeliers.

"There's a special light exhibition I'd like to see afterwards," Mom says, finishing her glass of champagne.

"Okay. Where is it?"

"It's near a place called Monument. Can we go?"

"Sure. Where did you hear about it? I want to Google it." I turn to pick my phone out of my purse.

"It's an old tradition," Colette interjects. "I'll show you. It'll be perfect in a couple of hours when the sun sets."

I shrug. "Okay. I'll follow you."

Jake sips his champagne quietly and raises his eyebrows when I glance up at him.

"You're coming too, right?" I ask.

He grins. "Of course. Can't miss an opportunity to watch you enjoy Christmas lights."

***

"Come on, up here," Colette calls out, her breath visible in the cold air. How is she so fast?

We round the corner and the old church ruins I showed Jake months ago come into view. The memories of us together on the bench are visceral and make me tingle with excitement.

If my mom and Colette weren't here, and it wasn't freezing cold, I'd suggest a repeat.

"Mom, look at this place. Isn't it beautiful?" I

look up; the spire is illuminated in a golden hue by the lamppost. The air is crisp and still. Will it snow?

"It is ..." Her voice is barely audible. She sounds awestruck.

"Where is this light exhibition, Colette?" I ask, but she's nowhere to be seen. "Colette?" I swivel on the spot.

When I turn back, Mom has disappeared as well. "Where the hell did they go?"

Jake smiles and points toward the door to the ruins.

"Did they sneak in there? Why?"

I push the heavy iron gate open and step inside. It's dark, and I can't see Mom or Colette.

Click.

I gasp.

Thousands of fairy lights cover the walls, vines, and bushes. It's a magical, wondrous sight.

"Oh, my word..." I whisper. "Look at this." I stare at the lights twinkling all around me. This isn't real. I don't want to blink, in case it disappears when I do.

There's a sound I don't recognize at first, but once I tune into it, I realize it's a violin. My stomach flip-flops with a sudden burst of butterflies. Something is happening.

A woman appears in the corner—the source of the sound—then two more, and a man with a cello takes a seat on the bench and starts playing. My brain is working hard but it can't compute. What's the song? Then I hear it, and the realization of what's going on hits me like a ton of bricks. Tears fill my eyes. I can't breathe.

"Jake," I whisper as I catch my breath and turn around to find him dropping to one knee. I gasp. I've imagined a range of different proposals and decided in the end it doesn't matter how he asks. But this is beyond what I could even dream up.

'Waterloo Sunset' plays cheerily in the background, and I wipe my tears, laughing.

"Nora," he says, his voice thick. He takes a small red box out of his jacket pocket. "I've lived many years, and in many countries. But it's only after I met you I understand what life is really about. You're my heart, my home, and the sweetest, dorkiest, sexiest, smartest, and most fun human I have ever met. I am the luckiest and happiest man alive, and I want to spend the rest of my days trying to make you as happy. Will you do me the greatest honor and be my wife?"

I yell out, "Yes!" and throw my arms around him, nearly toppling us both over. He folds his arms around me and stands up on shaky legs, holding me tight. Burying my face in the crook of his neck, I take a deep breath that fills me with his cedarwood scent and tears stream down my cheeks. How did I get so lucky?

"Do you want to see the ring?" he asks, chuckling, as I release my grip and find my feet. When he sees my wet face, he wipes the tears with a trembling thumb. He lets out a small laugh. "My heart is pounding so hard."

I put a hand on his face and take in the sight of him. His eyes sparkle with the reflection of the magical display around us. "No words can describe how I feel right now."

"I hoped you'd like it."

"I love it. I love you."

"Put the ring on." He laughs again and opens the box. The ring is a dazzling round diamond with three smaller diamonds on each side. It glitters with the most magnificent colors as I move it under the light. I take it out and he slides it onto my ring finger.

"Wow," I whisper, moving my hand so I can see it again. I look up at him again and he smiles the wide smile that makes my heart skip a beat. He's going to be my husband. "We're getting married. I'm going to be your wife. Mrs. Fielding. Or do I keep Gundersen?"

He chuckles lightly at my premature musings. "You choose. I'm not precious. You're my wife, either way." He beams.

Cheers erupt from behind us. I hadn't realized the music stopped and Mom and Colette had joined the string quartet in the corner. I wave my hand toward them, ring-side out, and gape at them exaggeratedly, receiving another cheer.

"So that's why Mom was so damned cheery today. You told her?"

"I did."

"Very cute." I wrap my arms around him

again. “So, what happens next?”

“Your Mom and Colette will go to jazz night at some old pub, so you and I can celebrate alone.”

I wiggle my eyebrows at him and he laughs, making my pulse race. Sigh, that smile.

“Excellent thinking. Can we stay here and dance for a while first? These lights ...”

“I thought you’d want that.” He waves at the string quartet and they start up. This time playing a slow version of ‘Take on Me.’

I run to hug my mom goodbye, and give her a playful jab in the arm.

“I can’t believe you knew about this all day,” I whisper with a giggle, before I rush back into the arms of my future husband. We sway in a tight embrace, and I keep my eyes open so I don’t miss a thing.

Glancing up at the climbing vines draped in fairy lights, I notice tiny flakes drifting in the air above us. Is it for real? The flakes grow larger, and I turn my face up toward the sky, laughing.

“Snow!”

We twirl together in the increasing flurry of winter. Cold flakes kiss my cheeks and land on Jake’s long eyelashes while he smile the widest smile yet.

My dreams fall short. ‘Happy’ doesn't even begin to describe how I feel.

THE END

Thank you for reading my debut novel!

Your support means the world to an indie author, and what helps a lot is a review on Amazon and Goodreads. Every rating and review matters!

Want more Nora and Jake? Sign up to my monthly newsletter and receive a bonus epilogue.

ABOUT THE AUTHOR

Ingrid Voss

Ingrid grew up in Norway, with her nose in a book, scabs on her knees, and Barbies with very little clothing. Living in London, she had beer in her glass, hearts in her eyes, and her very own office romance. Now in New Zealand, she lives her epilogue—babies and all—fueled by chocolate and coffee.

Exactly Me is Ingrid's debut novel, and she hopes it leaves you smiling. She adores lighthearted romance novels with relatable and flawed characters, happy endings, humor and a touch of spice—and that's what she aspires to write.

www.ingridvoss.com
www.instagram.com/ingrid.writes.romcoms

CHEERS

Firstly, thank *you* for reading Exactly Me! If you're still reading, I'm well impressed.

This novel would not exist if it wasn't for the unwavering support of my dear friend, 'Jane'. You know who you are. Thank you—sincerely, thank you sooo much—for taking the time to share your knowledge when I first mentioned I wanted to write a book. You didn't question my ability once, and so I didn't either. Even after that first draft! I don't know if you're aware of how big a deal that was.

Thank you to Ash, Anju, and everyone who read my various drafts. Your support and positivity mean the world to me, and I can't tell you enough how much I appreciate it. Cheers for you!

And to my dear husband: thank you for believing in me, for cheering me on, and for listening to all my ramblings about romance novels and self-publishing.

Cheers, Microsoft, for having Office on iPhone

so I could write the initial drafts of this book while my baby was feeding, and sleeping on top of me. Or is it thanks to Apple for having Office on iPhone? To whomever agreed to make that work—cheers. I know you find it hard to get along.

Oh, I can hear the music cue that my thank-you speech is too long. *gracefully bowing out*

Printed in Great Britain
by Amazon